RELENTLESS SOMMER

NORA SOMMER CARIBBEAN SUSPENSE - BOOK SIX

NICHOLAS HARVEY

For my uncle, Mike Golding.
Thank you for all your love and support over so many years.
1936–2024

1

TEA LEAF

Heather Lawson leaned over her bathroom counter, carefully applying mascara. Standing up straight, she looked in the mirror and sighed. Some people lost weight when they were stressed and unhappy, and she wondered why she couldn't be that lucky. Any upside to recent events would be welcome as Heather felt her life plummet farther off the tracks it had once happily rumbled along.

She'd never been a skinny woman, not even as a young girl in England, but sitting behind a desk at the bank all day had taken its toll on her waistline. Maybe she'd finally join a gym. She'd seen it before with friends who'd gone through a divorce. The fresh start inspired them to get in shape, make career changes, date again. But the thought of any of those things felt completely overwhelming to Heather. Perhaps she'd settle for low fat milk in her coffee and a salad for lunch, and see how it went from there. Losing a few pounds would definitely make her feel better about herself. She ran a hand over her tummy and groaned.

A purr emanated from her cat, Tea Leaf, as he rubbed against her leg. He was named after the cockney rhyming slang for thief, as he'd been the kitten who always stole the toys from the rest of the litter.

"I know, I know," she said to her dearest companion. "Mummy needs to lose more than a few pounds."

Heather looked in the mirror once more and stared into the reflection of her own eyes, brown and dulled by her cheating arsehole of a soon-to-be ex-husband. She noticed tiny lines that hadn't been there a few months back. Or perhaps they were, but she never took the time to worry about such things. They didn't seem important when the man she'd loved for over a decade told her he adored her. Conveniently leaving out the caveat that he also adored a twenty-four-year-old paralegal at his law firm. Heather had never seen the little harlot, but her brain had decided she looked a lot like Margot Robbie. Who didn't need to lose a few pounds. Or have crow's feet around her eyes.

"Come on, Tea," Heather breathed, tearing herself away from the evil mirror. "How about a spot of breakfast?"

The cat keenly followed her from the en-suite bathroom, through the bedroom to the tiled floor of the living area and kitchen. Heather paused to take in the view of the Caribbean Sea through the large windows and reminded herself that she still lived in paradise. Her husband had accepted a job with a law firm in Grand Cayman a year after their wedding, and the tropical island had been her home ever since. The divorce left her considering a move back to the UK where her family would surround her in love and support, but the view from the living room window would certainly not be the same.

Scooping Tea's favourite cat food from the can into a bowl, Heather tried not to breathe in while she stirred in the dry food the cat barely tolerated. Meowing around her feet, Tea eagerly crouched over the dish the moment the ceramic hit the floor. Heather smiled and picked up the matching white and blue dish sitting alongside on the paw print-decorated mat, washing it out in the sink and refilling it with fresh water.

"Don't pick around the bits you don't like, Tea," Heather instructed as she placed the water dish in its spot on the mat. "That stuff's good for your teeth."

And a myriad of other body parts and functions, according to the labels, and she wondered with an amused chuckle how pets ever survived without these mixtures and additives. Perhaps all that tasty goodness came handily packaged in mice and small birds.

Opening the fridge, Heather considered her breakfast options, glancing at her watch to see how much time she had before needing to leave. The bank was a ten-minute drive away in the busy morning commuter traffic from West Bay into the north end of Seven Mile Beach. She had fifteen minutes. Eggs would be a healthy option, but would require more work and clean-up. A coffee and a pastry on her way into the office sounded much better, but she could hear the mirror screaming at her from the bathroom. Maybe it would shut up if she made today the first day of her new life.

Heather closed the door and wandered back to the bedroom to find her handbag. The ex had moved out and left her with the home they'd recently built, but the downside was the memories. She looked around the room. Everything in their home reminded her of him. And when she saw him, she couldn't un-see Margot Robbie lying next to him in their bed. Which she knew was ridiculous, as her ex wasn't even close to being in Barbie's league. The home-wrecking paralegal was more likely to be a mousy girl who shrank into the crowd. A younger version of Heather. Which would make her easy prey for a confident lawyer with slightly crooked teeth and thinning hair.

Refusing to further wallow in self-pity, she decided to pick up a coffee from the shop near the bank, but with skimmed milk, and skip the pastry, thus removing a bundle of calories from her morning. But, with a stop on the way to work, she needed to leave sooner, and Heather quickly moved to the bedroom closet. For step two of her new life, the idea of getting in shape consumed her. There was a gym in amongst the shops at Camana Bay, not far from the cinema, so with the confidence that came with something she didn't have to actually do until later, Heather told herself she'd become a member after work. Grabbing leggings, a tank top, and her trainers, she stuffed them into a shopping bag.

From the kitchen, she heard Tea Leaf meow several times, which was odd. He rarely fussed unless he was asking for attention or food, both of which he'd do in her presence. Of course, she realised, with her being absent all day, it was possible her cat sat in the window from eight until five, meowing at everything that moved across the ironshore between the house and the rocky coastline. But she doubted it.

"What's all the noise about, Tea?" she asked, carrying her handbag and gym gear into the living room.

Her cat had stopped making any noise, and Heather looked over to his food dish, but he wasn't there.

"Tea? Where are you, sweetie? Mummy has to go to work now."

Walking into the kitchen, she looked around the island, but the cat was nowhere to be seen.

"Tea Leaf?" she called. "Where are you, love?"

From the coat room off the kitchen, leading to the side entrance to the house, Heather heard the muted cries from the cat. She walked over and opened the door to the little coat room, and stared in surprise at the pet carrier sitting on the bench. From behind the mesh top, Tea Leaf looked up forlornly and meowed in displeasure.

"How on earth did you get in there?" Heather said, completely perplexed.

And then a hand reached around her neck, and she felt a blade against her throat.

2

NEVER TRUST THE CAT

My body had no idea what time of day it was. I probably should have taken a day off between arriving back from Norway and going to work, but it didn't seem like a problem when I booked the flights. It was simply logistics. Times on a website. Oslo to Frankfurt, then Miami, and finally George Town Grand Cayman. Three flights encompassing nineteen hours of travel, arriving yesterday evening. I was completely knackered and crashed out until 3:00am when I was wide awake, as it was nine in the morning where I'd just come from.

We had just come from. I hadn't seen my parents in several years, so I decided to take my temporary foster kid, Jazzy, along. Temporary was a loose term we used to get around foster family rules about age and other *dritt*. It seemed I was stuck with the kid, and she was stuck with me. Jazzy had never been off the island, and I figured she'd be something my parents could fuss and talk about, so I wouldn't have to answer a million questions.

"More coffee," I said to my police partner, and checked my watch.

It was still only ten in the morning, with nine hours left on our shift. We worked four-day, twelve-hour shifts, two of which would be daytime, and two at night. I currently wished I'd started back with a night shift.

"Fancy style, or cheap?" he asked in his island sing-song accent.

"Closest," I replied, and he laughed.

He'd been laughing all morning at me. Jacob found most things in life either interesting or amusing. You couldn't find two more opposite personalities to put together in a police car. He's a really nice, fun guy, who people like. I'm less so.

"Vivo Cafe up ahead, or wait another minute and stop at Reg and AJ's dock?" Jacob offered.

I was about to repeat my last answer when I thought it over a little more. The trip had cost a small fortune and while I had backup funds I could call on if needed, my plan was to never do so. Fortunately, my little shack cost me nothing, but paying for two of us to live on one of the most expensive islands in the world with nothing more than a police salary meant making compromises.

"AJ's," I decided.

My friends AJ Bailey and Reg Moore ran their dive boat operations next door to the larger West Bay public dock. Their coffee pot was usually in constant use until lunchtime.

"Sure ting," Jacob replied, continuing on North West Point Road.

We were making our usual patrol around West Bay, the direction and exact route decided by coin tosses before we left the station. It kept our presence in any neighbourhood somewhat random and unpredictable, as we never knew ourselves until the beginning of our shift.

The other challenge I had, apart from jet lag, was the lack of big cases. Work life had become boring over the past few months, and while I didn't wish harm to come to anyone – well, almost anyone – I was ready for a case on which Detective Whittaker would let me be involved. He was the lead detective for the Royal Cayman Islands Police Service, and my mentor. Although I'd stretched our relationship pretty thin on occasion. I'd been in the doghouse for a few months now, so I hoped he'd let me be involved when a big case came up. Unfortunately, Grand Cayman was an incredibly safe place to live or visit, so no one had done anything really awful lately.

"Hey, mind if we stop for a minute?" Jacob asked.

Up ahead, an ambulance sat outside a newer oceanfront home, its lights on to make sure traffic took care while driving by. I didn't see a police car present and nothing had been called over our radio.

"Yes," I replied.

I didn't see any point in stopping if we weren't being called to a scene. It was probably a heart attack, or someone had tripped on the jagged ironshore which lined the coastline on this part of the island. Jacob slowed the car as we approached.

"Dat's my cousin, I tink," he said.

"Your cousin lives here?" I asked.

Jacob had about a million cousins, aunts, and uncles. The Tibbetts family were some of the early settlers, so his family tree was more like a forest. But we'd driven by this house most days for ages, yet he'd never mentioned his cousin lived there.

"No, no," he replied. "I don't know who live dere, but my cousin, she drives da ambulance."

That made more sense. I'd met her before, although I couldn't recall her name.

"She's working," I pointed out for purely selfish reasons. "Coffee."

"I'll only be a minute," he countered, parking behind the ambulance.

Jacob got out, and for a moment I considered switching to the driving seat and leaving him there while I went to get my caffeine fix, but decided a short delay probably wasn't the worst thing in the world. Anything which made the day pass faster was welcome. I got out and followed Jacob.

The home was nice, but not ostentatious, which was surprising based on the location. Waterfront land on the island had skyrocketed over the past few years, so rarely did anyone put a regular home on a lot which cost the price of a New York apartment.

Unless they'd owned that lot for a while, which I guessed was the case.

We entered through the front door into a hallway leading to an open living area with the kitchen on the right. I noticed a woman sitting on a sofa with a handkerchief held to her face. She didn't look surprised to see two police constables walking into the house.

"Maya, what happenin', girl?" Jacob said, keeping his voice quiet despite his enthusiastic greeting.

"Jacob, what ya doin' here, now? We called da coroner," his cousin replied.

I remembered her name once I heard it again. I also recalled her being a bubbly, happy woman, but her demeanour was far more subdued this morning. Which was understandable. Beyond the kitchen island lay the body of a woman who I guessed to be 40ish. It appeared she'd dressed for work, but hadn't made it out the door that morning. I took a few steps closer.

"We just drivin' by," Jacob said. "Saw da ambulance and came in to say hi."

"Looking for a cat?" Maya's partner said, and I looked his way.

The man was standing beyond the body, holding the pet in his arms.

"I have a kid and an iguana," I replied. "So, no."

I returned my attention to the body. A pool of blood encircled her head as she stared lifelessly up at the ceiling. By the streaked stains on the edge of the granite island top, it appeared she'd hit it with the back of her head as she'd fallen to the floor. A bowl lay tipped over nearby, and water had spread across the tiles. It looked like she'd slipped on the wet floor and crashed into the island. The innocent-looking cat in the male EMT's arms may well have caused the death of its owner. Maybe it didn't like the food she'd given it. At my feet was a mat with a silly paw print design and a barely touched dish of cat food. Next to it was an empty space where the water bowl should have been.

"Tough way to go out," the man said.

I nodded and looked up at him. He was about my height,

skinny, with brown hair and glasses. I think I remembered him from before as well, and I presumed he and Maya usually worked together. His name badge read Rowan. He was holding the cat like he'd be the one taking it home.

"Who is the lady in the living room?" I asked.

"House cleaner," he replied, and I noted a northern English accent. "She found the body when she let herself in to do her weekly cleaning."

Jacob was still chatting quietly with Maya. He didn't have a stomach for dead bodies and blood, so I knew he was deliberately staying at the opposite end of the kitchen island. They were chattering away about family and kids and whatever else people who like talking go on about. But I was overdue for my coffee. I took one more look at the poor woman on the floor and noticed two streaks of water leading from the main pool in the direction of her feet. I wouldn't have noticed if one of her legs hadn't been bent at the knee.

"Did you take pictures?" I asked Rowan.

"Coroner will do all that," he replied, petting the cat, who appeared to be tolerating the attention, although slightly unsettled.

Maybe it was starting to feel bad about killing its owner.

"The water is evaporating. You should take a few pictures in case he takes a while to get here."

"Probably a good idea," he agreed, and held out the cat.

"We have to leave," I said, as I had no interest in getting covered in cat hair, and I wanted my coffee now.

Besides, I couldn't be sure the cat was done with its killing spree.

"Jacob. We need to go," I said, nodding towards the front door.

"Okay, okay," he replied, shaking his head at his cousin. "You remember my partner, Nora?"

"I do," Maya said. "Hi."

"Nice to see you again," I replied politely. "Make sure one of you takes pictures before the water disappears," I added, not convinced Rowan would relinquish the killer cat in favour of snapping photographs.

Jacob gave Maya a quick hug, and we walked outside. The day was already heating up and the humidity hit me like a smothering blanket as we walked out of the cool, air-conditioned house. The contrasting weather from my homeland was jarring.

"Dat's a sad deal, right dere," Jacob commented as we got into the car.

"Never trust a cat," I replied.

Jacob laughed. "I tink da counter had more to do wit da head wound."

"Once the cat set the water trap," I pointed out.

He looked over at me, but I kept my eyes straight ahead. Jacob was too easy to mess with. It was barely worthwhile, but it passed the time.

"You kiddin', right?"

"It's no joke, Jacob."

"What you mean?" he said, pulling away from the house.

"I mean, if you don't get me coffee soon, there'll be another death in West Bay this morning."

Jacob laughed, but he drove a little faster than usual to Reg and AJ's dock.

3

A SCAM AND A BISCUIT

I leaned against the side of the pale blue hut Reg and AJ used as their office, storeroom, and loo. To call it an office was making it sound far larger and more grandiose than the little building deserved. There wasn't even room for a chair inside, but it worked for checking in their divers for the day's outings. AJ was out for the morning trip, as were Reg's three dive boats. He had crews running his boats and spent most days taking care of bookings and business at the 'office'. I liked Reg. He was a big bloke with broad shoulders and a mop of unruly salt and pepper hair which matched his bushy beard. If he donned a cable-knit sweater and yellow waterproof bib pants, he'd look like a Norwegian fisherman, fresh off the boat after a hard day on the frozen seas. But we were in the Cayman Islands, so he wore shorts and a Pearl Divers T-shirt advertising the name of his dive op.

One of the things I liked most about Reg was his desire to avoid needless chatter. I could drop by, enjoy a coffee with him for ten minutes, and we'd exchange a dozen words the whole time. But Jacob wasn't wired that way. So this morning, Reg had to converse for ten minutes about the weather, when his wife, Pearl, would be playing her music at the local pub again, and a bunch of other things, while I stood outside and tuned them out.

I looked over at West Bay Public Dock, which was quiet as all the dive boats were scattered over the reefs off Seven Mile Beach for their morning excursions. An old man sat in the shade of a casuarina tree with a pile of coconuts at his feet, ready to cut them open for the tourists stepping off the tour boats. It was a beautiful, peaceful morning on the island.

"We should go," I said to Jacob again, and he wrapped up a story he was telling Reg about a family member who'd done something at a school sports event. Or maybe it was a spelling competition thing.

I refilled my coffee from the pot inside the hut and nodded to Reg. "*Takk.*"

"Any time," he replied, grinning behind his thick beard.

"Take care now, Reg," Jacob told him as I shoved him towards our car. "Tell your lovely wife I said hi."

We'd just got in and Jacob started the engine when his mobile rang. He answered, and I knew it was a local friend or family member as he spoke in his full island accent. Like most Caymanians, he tones it down when dealing with people who weren't raised on the island, which is good, as I struggle to understand their dialect. My English is pretty good, but I find their local sayings and contractions confusing. Some days, I have taught Jacob a word in Norwegian and he's taught me a local saying, but I don't think either of us would be fluent in the other's tongue anytime soon.

I caught bits and pieces from his side of the conversation, and whatever they were talking about sounded serious. Jacob didn't fret over much, but he was clearly aggravated by this call. After a few minutes, he finished and hung up.

"We gotta go see my grandma," he said, pulling the car up to North West Point Road. "Some guy done ripped her off."

"Ripped her off how?"

"Wit some kinda internet email scam ting," he said, turning right and then right again to head south on West Bay Road.

"We have a cybercrimes unit," I pointed out. "I'm not sure we can do much to help her."

Jacob didn't slow and even put the lights on.

"You know computer stuff pretty good," he countered. "We at least gotta take a look and see what happened."

He was determined and at the very least I figured his grandmother would be comforted by Jacob making a point of going by, but I doubted even the cybercrimes team could help. Most of these things were from hackers and scam artists in foreign countries where we had no chance of doing anything about them.

"Okay," was all I replied, and he sped on, turning left down a narrow lane called Genevieve Bodden Drive.

His grandmother's house was a small traditional cottage painted pale white with green accents and a metal roof. The front porch sat in shade under the extended roof, with carved posts and a decorative wooden balustrade railing. The door opened before we'd walked up the steps, and an older dark-skinned lady appeared.

"Grandma, we gonna try our best to sort dis out now," Jacob said, leaping onto the porch and hugging the woman.

She was a good twenty centimetres shorter than her grandson, so she disappeared from view for a moment in his embrace.

"Show us what happened," he said, releasing her and shepherding the woman into her own home. "Dis is my partner, Nora," he added, waving a hand at me as I followed them inside.

"Hello Mrs Tibbetts."

"I ain't been a Tibbetts for forty-five years, dear. I married a Rivers."

I thought I remembered Jacob telling me once that one of his grandfathers had passed away, so I didn't say anything more. Another good reason for not talking much was the reduction in incidents of saying the wrong thing. I did enough of that already.

The inside was as clean and tidy as the outside, with simple furnishings and lots of family pictures on the walls and shelves. She led us into a small dining room off the kitchen and pointed to an ancient-looking laptop on the table.

"Dats da email message I got, right dere," she said, stopping and staring at me. Her face broke into a smile. "Da boy say you from anudder country," she said, looking me up and down. "Where dat now?"

"Norway," I replied.

"Oh, my husband bin dere," she said, as though Scandinavian countries were a natural destination for any Caymanian. "Merchant navy," she added as an explanation, which made more sense.

"How you end up here?" she asked.

"A boat," I replied.

Grandma frowned at me until I grinned, and then she waved her hand and burst out laughing. Her entire face lit up when she did, and I could see where Jacob got it from. I hoped I could give her a moment of levity, as I was pretty certain we wouldn't be able to do much for her regarding her scammer problem.

"Nora's good wit da computers, Grandma," Jacob said, and then busied himself with her laptop so he couldn't see the glare I gave him.

"I got fresh mango juice in da fridge," Grandma said, and beetled off to fix us drinks, whether we wanted them or not.

Unless they were growing mangos containing caffeine these days, it wasn't what I needed, but I rarely turned away fresh fruit juice.

"Looka here, Nora," Jacob said, beckoning me over, and I reluctantly pulled up a chair alongside him.

"Dis guy sent an email sayin' her bank security been compromised and she need to reply to da email so dey can call her." Jacob turned in his chair. "Dey call you, Grandma?"

"Yes. I do what dey tell me to do," she called back from the kitchen where I could hear glasses clinking and the fridge door opening and closing. "He call me right quick yesterday afternoon after I reply to dat email."

"What dey say on da phone?"

"He nice fella and all," she replied, walking back in with glasses of mango juice. "He said he gonna help me get it sorted before anyting bad happen."

"Den what?" Jacob asked.

"Den I guess *he gone done* someting bad."

"How'd he get into your account?" Jacob asked.

"He did someting so he on my computer too, and we log into da bank," she said, setting the drinks down. "I just sittin' dere, and he click around some, den say it's all good now, and dat's it."

"Then when you checked later," I interjected, keen to get on with this. "Some of your money was gone."

The old lady nodded. "Yeah. Dis morning. Bank say I transfer my own money away using someting I ain't never heard of. But I didn't do nuttin of da sort. Dat man musta done it."

"How come he didn't take it all?" Jacob asked, looking at me.

"Because it would flag a call or another security check," I replied. "He probably made a series of Venmo or PayPal payments for a few thousand each time. He would have done it afterwards. All he did while screen sharing was get her login and password and check the balance."

"Dat's right," grandma confirmed. "Da bank say dere eight of dem. Took twenty tousand dollars from me."

Jacob jumped up and put his arm around his grandmother. "Don't worry, now. We gonna get dis sorted out for you, ain't we, Nora?"

I opened my mouth to explain how I doubted we would, but Jacob didn't give me time.

"Got a biscuit or two, Grandma?" he asked, sitting back down.

Once she'd wandered off to the kitchen, he turned to me. "I don't know what we can do, Nora, but we gotta try someting. Twenty tousand dollars is a lot of money to her."

"It's a lot of money to most people," I muttered. "But I don't know how to track this guy down. He's probably in Eastern Europe or Asia."

"I know we can send it in to da cybercrimes guys, but dey

always buried," Jacob whispered. "It'll go to da bottom of deir list and get forgotten."

I thought for a moment. "Mrs Rivers?" I called out. "Can you show me your phone?"

Grandma reappeared with a tin of digestive biscuits and placed them on the table, then pulled her smartphone from her pocket. It was an older iPhone, but still newer than the model I'd reluctantly succumbed to using. She unlocked the screen and handed it to me. I quickly found the incoming call and noted down the number and time of day. The number was a long string of digits.

"Dat ain't no local number," Jacob said as he watched me write in my pocket notebook. "Don't even look like any phone number I ever seen."

"It's a VoIP call," I replied.

"A what now?" he asked.

"Voice over internet protocol," I explained. "He called from a computer."

"So we can trace dat back to a... what do you call it?"

"IP address," I filled in for him. "But no. If he's smart, he would have originated from a private VPN and then bounced it off several IP addresses."

Jacob and Grandma looked at each other, then back at me.

"We can't trace it," I said, unwilling to further explain a procedure I wasn't altogether sure of myself. "Did the man have an accent?" I asked in another attempt to move things along.

"He did, but I don't much know what kind," Grandma replied.

"Was it Caymanian?" I asked.

She shook her head. "No, definitely wasn't local. Didn't sound nuttin' like you, neither."

I finished my bite of digestive, which made me crave more coffee.

"Hispanic?" I asked, almost certain he wouldn't have been.

She shook her head again. "More like da man who work in da post office."

I looked at Jacob. I couldn't remember the last time I'd been to the post office.

"Dat nice fella who bin dere for a few years now?" Jacob asked.

"I reckon so," she replied, and I waited for Jacob to explain.

"He's from England. But his family's from India, I tink."

That wasn't good news. We had zero chance of tracing anyone down in India.

"We have a cybercrimes unit who specialise in this sort of thing," I said, hoping to steer things that way before Jacob over-promised her the moon. "They may already be after this guy. I doubt you're his first victim. The bank should also have reported him once you told them what happened."

"Can't be too many people on da island goin' round doin' tings like dis," Grandma responded.

I'm sure she felt naïve and embarrassed, and I felt awful for her. These *drittsekk* were good at what they did. They preyed on the elderly who were more likely to believe their lies and trust someone who appeared helpful.

"I doubt he's on the island, Mrs Rivers. Most of these people are in countries we have no jurisdiction in or ability to do much about."

"No, da man 'ere on da island," Grandma replied. "He say what a nice day it be."

"He'd be right 340 days out of 365, Mrs Rivers. That just means he looked up the weather on the internet."

Grandma stared at me, her brow furrowed. "But I heard da ting."

By Jacob's expression, I could tell he was as perplexed as me.

"Heard what?" he asked her.

"Da cruise ship," she replied, as though the answer was obvious.

"How do ya hear a cruise ship, Grandma?" Jacob questioned.

"Da horn dey honk when da people s'pposed to come back. I hear it while we talkin'."

"Okay," I said.

But I was still sceptical. Cruise ships weren't the only things making honking noises in the world. I'm sure the streets of Delhi were filled with the sounds of honking horns.

4

JOHN LENNON'S RABBIT

We left with Grandma's laptop, because Jacob insisted. Sergeant Redburn, our immediate boss at West Bay station, gave us permission to visit the cybercrimes unit in George Town, so I spent most of the drive answering a million questions from my partner about internet scams. I wasn't an expert, but I'd learnt a thing or two during the two times I'd spent on the run in the Caribbean. YouTube could provide an impressive education on almost anything.

I called a lady named Eileen, as she was the only person I knew in the technology divisions of the Royal Cayman Islands Police Service, and it gave me an excuse to stop answering Jacob's questions. She was with the Technical Support Unit, which wasn't cybercrimes, but a place to start.

"TSU, Eileen, how can I help you?" she answered through the car's hands-free speaker.

"This is Constable Sommer."

"Okay. How can I help you?"

I might know her, but apparently it didn't mean she remembered me.

"You were really helpful to Detective Whittaker and me on a case last year, so I hoped you could advise us on a new case."

"Okay. I'll try."

"It involves internet fraud, so I'm guessing it falls under cyber-crimes. Who should I speak to in the unit?"

"Hold on and I'll transfer you."

"No, wait a moment," I quickly stopped her. "This case involves the family member of my partner, so I was hoping you'd recommend someone we can speak with so this doesn't get lost."

There was a pause on the line, and I waited.

"I know they're swamped," Eileen finally replied. "So I don't know how quickly they can get to anything new, but ask for Luke. He's... umm, let's say quirky. But he'll be straight with you on what can be done or not done."

"Thanks. I'll ask for him."

"Good luck," Eileen said, and I heard a click as she transferred the call.

"Cybercrimes," a female voice answered.

"Luke please."

"Who's calling?"

"Constables Sommer and Tibbetts."

"Does he know what this is regarding?"

"A cybercrimes case," I replied.

"Okay. But specifically?" she asked. "Have you spoken with Luke before?"

I wondered if this guy was a police employee or a mob boss.

"How can Luke talk to anyone if he only talks to people he's spoken to before?" I asked, and Jacob smacked me on the arm.

"He's busy at the moment," she replied snarkily. "I'll have him call you."

"Eileen told us we have to talk to Luke," I got in before she hung up.

The line didn't go dead.

"Wait a minute."

We sat on hold while Jacob found a parking spot at central station.

"Why you gotta antagonise da woman?" he hissed at me.

"Because she made no sense…" I rebutted until a voice came on the line.

"Who's this?" an irritated Englishmen asked in an accent I thought was from Birmingham.

"Constables Sommer and Tibbetts."

"What do you want?" he snapped.

"Someone scammed my partner's grandmother with an email and a phone call and we're coming to see you about it. We're at central now."

"I don't do that stuff. Submit it into the system like anyone else."

"You're cybercrimes, aren't you?" I asked, getting instantly pissed off with the bloke.

"Not that kind."

"And what kind is dis?" Jacob asked, sounding equally annoyed.

"The petty kind which I don't deal with."

"It ain't petty to my grandma, mister!" Jacob blasted back, and for once it was *me* who reached out to calm *him* down.

"Look, we were told to talk to you because supposedly you're the best," I said, expecting the man to hang up at any moment. "But if you don't think you can figure this out, that's fine. We'll have one of the others do it and they can prove you're not the best."

I heard a weird chuckling sort of noise over the line. Jacob and I looked at each other, unsure what the noise meant. It was possible Luke was amused, or he could be choking on a peanut.

"That's a bunch of BS, but I like your style," he said, so I guessed he was amused. "You're the blonde from Sweden, right? You were the one in the livestreaming kidnap mess."

"Norway," I corrected him.

"You're pretty tasty," he said, and he was lucky he wasn't

standing in front of me. I'd have broken his nose. "I'll give you five minutes."

He hung up.

"*Drittsekk*," I muttered.

"Nora," Jacob said, grabbing the laptop and racing out of the car to keep up with me. "He can help us. Please wait until he's found my grandma's money before you kill da guy."

"No promises," I replied, flinging the front door to the station open, which almost hit Detective Whittaker, who happened to be about to leave the building.

"Woah," he said, startled. "What's the big hurry, constables?"

"Sorry, sir," I replied, stepping out of his way. "We're going to cybercrimes. They gave us a small window of time."

"You mean *he* gave you a small window of time," Whittaker replied, with a grin on his face.

"Luke," I said, to confirm we were talking about the same person.

Whittaker smiled. "You better not keep his holiness waiting."

I started to walk away, but paused when the detective spoke again.

"What case is this?"

"My grandma, sir," Jacob offered. "Beatrice Rivers. She bin scammed by some guy."

Whittaker nodded. "That's too bad. I'm sorry to hear it. I know your grandma from church. Lovely lady."

"Tank you, sir," Jacob replied.

"Let me know if I can be of any help," Whittaker said, and turned to me. "Probably time to get you on another case, Constable Sommer."

"I'm ready, sir," I replied, pleased to hear I was out of the doghouse. Again.

The detective continued out the door, so we hurried across the reception and down a few hallways to the cybercrimes unit. When we entered the office, I expected to see banks of supercomputers and servers, but it was nothing like that. The room was divided into four cubicles and each one that I could see had a pair of monitors on a desk which looked like any other standard office in the building. A woman sat at the closest one with earbuds in, and if she knew we'd entered, she chose to ignore us. I stepped forward and plucked an earbud out of one side.

"Where's Luke?"

The woman jumped in her seat and scowled at me, pointing to the only office off the main room. We walked over and entered. The place looked like fifty computers had exploded their componentry, with parts landing on any available surface.

"Got the computer?" Luke's voice came from behind a bank of three monitors.

"Ja," I replied, and Jacob held out the laptop.

A hand reached up and snatched it from him. I walked to the side of the desk to see this bloke. It was rare to meet someone who was more keen to avoid human interaction than me. Luke was short, skinny, and incredibly pale. I don't know how someone could live on a tropical island and remain so pasty looking. He had a curly mop of ginger hair, freckles, and round glasses like the guy from the Beatles used to wear. The one who was shot for no good reason.

I've always wondered why nutjobs shoot innocent people. There's plenty of *drittsekker* around whose absence would better the world. *Why not take them out?* Not that I support shooting anyone, but if you must, at least pick someone who their own mother might give you a slap on the back for eliminating. Two stones with one bird, as I'm pretty sure the saying goes. Anyway, Luke wore those glasses, but I doubted he could write songs, and probably didn't want to get shot. Although if he kept being rude, he might get punched by a girl.

"Password?" he demanded, glaring at me.

Jacob gave him his grandma's simple password, which Luke scoffed at as he typed it in. The offending email was still open on the screen, and Luke's fingers clattered angrily on his keyboard, followed by a swirling movement of his mouse, which looked more like a small, futuristic car than any computer mouse I'd ever seen.

He paused and looked up at me. "Number the call came from?"

I tore out the page from my notebook and handed it to him.

"VoIP call," he said, and tossed the paper aside.

"Obviously," I responded, and he glared at me again.

"Okay, Miss Not From Sweden, then you know it'll be untraceable."

"Not entirely," I replied.

"Of course not," he countered, growing more annoyed. "But finding the first location it was routed through does nothing to track the origination, does it?"

He pushed his glasses up his nose as though the gesture put an exclamation point on his statement. Which happened to be true. His statement, not the gesture. I watched him tap, click, and scroll and waited for his next words of enlightenment.

"I was wondering, "Jacob whispered to me. "Why do people always think you're from Sweden?"

"They have better PR," I replied.

After another thirty seconds, Luke slapped the laptop closed and held it aloft for someone to take it from him. I obliged.

"Well?"

"I've added Granny's case to the others. We're working on it, but I doubt we'll get to it until after this bank fraud case."

"Isn't this a bank fraud case?" I asked, to which I received yet another impatient glare.

"No, this is a *Granny clicked on an obvious scam email and paid the price* case. The one we're swamped with is a ransomware extortionist from Brazil who's hacked into a major financial house's system. Not the same."

"So you don't know how to figure this out?" I challenged.

"That's not what I said, and your five minutes are up."

"We haven't bin 'ere five minutes," Jacob complained.

"Clock started when you entered the department and ends

when you leave through the door. Which you're about to do. We'll get to it when we can."

"Not if we solve it first," I rebutted, and headed out of his office.

I heard Luke scoff from behind his kingdom of monitors. "In your dreams, blondie."

I resisted the urge to turn around and launch the nearest piece of dead computer at him, and kept walking.

"We'll see," I called over my shoulder.

A few minutes later, I directed Jacob to drive out of George Town on South Church Street. I had no doubt that Luke, the self-proclaimed computer genius, knew far more about tracking down hackers and online scammers than I did, but I had an ace in my shoe.

A couple of kilometres out of town, I pointed to the small apartment complex I remembered visiting before, and Jacob pulled into the gravel car park. We trotted up the wooden steps to the second floor and banged on the first door we came to. There was no response. I banged again even harder, then peeked through the front window, finding a tiny gap at the edge of the blinds. The person I was looking for sat at a desk with headphones on.

"Dey in dere?" Jacob asked, and I nodded, taking out a small, soft case from my back pocket.

"No, no, no!" Jacob hissed at me. "You can't do dat now!"

Using two of the lock picks in the keyhole, I quickly undid the mechanism and eased the door open. A security chain stopped it opening all the way. While Jacob continued muttering and fretting behind me, I slipped my long, slender fingers around the door and unhooked the chain.

The door swinging open threw a burst of light sunlight into the room, and the woman at the desk jumped up, the cord pulling the headphones from her head. I smiled.

"Hello, Rabbit," I greeted her. "I need your help with something."

5

KNOCKING BEFORE BREAKING AND ENTERING

"Did you just break in?" Rabbit asked, her mouth agape.

"You didn't hear us knocking," I pointed out.

Rabbit, whose real name was Rebecca Thompson, stood barely 150 centimetres tall with a frizzy, red-tinted afro, dented where her headphones had rested. Her black T-shirt had Nirvana written across her chest and a goofy smiling face drawing. It was probably something hip and cool, but I had no idea.

She looked at the door, which Jacob closed to keep the air conditioning contained, then back at me.

"It was locked."

"We're the police," I responded. "We're allowed to do it."

"Not without cause or a warrant," Rabbit protested.

"That's true," Jacob muttered, and I glared at him.

"It's good we're here then, as you should tell the police," I joked.

She didn't look impressed. In all honesty, if I were in her shoes, I wouldn't be either, but I didn't have time to mess about. The sergeant would be getting impatient for us to continue our West Bay patrol soon.

"The door isn't important, Rabbit. I have a problem for you."

"I have enough problems, thank you," she replied.

I recalled from our earlier dealings that her accent was slight. She'd been educated at a university in America and returned to the island with a degree in computer wizardry. Or whatever they called it. She was a twenty-four-year-old with the face of a fifteen-year-old and the brain of a genius.

"Take a look at this," I urged and gesticulated for Jacob to hand over the laptop.

He set it down on a small open space on her desk, lifted the lid and typed in Grandma's password. Rabbit gave the door one more glance as if to say she wasn't forgetting about it, then studied the email.

"Looks like a pretty standard email scam," she commented. "I hope whoever received this didn't reply."

"She replied," I said. "And he called. Now she's twenty K poorer."

Rabbit shook her head. "Who is Beatrice Rivers?"

"My grandma," Jacob replied.

"This is my partner, Jacob," I said, realising I hadn't introduced him.

I'd forgotten I'd been with Detective Whittaker when I'd first met Rabbit. She nodded to Jacob.

"Sorry about your grandma, but not sure what you want from me."

"We need to figure out who did dis," Jacob said. "I gotta get her dat money back."

Rabbit shook her head again. "Ain't much chance of that," she began, but I cut her off.

"We have a challenge for you."

"What do you mean?" Rabbit asked, and Jacob's face looked just as quizzical.

"Get the money back and you get twenty-five percent."

"What?" Jacob blurted.

"And," I continued, ignoring my partner. "I assume you know Luke in the cybercrimes unit?"

Rabbit rolled her eyes. "Sure. I know him."

I grinned. "He says he's better than you."

Rabbit raised one eyebrow. "I bet he did."

"That true?" I asked.

The corner of the young woman's mouth twitched. "Nope."

"Then here's your chance to prove it," I told her. "It's next up on his agenda. You help us catch this guy first, and you get twenty-five percent. He beats you to it, then he gets bragging rights."

"Why should I care what he does or thinks?" Rabbit asked nonchalantly. "Besides, you have no way of catching this guy. He'll be in China or Russia."

"What if I told you he's on the island?" I teased.

"Then I'd say he bounced it off a local number, and he's still in China or Russia."

"He used VoIP," I mentioned.

Rabbit shrugged her shoulders. "Then you have no idea where the call originated, and no way to find out."

"Except we know he's here on the island," I reiterated.

"How could you know that?" Rabbit asked, tilting her head to one side, which made her mass of hair bounce.

"Because he knew things about the island and Jacob's grandma heard the cruise ship horn in the background."

"Hmm," Rabbit murmured, thinking for a moment. "Could have been any horn honking, anywhere," she countered.

"Except his grandma heard it at exactly the same time out of her window," I rebutted.

Jacob opened his mouth, undoubtedly ready to dispute the point, but my glare kept him quiet. We both knew Grandma had no way of hearing a cruise ship horn on the south side of George Town, all the way from West Bay, but Rabbit didn't know where Grandma lived.

She considered the new information for a moment. "Okay. I'm kinda slammed with a few projects right now, so no promises, but I'll look into it. Twenty-five percent though, right? And the dude took twenty K?"

"Twenty K," I confirmed.

Rabbit forwarded the email to her computer, and I used the old pencil over the imprint method to give her the VoIP number off the page below the one I'd given Luke. I also took a picture of it this time with my phone so I wouldn't have that problem again. Once we reached the car, Jacob finally spoke up.

"I don't know we can give her twenty-five percent of what she get back, Nora. We shoulda asked Grandma first."

"How much is she getting if no one tries to track the *drittsekk* down?"

"I get dat," he replied, pulling out of the car park onto South Church Street. "Just da whole ting got me upset, man. It ain't right dis guy takin' her money like dat."

I felt the same way, and I'd like to make whoever it was pay, but I doubted we'd ever find them. I'd sold Rabbit on the fact the guy was here in Grand Cayman, but I also doubted that was true. Lying didn't feel right, but I figured it wouldn't take her long to discover whether or not the thread was digitally trackable, and then we'd know if we had a chance.

"We'll see if Rabbit gets anywhere," I said, because it felt like I should say something.

Jacob stayed quiet until we were back on patrol in West Bay. I could tell something was still on his mind, but I was happy to carry on in silence, so I wasn't about to ask. He knew that about me, so if it was important enough to him, he'd eventually bring it up. Which he did. Or at least started talking.

"When do you think you'll get into the training program?"

That wasn't what I was expecting. I'd figured it would have something to do with his grandma, not my indiscretions hampering my career advancement. Which had been delayed another six months, at least, after a hearing about my conduct.

"It's up to them, not me," I replied.

"But you still gonna do dat when you can, right?"

"Ja."

I wasn't sure why this was coming up after his prolonged silence, but maybe he'd worked out whatever had been bugging him and moved on. This could be the next thing he happened to think of to talk about. I wasn't sure, as he went quiet again for another few minutes.

"When does da next training start?" he asked.

"In a few months."

"You get into dat, you tink?"

"It's up to them," I repeated.

"What does Detective Whittaker say about it?"

"Only what you heard him say earlier," I replied, which was true.

I hadn't had cause to speak with the detective in a while. Perhaps even a month or more, which hadn't struck me as odd until Jacob brought it up. I usually crossed paths with Whittaker on a somewhat regular basis, through work, or I'd see him Friday evenings at the Fox and Hare pub when Reg's wife Pearl played. I had done a good job of giving the detective reasons to dissociate himself from me, but I didn't think he was actually doing that.

"Why?" I asked, which I wouldn't normally do, and wasn't sure why I did now.

"Just tinkin' about what's comin' down da road," Jacob replied.

"You could always apply too."

Jacob shook his head. "That ain't for me."

He'd said the same thing in the past, but I still couldn't understand why. Jacob was a smart guy, and he knew so many people on the island, he could converse with someone wherever we went. I thought he'd make an outstanding detective if he chose to do it. His problem was his family. He was a devoted husband and father. Jacob almost never missed his children's games, events, or meetings at their school. He'd trade or move shifts around to make sure he was there.

I was about to quiz him again on why he didn't want to do it, but I stopped myself. Jacob worked hard and focused on the job while on duty, but his priority was his family, and when he finished work, he was all theirs. We were just different. And that notion made me think again. I had someone at home, too. So maybe his problem wasn't really a problem. But of course, my situation was different. I hadn't chosen to have someone I was responsible for. It had just turned out that way. And Jazzy was independent enough to deal with my shitty parenting skills. At least that's what I continually told myself.

The day felt like it had already been thirty-six hours long as I trudged from Conch Point Road through the woods to my shack. Using the torch on my mobile, I picked my way in the darkness until I reached the house where the porch light illuminated the steps and the coastline. In daylight, it was a beautiful view of the ocean from the front of my little home, which I'd missed while we were away. I unlocked the door, walked inside, and turned off the outside light.

"Hey," Jazzy said, looking up from the book she was reading on the sofa.

"Hey. Did you eat?" I asked, unsure whether I had the energy to chew.

She nodded without looking up.

"Edvard come around?" I asked, wondering if the blue iguana who'd adopted us had figured out we were back.

I'd deny it if anyone dared accuse me of caring about the ugly lizard, but I was secretly worried he'd given up on us while we were away.

"Didn't see him," she replied.

Jazzy's focus was on her reading, so I didn't know why I asked the next question. I wouldn't usually, as it constituted small talk, which I was allergic to, but I guess it was some kind of intuition.

"How was school?"

Jazzy's shoulders dropped, and her hand holding the book fell to her lap. She gave me one of those teenager's you're-ruining-my-life glares, which she saved for special occasions.

"There's a letter on the counter for you."

I spotted an envelope by the coffee maker where she'd probably put it, hoping I wouldn't notice until the morning. I could see it was from her school. That meant one of two things. They wanted money for a trip or event, or she was in trouble. I was about to ask her what she had done, as I could tell from her demeanour which of the options the letter was about, but I stopped myself. Six or seven years ago, I would have been pissed off at my parents if they immediately assumed I'd been in trouble, even if we all knew that's what it was. I opened the envelope instead and read the letter. When I finished, I looked over at the kid. She was curled up on the sofa doing her best to make all 45 kilograms of her little body appear innocent.

"Did he deserve it?" I asked.

"Big time," she replied.

"Did he hit you back?"

Jazzy shook her head. "He stayed down. I got him good."

"Okay," I said, trying not to let her see how proud I felt. "I'll take care of it in the morning."

6

GEOGRAPHICALLY INEPT

There was no way this day wouldn't suck. A twelve-hour day shift running into another twelve hours on night shift was going to be brutal. And to kick the whole thing off, I had to drop by Jazzy's school and discuss her punching out some kid.

Sergeant Redburn gave me permission to detour from our patrol to take care of it, so we made a quick loop of West Bay before heading to George Town. With Jazzy riding in the back of the patrol car, much to her amusement. She had all kinds of ideas of how she'd like to be dropped outside her school so it would appear her attendance came straight from a night in jail. While I found her ideas amusing and creative, I settled for parking around the corner and walking in with her. Something told me there was no point throwing petrol on the fire. Marching in with a RCIPS constable still won her a lot of staring and pointing.

The headmaster's secretary made us wait a while before finally being summoned into his office.

"Thank you for coming by Miss Sommer, Miss Holder," Mr Geoffreys greeted us. "Please take a seat."

We sat, and I placed the letter on his large wooden desk.

"Where's the other kid?" I asked.

"He's in class," the man replied. "I'd like to see if we can get to the bottom of Jasmine's behaviour, Miss Sommer. Needless to say, we can't have students resorting to physical altercations in the classroom."

"She told me it was outside the classroom," I responded, wondering why anyone would use the term 'Needless to say' right before they said something they clearly felt the need to say.

"That's true," he said, taken aback that I'd challenge a detail. "I mean on school grounds."

"Where's the teacher?" I asked.

"Miss Parsons isn't in this morning," he replied. "But she doesn't need to be here for this discussion."

"How come?" I asked.

Geoffreys shuffled a few papers on his desk, none of which he looked at, so I guessed they weren't anything to do with Jazzy.

"Because we know what happened, and we're here to discuss how we move forward from here."

"We're not moving anywhere until you present me with the facts and witnesses to what took place."

Geoffreys stared at me, looking bewildered. "This isn't a court of law, Miss Sommers. I'm sure you want to do what's best for Jasmine, so I really think we should stick to discussing next steps."

"Who witnessed what happened?" I pressed on.

Maybe as headmaster, he was used to everybody lying down and taking whatever he deemed appropriate, but I wanted to know the facts first.

"It was right outside the classroom," he replied.

"Okay. So who saw what happened and heard what was said?"

He now looked at Jazzy, no doubt wondering what she'd told me. I didn't want to look her way but hoped she wasn't grinning at him.

"I don't believe there's any doubt Jasmine punched the boy, Miss Sommer."

Now I did turn, and was pleased to see an expression somewhere between concern and innocence on her face. I knew that look. She pulled that *dritt* on me too. But it was good in this instance.

"Jazzy. Did you punch the kid?"

"Yes, I did," she replied.

"Why did you feel the need to do that?" I asked her.

"Miss Sommer," Geoffreys tried interrupting, "Miss Parsons already went through all the…"

"You can cross-examine in a minute," I said, cutting him off. "And Miss Parsons isn't here to present her testimony, so answer the question, Jazzy."

The headmaster grunted something in complaint, but didn't offer a verbal argument.

"He taunted me and called me names," Jazzy said.

"Then you should have told Miss Parsons about it, instead of hitting him, Jasmine." Geoffreys interjected.

"I'm not done," I said firmly, frowning at the man. "What did he say to you, Jazzy?"

"He started by calling me Homeless Holder," Jazzy said. "But he calls me that all the time."

"So what was different about yesterday?" I asked.

Jazzy turned to me. "He started being rude about you."

"I really…" Geoffreys began meekly, but I held up a hand and he stopped.

"What did he say?"

"He said the only person who'd take me in was a Russian rental mother."

"I get that the boy did some name calling," Geoffreys jumped in, summoning more conviction in his voice. "And I apologise to you both for the words he said. That will certainly be addressed with him, but it doesn't justify a physical altercation."

"Will be?" I challenged. "Or has been?"

Geoffreys nervously shuffled papers again. "That's between the young man, his family, and the school, Miss Sommers."

"You just told me he's in class like any other day, but we're in here with you. I hope you have him in geography, as he doesn't know the difference between an authoritarian state dictatorship country occupying the largest land mass of any nation from a truly democratic monarchy in Scandinavia."

"Sweden has a monarchy?" Geoffreys asked. "I'm embarrassed to say I didn't know that."

"Sweden does have a king. As does Norway, which is where I'm from," I replied. "So there's another thing for you to be embarrassed about, Mr Geoffreys."

I turned to Jazzy once again. "Did you give the kid any warning?"

Jazzy nodded. "I told him to shut up, or I was gonna deck him."

"And what was his response?" I asked.

"He said the thing about you."

"We don't use terms like shut up, Jasmine, you know that," Geoffreys said.

"So calling her homeless and insulting her foster parent gets rewarded with class as usual," I responded. "But shut up crosses the line?"

He began to defend his position, but I waved him off.

"Seeing as Parsons isn't here to explain why she didn't establish all the facts before sending Jazzy to be sentenced, I suggest we settle this manner so you and the name-calling kid can spend some time studying world geography together."

Geoffreys' mouth opened and closed a few times like a goldfish, so I continued.

"Jazzy will apologise for hitting the geographically challenged idiot, and he'll apologise for being a little shit. On top of that, Jazzy will agree not to punch him again and report him to a teacher if she's provoked and insulted again. Deal?"

"She shouldn't be hitting anyone," Geoffreys muttered.

"Well, they know what they'll get if they pick on her now, so I doubt she'll have any more problems," I said, stood, and extended my hand.

The headmaster stood and shook my hand.

"We have a deal?" I confirmed.

"Well, I…" he mumbled.

Maybe he thought I was simply leaving, but he'd just shaken my hand.

"You just agreed to the deal. Are you backing out already?"

"No, no," he said, shaking his head. "I'll supervise the apologies myself. Thank you for coming by, Miss Sommer."

"I hope I don't have to come back," I told him and nodded towards the door, letting Jazzy know we were leaving.

"I hope you don't either," I heard Geoffreys saying under his breath as we left.

"Thanks," Jazzy said, once we were outside the hallway in the courtyard. "That was cool."

"I wish the teacher had been there. She needs an arse-kicking, too."

"Miss Parsons isn't so bad," Jazzy replied. "I don't think she really knew what to do."

"Okay," I said, although it didn't seem like the woman had done much to find out what really happened. "Get to class and don't hit anyone."

Jazzy grinned. "I'll try."

I took a few steps away, then stopped and turned around. "Don't forget, you're on your own tonight. I have a double shift."

Jazzy nodded. "I know."

"Make sure you put something out for Edvard."

She nodded again and waved as she strode towards her class. I stood alone for a moment in the courtyard, wondering how I'd ended up responsible for a teenager and an endangered lizard.

We'd barely made it back to West Bay when my phone rang. It wasn't a number stored in my contacts, but that wasn't surprising, as I only saved about a dozen in there.

"Hallo," I answered.

"It's Rabbit."

"Hey. What did you find?"

"You sure this guy's on the island?" she asked.

I felt Jacob's eyes burning into the side of my head, so I put the call through the car's speakers.

"We believe so, yes," I replied.

"Then he's doing a good job bouncing his call through a server in Croatia," Rabbit replied. "That's as far as I could trace."

"So what do you need to do next?" I asked.

"I'm doing it," Rabbit replied.

"Which is?"

"Calling and telling you I could track it as far as Croatia. That's it."

"You're giving up?" I asked, deliberately sounding surprised and disappointed.

At least that was my intention, but I've no idea how I actually sounded to someone else. I'm not very good at pretending anything.

"Call it what you will, but I'm telling you, without more information, no one can track this guy from what you've given me."

"Not even Luke?" I taunted.

Rabbit grunted. "If I can't, I guarantee he can't."

I liked Rabbit. She was confident without being arrogant, which I appreciated.

"Okay. I'll see if we can get you more to work with," I said and hung up.

"How we gonna find out anyting more?" Jacob asked. "All we have is da email and dat number that ain't really a phone number."

An idea hit me, and ignoring Jacob, I turned the car around and returned to West Bay Road.

"Where we going now?" he asked.

"We have another computer geek we'll try," I replied, turning left.

"We do?"

"We do," I said, turning left again on Earnest Jackson Road, which led to a housing estate adjacent to Jackson's Pond.

I parked in the street by a sprawling, modern, single-storey home which fronted a smaller pond. We walked to the front door, and I rang the bell. After a few moments, the door swung open, but nobody greeted us. I walked in, turning left when the hallway met a large living room.

"It'll take me a few minutes to get ready for our date, Miss Sommer," a young man said from across the room.

I smiled. "How are you doing, Robbie?"

A whirring sound came from the motor inside the wheelchair, and a thin, drawn, dark-skinned face beamed back at me.

Robbie Barker's body had failed him, but his mind was razor sharp. He'd helped us on another case, and I'd learnt to respect him as a human as well as a computer wizard. There was no way I'd have his outlook on life if I was in his position. I was pretty sure he was sixteen now, and he had to weigh ten kilos less than Jazzy, who was tiny. He wore grey tracksuit bottoms, as he had done when I'd first met him, and his black sweatshirt had a character from a computer game on it. At least, that's what I guessed it was.

"Better after my jog this morning," he replied, and his smile got wider.

"This is Jacob," I said. "We need your help."

"I'll clear my schedule," Robbie replied. "But it better not be something easy."

I shook my head. "No, this one isn't easy. It's stumped two people already."

"I'm insulted that I'm third on your list, Constable."

"I didn't think it was challenging enough, but turns out it is," I quipped in return.

"In that case, what you got?"

Jacob placed the laptop on Robbie's desk in front of his bank of monitors, and I held out the VoIP number so he could see it.

"Hmm," Robbie muttered. "VoIP call. I bet he bounced it off an overseas server. You know this guy's a few thousand miles from here, right?"

"We think he called from the island," I replied, less inclined to embellish the theory with Robbie.

"He still bounced it through an overseas server somewhere," Robbie countered.

I nodded. "Croatia."

"Hmm. In that case, I'd say that's a dead end. We should focus on the origination of the email. Can you forward it to me so I can look at it on my computer?"

He gave Jacob his email address, and my partner did as requested. Jacob then moved the laptop out of Robbie's way. I watched him stare in amazement as the kid started using his own computer system. With the limited mobility of his fingers, Robbie used a small joystick on the arm of his wheelchair, combined with eye-tracking software to work at an amazing speed. I could barely keep up with what kept opening on any one of his three screens. Occasionally, Robbie would pause and study an IP address or datasheet, then off he'd go again.

After a few minutes, he turned his chair to face me. "Why do you think this guy is on the island?"

"It's Jacob's grandmother who's been scammed. The guy took a bunch of her money. She's sure that in the background she heard the cruise ship horn."

"The cruise ship horn, or *a horn*?" Robbie asked, sounding as dubious as I felt.

"She lived 'ere her whole life," Jacob replied. "I reckon she right about it bein' a cruise ship horn. Question is whether it was 'ere, or some place else."

He made a good point. Even if the guy wasn't in Grand Cayman, perhaps we could narrow our search down to cruise ship ports of call. Which really didn't help much, as we didn't have any jurisdiction away from these shores.

"I'll need some time," Robbie said, and turned his chair around to face his computers. "I have a paper to write first."

"School?" I asked.

"University," he replied.

"You're already at university?"

"Sophomore."

"Cool."

"I want to be like Stephen Hawking," Robbie said, as though everyone could aspire to be a genius.

"I'm sure you'll be just like him."

"I'm halfway there," Robbie replied, and I noticed his fingers tapping on the arm of his wheelchair.

I could also see his grin widening once again.

"*Ikke vær fjols,*" I said, shaking my head.

"I know. But you gotta love me," Robbie replied.

"I might if you figure this out," I teased, and gently squeezed his bony shoulder before we left.

7

IDCS

Back on patrol, the day dragged on. We stopped by and gave Grandma Rivers her laptop back, and Jacob made it sound like we had every law enforcement agency on the planet working to find the *drittsekk* who stole her money. I didn't say anything as I wouldn't be the one who had to deliver her the bad news down the road. I figured Luke, despite his abrasive delivery, was right, so I'd included Rabbit and Robbie to put up a good show for Jacob, so he in turn could feel good about telling his grandma he'd tried. But three clever computer geeks saying it probably wasn't possible hadn't tempered his promises.

One thing I'd learnt over the past few years was that if we wanted to, we could hand out tickets as fast as we could write them. Traffic violations happened all around us, all day long, despite the fact we were driving a black and white police car with lights on the roof. Speeding and rolling stop signs were easy pickings, but unless the people were really being dangerous, I didn't see the point. I preferred catching the serial offenders of what I considered to be the more serious crimes in the inconsiderate douchebag category. Jacob wouldn't say douchebag, as apparently it's a bad word, but I thought it sounded appropriate. He said IDC instead.

Jacob had been slow to come around to my way of thinking on the matter, as our compatriots tended to take the easy pickings, so it had become the norm. But he now embraced the opportunity to point out and pursue IDCs whenever possible. He'd even begun using my opening line, 'Your right-hand indicator doesn't seem to be working', to those who failed to push on the stalk within fingertip reach of their steering wheels. I really enjoyed pulling over those who pushed the stalk *as* they turned the wheel. The ultimate testament to laziness. My explanation was always the same, and usually met with a blank stare. 'Indicating is to show what your vehicle is about to do, not what it is in the process of doing.'

Loud music from a car, golf cart, motorcycle, bicycle, or human walking along the street always grabbed my attention. Motorcycles were especially irritating. They played their music ridiculously loud to hear it over the engine noise and through a helmet, leaving a trail of noise pollution behind them. I liked to point out that the convenience store at the four-way stop on West Bay Road and Church have earbuds for $9.99. Far cheaper than the ticket I just gave them.

The Cayman Islands were a safe place to live or visit, so most crimes were petty crimes. Domestic disturbances, DUIs, bar fights, and opportunistic thefts were the majority of calls we received to either handle or provide support. People died every day of natural causes or illness, just like everywhere else in the world, but reports of dead bodies weren't common. So when dispatch asked for officers near Shorelink Terrace, a neighbourhood street on the east side of town, to attend the scene of an unresponsive adult, we put the lights on and sped that way.

We were only a half mile away and the first to arrive on scene. Initially, I thought we had the wrong house, as everything looked quiet and normal, but dispatch verified the house number and I noticed the gate to the backyard was open. We parked, and I jogged through the gate to a small but neat and tidy, simply landscaped area surrounding a rectangular pool. On the patio next to the water, a man kneeled over a soaking wet, fully clothed woman, giving her CPR.

"How long has she been out of the water?" I asked, rushing over.

"Two, three, maybe five minutes," the man replied in a panic. He had an English accent. "I can't get her breathing again. She's so cold."

I knelt next to him and took over chest compressions while he continued with the mouth-to-mouth portion. By the pallor of her skin and the lifeless stare from her eyes, I knew it was too late, but we had to keep trying. I could hear more sirens, so the EMTs would be here soon. It was up to them to decide once they arrived.

"Are you related to the victim, sir?" I asked.

"No, no," he said as I pumped her chest. "I live next door. Came home from work and happened to look out my bedroom window. I saw Zara face down in her pool."

The in-ground pool had a cover stretched across its surface, held in place by weighted bags around the perimeter. Except for where the woman had plunged in, pulling the thick plastic sheet with her and forming a flooded indent not much longer than her own height.

"She musta tripped and fallen in," Jacob commented, nodding his head towards a brush on an extendable pole, which lay by the edge.

"Zara doesn't swim," the man said, sitting back as Jacob's cousin and another EMT came through the gate.

"Maya," Jacob called out. "Dis lady been pulled from da pool. Not sure how long she bin in dere. Dis fella been given her CPR for a while now."

I continued giving the victim chest compressions while Maya took over from the neighbour. She felt the woman's neck for a pulse, and as soon as she touched her skin, she shook her head.

"I'm sorry. Dere's no point. She bin dead a while. I'm afraid she gone."

I stopped compressions, feeling bad that I'd probably cracked a few ribs of a corpse.

"You sure now?" Jacob asked.

Maya gave him a look which told him not to question her, and he held up both hands.

"Sorry. I know you know what you're doin'."

"I'll get what we'll need from the ambulance," Maya's partner offered, and walked that way.

He was older than Maya and spoke with a regional English accent I couldn't place.

"Where's dat udder guy you usually work wit?" Jacob asked.

"Someone out sick," Maya replied. "Dey put him with anudder wagon down south. I worked wit Jimmy a bunch though. He ain't da happiest sort, but he's good."

I stood and looked at the neighbour. "Your name, sir?"

I realised we'd fallen into small talk around the body of someone he knew.

"Joseph. Joseph Taylor," he replied, unsure what he should do now.

The shock and disbelief were just hitting him.

"Who else lives with the deceased, sir?" I asked.

His hands began shaking, and he clutched them together. I took his arm and led him away from the pool so he didn't have to stand next to the body.

"Zara lived alone since her divorce last year," Joseph replied.

"Does she have family here on the island?"

He nodded. "She was local. Lived here her whole life apart from university abroad."

Behind me, I heard Jacob calling dispatch over the radio, requesting the coroner. We'd have to stay until he arrived, which I hoped wouldn't be long. Handing out IDC tickets was better than hanging out with an unfortunate dead person and a distraught neighbour. Things would only get worse if the family showed up. I wasn't the best deliverer of bad news. In all honesty, I really wasn't good at delivering any news.

"Why was her pool covered?" I asked, wondering what the point of having one would be if she left it covered all summer.

"She didn't swim," Joseph replied. "It's been covered since her husband left. He was the only one who used it."

"Didn't, or couldn't," I asked.

"Zara was scared of the water," he replied. "She never learnt to swim."

I looked over again at the pool and the woman's body. It seemed horribly ironic. Especially in her own backyard.

"We'll need a full statement from you, but you're welcome to go home for now," I told him. "But please don't leave until we've spoken again."

"Okay," Joseph replied, and started towards the back gate.

Which made me think of something. "Mr Taylor," I said, and he stopped. "Was the gate open or closed when you came around?"

He thought for a few moments. "It was pulled to, but wasn't latched."

I nodded. "Thanks."

Joseph left, and I walked to the back door of the house. It was unlocked, and I entered carefully, wishing I'd asked the neighbour whether Zara had any pets. Nothing jumped, barked, or ran my way, so I closed the door behind me and looked around. The door led into the kitchen, which opened on my left into a dining area. Beyond that, towards the front of the house, was the living room. A large leather tote bag sat on the kitchen counter next to a set of car keys. By the sink, a coffee cup and bowl rested in a drying rack.

I walked to a door on the far side of the kitchen, which opened into a double garage. A mid-size car was parked down the middle. Zara clearly didn't leave room for another vehicle. I closed the door and walked through the living room to the front door. It was locked. Hearing the back door open, I turned and saw my partner.

"Coroner on da way," Jacob said, looking at the bag and keys, as I had. "Looks like she was gettin' ready to go somewhere."

I nodded, walking over to join him. "Probably work."

"You tink she bin in dere since dis mornin'?" he asked.

"Did you feel her body temperature?"

Jacob winced. He was squeamish around bodies.

"Her core is cold. And she's been lying in the sun all day."

Jacob stared out the kitchen window as his cousin and her partner prepared a body bag to remove Zara once the coroner had cleared them to do so.

"You tink she went out back to maybe clear someting off da pool cover wit da brush, and fell in?"

"Looks that way."

I exited the house, walking back to the pool, and Jacob followed. Maya introduced us to the guy she was working with today. I think she said his name was John, or Jim. I wasn't really paying attention. Obviously, the woman had fallen in her own pool, but I couldn't help wondering why she hadn't managed to climb out. Swimming didn't have much to do with it when the pool was only four-foot deep according to the lettering near where the cover was pulled in. Although, by the way the cover had partially pulled in, it might not have been enough for her to drop into the pool itself where she would have been able to stand. The idea that Zara had floundered around in no more than ten or fifteen centimetres of water held in the cover, until she'd worn herself out and drowned, wasn't pleasant.

The coroner arrived, and I let Jacob explain what we knew. I'd met the guy a few times before at various crime scenes involving a body. He was a gruff-mannered man in his fifties, with thin grey hair and slight paunch despite his slim build. He was one of those Englishmen who lived in the tropics yet their skin tone remained remarkably pale. Maybe Cybercrimes Luke would look like him when he got older.

"Where's the witness?" the coroner asked, and I remembered he was actually Welsh, not English.

"Next door," I replied. "I told him not to leave until we said."

He grunted in response. "You need to get a written statement."

"I know."

He frowned at me. "Then go get the written statement, Constable Sommer."

"Want to know what we've found first?" I rebutted. "Mr..?"

"Gareth Davies," he replied tersely. "I'm sure your partner can tell me *while you're* getting the written statement."

I shrugged my shoulders and left. I was usually more observant than Jacob, but he sometimes picked up things I missed. Either way, it didn't matter. Zara had tripped and fallen into her own swimming pool, which she never used, and Coroner Davies had the right to conduct his investigation however he saw fit. So I walked next door.

"I need to take your statement now," I told Joseph when he answered the door.

He nodded and let me in. "I was just making a cup of tea," he said as we walked to his kitchen. "Would you like one?"

"Got coffee?" I asked.

"Instant, I'm afraid, but you're welcome to it."

"As long as it has caffeine," I responded, trying not to think about the next shift, which wouldn't even start for several hours.

While Joseph made the drinks, I took out my notebook and thought about questions I still didn't have answers to.

"What time did you leave your house this morning?"

"5:30. I go to the gym before work," he replied.

"So it's still dark?"

"Yes. So I didn't see anything out of the ordinary, but I suppose she could have been in the pool already," he said, pausing what he was doing. "That's an awful thought. Poor Zara, lying in the water all day."

"What's Zara's full name? Is Zara short for something?"

"No. At least not to the best of my knowledge," he replied. "And I believe she's still going by her married surname. Which is Parsons."

I looked up. "Parsons?"

He nodded.

"Is she a schoolteacher?"

"That's correct, yes. Teaches at the secondary school in George Town."

"*Dritt,*" I muttered.

That explained why Jazzy's teacher hadn't shown up today.

8

RESISTANCE AND RESTRAINT

It was dark and our night shift had begun before I could drop by the shack and see Jazzy. By the time I'd make it home in the morning, she'd probably be gone, and I wanted her to hear it from me about her teacher. Even if I wasn't the best deliverer of bad news.

"Thought you had work?" she asked when I walked in the door.

She was reading on the sofa. She'd probably watch TV, given the choice, but I didn't have one and had no plans to get one.

"I do," I replied, and headed for the coffee maker. "Wanted to check on you."

"Check on me for what?" she asked, tipping her head to one side. "Thought I had friends over for a raging party?"

"No."

"Well, you just missed them. We had fun."

I wasn't sure whether her being in a fun, joking mood was a good or bad thing to get the news I was bringing her. I hated to ruin her evening, but in the morning, rumour and bullshit stories would be circulating, and I wanted her to be aware of the truth.

"Your teacher is Zara Parsons, right?" I asked, double checking before I did the ruining.

"Yup. She was out all day today."

"Yeah," I said, hitting start on the coffee maker after getting it ready. "I can tell you why."

Jazzy put her book down when I walked over and sat next to her.

"We found her dead this afternoon."

"What?" she replied, with her jaw hanging open.

"She had an accident at home. I wanted to make sure you knew before school tomorrow."

"An accident? What happened?"

"I can't say, as I don't know that all the family members have been told yet."

"I won't say anything," Jazzy assured me.

And I believed her. But I still didn't want to put either of us in that position, just in case she slipped. Or more likely, someone accused her or me of saying something. This way, we could honestly respond.

"Accident. No one else involved. Nothing sinister," I said. "That's all I can tell you, and all you need to know."

"You don't trust me?" she responded.

Her tone was more interested than accusatory.

"I do trust you, but it would be wrong to say anything more, and this way you don't have to lie if you're asked for details."

"Why would anyone ask me for details?"

"Duh..." I replied.

She nodded. "Yeah, I guess. But most people don't know I live with a copper."

"Probably better they don't."

"Why?"

"Because most people act differently around police."

She thought for a moment. "I suppose. I guess I used to act differently around the police."

"That's because you were stealing things and hiding," I replied with a grin. "I think that's different."

She stuck her tongue out at me.

"You gonna be okay?" I asked.

Jazzy nodded again. "Yeah. I'm sad, but I'll be okay."

I went back to the kitchen to pour my coffee. "I gotta get back. Jacob's waiting in the car."

"Hey, one more thing," Jazzy said, and I looked up once I'd filled my travel mug.

"What?"

"I got onto the track and field team."

"You did? That's cool. I didn't know you were trying out."

She shrugged her shoulders. "No biggie. Thought it might be fun."

"What event?"

"100 and 200 metres."

Jazzy was small, but she was quick on her feet. Probably had plenty of practice when she lived on the streets before we adopted each other.

"Just fun, or are you serious about it?" I asked, thinking about all the time I'd put in to the swim team when I was a kid.

"We'll see," she replied.

"You're a shitty loser," I pointed out.

"Good job I don't plan on losing then," she replied with a grin.

I smiled. There was no way she'd be doing it just for fun.

"We have our first meet tomorrow after school. I know you're probably working, so no big deal."

I had night shift again to finish out my four days. "I'll be there."

Jazzy went back to her book, and I picked my way through the woods to the road where Jacob waited for me. On one hand, I was excited Jazzy was taking part in sports. But on the other, it was one more obligation on my list, and another opportunity for me to screw it up.

Night shifts were usually busy between 7:00pm, when they began, through 2:00am when even the latest nightclubs closed. After that, it sucked until people woke up and started their days around

6:00am, and then we were off at 7:00. Anyone out and about in the middle of the night was generally sneaking home after an unplanned late night tryst or up to no good. We often ran across folks from the Department of Environment on the prowl in one of their pickup trucks, looking for poachers, and sometimes met them for breakfast near the end of our shifts.

We parked and walked inside Eats Cafe at the top of Seven Mile Beach. It was the only option open at six-thirty in the morning. A DOE pickup was one of two vehicles in the car park. I spotted my friend Casey at a booth, so we joined her. The other two people in the restaurant looked like tourists, probably grabbing an early meal before diving. Casey and her husband used to run a pair of dive boats for many years, which made her the perfect DOE officer patrolling by road or boat. She was also a no-nonsense lady, so I liked her.

"Hey," I said as we sat down.

"Are you starting or ending?" Casey asked.

"Gettin' done in half an hour," Jacob replied. "You?"

"Same. Just dropped my co-worker off and figured I'd have a bite before I go home and crash."

The server, a woman named Mariah who usually worked mornings, came by and we ordered coffee. I chose an omelette, and Jacob went for pancakes, which sounded tasty, but I couldn't face the idea of sleeping with all that food in my stomach.

"Busy night?" I asked Casey.

"Wasn't until early. We caught a guy pulling in lobster out by Barker's National Park. He wouldn't talk, but pretty sure he's got traps along the North Sound reef. We'll look by boat tomorrow. Or today, I guess. Or whenever the hell I wake up next."

"How d'you spot him?" Jacob asked.

"Pure dumb luck," Casey chuckled. "He must've been about to leave in his truck. When he started it, he'd left his stereo cranked up, so the music blasted and he had his window down. We happened to be a few hundred yards away, making a lap around the park, and heard him."

"IDC," I said, and grinned.

"Huh?" Casey reacted, looking up at me.

"Inconsiderate d-word category," Jacob explained. "It's Nora's term for people not bein' respectful to others."

Casey laughed. "I'm using that. We deal with plenty of IDCs every day."

Mariah brought us coffee, and I was about to take a sip when the door opened and loud voices made me turn around. A group of three young men stumbled in, laughing and playfully pushing each other around. No doubt they'd started their evening smartly dressed, but now their shirts were unbuttoned at the top and their ties were all over the place, hanging low around their necks. My guess was rich kids from Florida.

Mariah was the only person working out front and she walked over to them and offered them a booth near the back. The three settled down as they followed her, but one looked our way and nudged his mates.

"Check out blondie over there," he said in what he probably thought was a whisper, but we could all hear.

Jacob put a hand on my arm. "Just lads havin' harmless fun, right now."

I nodded and sipped my drink. The three dropped into the booth and all asked for coffee, which was a good sign. I didn't see a car pull up, so I hoped they'd walked here, which was also good. Or staggered. I couldn't think of anywhere they could have been all night as everything closed by 2:00am at the latest, so they'd probably come from their hotel room close by. It was hard to tell exactly, as they were giggling and slurring, but the three sounded American, supporting my Florida guess.

"How about you two?" Casey asked. "Busy night?"

"*Nei*," I replied. "Long. At least it wasn't a double like the night before."

"Yuck. I couldn't do that crap. Messes me up enough when we do these night sessions."

A clattering sound and a cup smashing echoed from the back of the cafe, followed by raucous laughter. I turned and one of the young men was on the floor with the other two pointing and cackling.

"Shit, man, I fell off the seat," the one on the floor muttered.

I looked at Mariah, who gathered up a cloth and walked their way. She caught my eye and gave me a soft shake of the head, so I stayed put. I really wanted a quiet breakfast before heading home, but these idiots were ruining one and threatened to delay the other.

"Twenty-four hours straight is tough," Jacob said. "But four days off makes up for dat. Works out perfect for me dis weekend. Gotta a school event on Saturday and a big family ting on Sunday."

"A birthday?" Casey asked.

"Yeah. Not sure whose, but it's all da ones for da month. Tibbetts somewhere always havin' a birthday, so we do one big celebration each month."

Mariah yelped, and I couldn't stand it any longer. Leaping to my feet, I saw Mariah walk away, and this time she nodded towards the booth, letting me know she'd had enough.

"Nora!" Jacob hissed from behind me, but I was already moving.

The three men nudged each other and chuckled as I approached.

"We were hoping you'd come join us," one of them said, patting the open spot on the bench next to him. "Slide on in, cutie."

"Good morning," I greeted them. "Had a good night?"

That set them all off high-fiving and bragging about how totally awesome their party had been.

"That's very impressive," I continued. "Obviously you're cool guys, so I'm sure you'll be respectful to Mariah while she brings you your food, right?"

"Heck yeah, we're getting along great with her," the one who seemed to be the mouthy leader replied. "She's invited to our party tonight. And so are you, gorgeous. You can bring that sexy accent with you," he added, to noisy approval from his cohorts.

"We'll both pass," I replied. "Enjoy your breakfast, and remember to be respectful, okay?"

I turned around and walked away, feeling a mixture of pride for being chill with them, and disgust for the same reason. They were IDCs, but the last thing I wanted was to get caught up in busting and processing these *drittsekker* instead of being home in twenty minutes.

"You don't know what you're missing," one of them said, but I kept walking.

"You can bring your handcuffs," another added. And their laughter grew.

"I always wanted me a Swedish piece of ass," the mouthy one shouted.

I'd just made it to the booth. I took a deep breath, looking at Jacob.

"Let it go, Nora," he said quietly.

I was about to sit when I heard them switch their attention back to Mariah, who stopped by to top off their coffee.

"You're gonna party with us, ain't you?" I heard one of them say. "We take 'em curvy too."

"Oh, that's it," Casey groaned, jumping up.

I flipped the safety strap on my Taser as I whipped around and strode back to the table of idiots, Casey hot on my heels. Scrambling to keep up was Jacob, but he wasn't trying to hold me back anymore. I glanced at Mariah, who flicked her eyes towards the door. I didn't need telling twice.

"Step out of the booth, you're coming with us," I demanded.

The three men laughed until I stood before them with Casey and Jacob flanking me.

"Whoa, whoa, whoa," Mouthy said, holding his hands up. "We're just having some fun. No reason to get all excited."

"Step out of the booth," I repeated.

None of them moved, the two sheep looking at Mouthy.

"Or what?" he replied. "We haven't done anything wrong."

"Drunk and disorderly, causing a public disturbance, and resisting arrest."

"We haven't resisted anything, bitch. This is bullshit!"

"Third time. Please step out of the booth," I insisted, hoping they would so we could put the scare to them and send them on their way.

But of course, that wasn't the option the drunken idiots chose.

"No way, we're trying to eat breakfast here, minding our own business," Mouthy continued, and I stepped forward, seizing his waving arm.

"Step out. Now."

He reached out towards my chest, attempting to shove me away, but I twisted the wrist I held and he yelped like an eight-year-old. I pulled him from the booth until he fell to his knees on the floor. One of his buddies decided to come to his rescue and lunged across the table. Casey had the guy's arm behind his back in a second, sending his face into the tabletop, scattering cutlery and coffee cups. She quickly dragged him from the booth and laid him on the floor with a knee in his back.

"You want da same ting?" Jacob said to the third guy.

He shook his head and held his hands up. "I'm cool."

Jacob then looked at me, shaking his head. "Ten minutes, Nora. Ten minutes, and we'd a been outta here wit a full stomach."

"Good point," I replied, cuffing Mouthy and pulling him to his feet.

I guided him back into his booth, where he plonked down and looked at me strangely.

"Sit there and shut up," I instructed.

I turned to Mariah, who watched the show from a safe distance. The cook had joined her.

"Our food about ready?" I asked.

The cook, a tall local man in his fifties, laughed. "Coming right up, miss."

Mariah gave me a nod.

"These *drittsekk* can wait a few minutes," I said.

Casey grinned and shoved her guy back in the booth. "Not a word out of any of you."

We walked back to our table.

"Actually, I'm proud of you, Nora," Jacob said as we sat.

I looked at him questioningly.

"You didn't taser anyone."

I glared at the three idiots. "They're not worth me getting another hearing."

9

IKKE VÆR FJOLS (DON'T BE A FOOL)

I was too tired to think about much by the time I got home and went to bed. One of the things I left out of my thinking was silencing my stupid phone. I'd been asleep for two hours when it buzzed and I sprang up in bed. Another downside of having a kid living with me was the chance that a call could be about her, so I answered.

"Ja?"

"Miss Sommer. It's Robbie. Are you okay?"

I'd noticed Robbie always started with Miss Sommer, and after a while moved on to calling me Nora as I'd told him ages ago he could. But the kid was polite.

"I was asleep," I groaned.

"Oh, I'm sorry. But it's nearly lunchtime."

"I worked the night shift," I explained. "What's up? Did you trace the scammer?"

"No. I don't think we can. He's pretty good."

"You woke me up to give me bad news?"

"I'm really sorry," Robbie said. "But, A: I had no way of knowing you were sleeping in the middle of the day, and, B: I have an idea."

"Okay," I grunted. "Tell me the idea and I'll decide whether I'll taser your skinny arse or not."

Robbie laughed. "You know I probably wouldn't feel that, right?"

He made me chuckle. "*Ikke vær fjols*. What's your idea?"

"Do you really think he's here on the island?" Robbie asked.

"I think there's a slim chance he is. But there is a chance. Why?"

I sat up now as I was fully awake.

"Anyone this smart at computer tech is online in forums, groups, and probably a gamer," Robbie explained. "You can't stay current on this stuff if you're not involved or at least observing the community."

"So you think we can reach him that way?"

"Maybe. There are only a few people who I know are here in Cayman that are this good, and generally we all know each other, or at least know our online handles."

"Handles?"

"Yeah, you know? Gamer tags. The name they use online. Most serious people have a handle they use everywhere. It's how they pick up a reputation."

"Okay, so can we start with the ones you know?"

"I'm pretty sure one of them works for you," Robbie replied.

"Nobody works for me," I replied, slightly confused.

"I mean, he works for the police."

"Oh, that could be Luke."

"Ah, that makes sense," Robbie replied. "This guy's handle is Skywalker Five-O."

"How does that make sense?" I asked.

I had no clue what a sky walker was. *Some kind of comic super hero BS?*

"Seriously?" Robbie laughed. "*Luke* Skywalker. *Star Wars*."

"Oh, that's an old movie, isn't it?"

"We gotta hang out sometime and get you up to speed, Nora."

I wouldn't mind hanging out with Robbie, but I didn't really want to watch movies, and I didn't want the teenager to get the wrong idea, either.

"What does the five-O part mean?"

He laughed again. Apparently, I was out of touch.

"*Hawaii Five-O*. It's a cop show on TV."

"I don't own a TV."

"It shows," he said, laughing some more.

"Okay, so we can presume that's Luke, and he knows we're investigating this because I've met with him. But I don't think he's the scammer."

"He's pretty much an ass online," Robbie said. "Sure you can rule him out?"

"He's definitely an arse in person, but I doubt it's him. Either that or he did a good job of covering it up when I spoke with him. Who else?"

"El Conejo is another one. He's involved in a lot of chat rooms, and he's super smart."

Now it was my turn to laugh. "That's a she. Rabbit."

"I know what El Conejo means, Nora."

"I'm sure you do, but I'm telling you it's a girl, and she's called Rabbit."

"Wait, I've heard of a woman who does IT stuff on the island who goes by Rabbit," Robbie replied. "Duh. I should've put that together."

"Who else?" I asked.

"They're the two I know are here in Cayman and have the skills. There has to be a lot more with all the IT departments in the law firms, banks, and stuff, but we'll have to figure them out."

"How do we do that?" I asked.

"I dunno," Robbie replied. "Get talking to them online, I suppose."

I got out of bed, trudged to the kitchen, and started preparing the coffee maker. I was wide awake now with little chance of going back to sleep for a while.

"Why don't I put you together with Rabbit? Maybe the two of you can figure something out."

"Is she one of the two you went to first?" Robbie asked.

"Yeah. Luke, then her," I admitted.

"And it couldn't be this Rabbit lady, right? She's not the scammer?"

"No. I know her. She wouldn't," I said firmly. "Besides, we know it was a guy who called Jacob's grandma."

"Okay, sure. I'm cool with that. But you'll have to set something up. She never responds to anyone online."

"Okay. I'll get back to you."

I hung up the phone and yawned. My four days off weren't starting the way I'd planned. Sleep and diving had been my only goals for the next four days, but somehow I'd found myself in the middle of Grandma's missing 20k case. I poured a cup of coffee, found a big leaf of lettuce in the fridge, picked up my phone, and went to the deck. Maybe Edvard the elusive and endangered blue iguana would have good news for me.

Rabbit almost never answered her phone. She was one of those people who ignored calls until she poked her head up from whatever she was working on long enough to see who she deemed worthy of calling back. I left her a message and gave myself a 50/50 chance of falling into the *worthy* category.

I texted my friend, AJ, then ate lunch while I waited to hear back. By the time I'd finished my *gudbrandsdalsost* and toast, a Norwegian cheese I'd brought back from the trip, she returned my text and told me she was heading for the *Kittiwake* wreck for her afternoon trip. I contemplated freediving, but based on the lack of sleep I'd had lately, I decided to scuba dive instead. All my gear was stored on her boat, so I changed into my dive leggings over a bathing suit, threw shorts, sun-shirt, and sweatshirt into a gym bag, and left the house.

It was a beautiful day, with a lighter than usual breeze keeping the water calm, but the sun and humidity felt more intense with little air moving around. I parked my Jeep over the road from the dock and walked across to their little office.

"Hey," I greeted AJ, who was eating her lunch as she finished her trip paperwork.

She looked up and smiled. "Hey. Are you off for a few days?"

I nodded. "*Ja*. Through Sunday."

"Great. Well, we're full most days, but there's always room for an extra guide."

AJ was like a big sister to me, although we were polar opposites in most ways. She was nice, people liked her, and she usually had her shit together. She was twelve years older than me, but it didn't feel that way. Probably because I'd had to grow up fast in my mid-to-late teenage years, but partly because AJ had one of those positive auras which made her seem younger.

"Okay if I dive?" I asked, figuring she'd expect me to freedive without a tank.

"Of course. We have enough tanks filled on board. Thomas just finished topping them off."

"I'll see if he needs a hand with anything," I offered, turning to walk away, but I stopped. "Hey, don't let me forget I have to be at Jazzy's school by four-thirty."

AJ cringed. "You know I'm naff at remembering things, but I'll try. Tell Thomas I'll be there in a jiff," AJ said as I walked away.

She was English, like Reg, and I was used to most of their quirky phrases and sayings, but I still got them mixed up occasionally. I knew *jiff* meant she'd be there shortly, rather than arriving in some obscure mode of transport. Naff seemed obvious, but I was worried I'd mix them up. Be there in a *naff* probably meant something completely different.

"Can I help?" I asked Thomas, AJ's only full-time employee.

He was one of the few locals who chose to work for the numerous dive operations on the island. His outgoing, happy and easy-going nature made even AJ seem pessimistic. When we'd first met, he'd had a hard time understanding why I didn't want to talk much, but he'd learnt to deal with me over time and I enjoyed being around him. Occasionally, I'd work the boat with one of them to give the other a day off, which I usually liked. As long as the customers didn't suck. Which most of them didn't.

"Want to bring your gear up?" Thomas replied. "Set up near the stern and you can get in first."

I hopped aboard and went down the three steps to the storage cabin below the bow. By the time I brought my gear out, AJ was joining us with her six clients, and I helped them get situated so Thomas could start the twin engines and prepare to leave. I then set up my own gear on a tank once we were motoring across the calm, turquoise waters towards the wreck.

Grand Cayman's Seven Mile Beach was simply stunning, even if it wasn't seven miles long, or a beach from end to end. Despite the erosion and rising seas, the sand stretched for miles, and the outer reef flattened out the deep water swells, until a gentle tide tickled up the beach where people sunned themselves. I found the idea of lying down to present my whole body to the scorching sun a puzzling concept, but apparently I was in the minority.

Thomas brought the Newton dive boat to a stop and I looped our line through the mooring pendant on the wreck buoy, then tied it to a bow cleat while AJ briefed the customers. We were earlier than most of the afternoon crowd, so only one other dive boat was currently moored to another of the multiple buoys at the site. The USS *Kittiwake* was a 251-foot, decommissioned, United States Navy submarine rescue vessel, sunk as an artificial reef and dive attraction. It had originally been carefully scuttled, upright in a stretch of sand between the outer and inner reefs. Tropical Storm Nate had other ideas and the ship now leaned steeply over on its port side, nestled against the outer reef.

I geared up while AJ and Thomas helped the customers prepare, and I was about to splash in when AJ grabbed my arm.

"Hold up a second. I almost forgot, I have something for you."

She hustled to the cabin, disappeared down the steps for a few moments, then reappeared. I was expecting her to bring a sling spear and a container, telling me someone had reported an invasive lionfish inside the wreck somewhere, but I couldn't see anything in her hands.

"Here," she said, and held out a wrist-mounted dive computer.

"I have mine," I told her, holding up my arm.

It was cheap when I'd bought it second hand a few years ago, but the computer still worked.

"I'm giving this to you, you silly bugger, not loaning it."

I stared at the sparkling new Tern, which looked more like a fancy wristwatch than a high-tech, multi-functional computer by Shearwater, who were generally considered the best in the business.

"How come?" I said, because that's what I was wondering.

It wasn't my birthday for several months, and besides, this was a far too extravagant present.

"Mermaid Divers are official brand ambassadors," AJ explained. "So anyone working on the boat gets a computer."

"You mean you're a brand ambassador for Shearwater," I replied, knowing my friend was playing down the honour.

She shrugged her shoulders and grinned. "Take the bloody thing, Viking."

So I did. "*Takk.*"

AJ nodded, still grinning. "Now get off my boat."

I wished I had more time to play around with all the menus, but I strapped it around my wrist and took a diver's giant stride into the ocean. I did a final gear check on the surface, and while AJ and Thomas shepherded their customers into the water, I dropped below, descending five metres to wait for them.

One of the things I loved about freediving was the silence, but scuba was a close second. My inhales and exhales through the regulator disturbed the perfect serenity, but the sound of my own breathing also had a comforting rhythm to it. I glanced down at the huge ship below me and began thinking about where I'd explore in a few minutes, but then spotted something out of place. Or rather, someone out of place.

A stream of bubbles blasted from behind the diver's neck and they writhed around, trying to reach the valve at the top of their tank. I had no way to know what they were thinking, but it looked like the guy was about to shut off his own air supply. I kicked hard to reach him on the slanted deck of the sunken ship, tipped over as though it had fallen over in the sand. The man appeared to be alone without a dive buddy nearby.

As I reached him, his hand had found the valve, and he kicked and rolled about, trying desperately to twist the knob to close the leaking first stage. I took hold of his buoyancy control device shoulder strap, the vest-like piece of gear which held the scuba tank on his back and contained an air bladder for adjusting buoyancy at depth. His eyes were wide and frenzied, staring back at me in panic. Taking my octopus, the name given to a diver's backup regulator, I offered it to the diver, letting him remove his own primary reg and replace it with my spare. He did, and immediately calmed down, sucking heavy breaths from my tank. I placed his hands on my BCD straps and pointed my thumb towards the surface, the hand signal for surfacing. He nodded.

Tugging lightly on his harness, I finned off the deck, holding his strap tightly in case he tried to bolt, and began a slow ascent. Reaching down, I turned his computer console around to see how long he'd been underwater. His dive time read 16 minutes at a maximum depth of 49 feet. He had 1400 psi left from a tank which would have started with around 3000. From those figures, I knew we were fine to go straight to the surface without any decompression stops.

I reached back and turned his tank valve off the rest of the way, then looked up. AJ was now in the water and staring back at me, holding up an okay hand signal. It was a question, and I answered with a similar signal. I then made a swirling circle with my finger, pointed to the wreck below, and repeated the okay sign. She was good to take her group down. One more okay hand signal from AJ, and she gathered her divers and descended past us.

When we broke through the surface, I cracked the valve open once more on the guy's tank, and air hissed into the atmosphere. I hit his inflation button, filled his BCD bladder with air, then shut the valve off again. Once he was comfortable floating, he took my octopus out and handed it back to me.

"Thank you," he said in a New York accent. "What the hell happened to my regulator?"

"First stage blew out," I replied, looking over at another dive boat moored a hundred feet away. One of their crew was waving to us. "You okay to swim to your boat?"

"Yeah, I can do that," he replied. "I didn't know what to do," he continued, finally letting go of my strap. "I couldn't get it to stop leaking air."

"Good thing you didn't," I pointed out.

He thought for a moment. "Jeez. I was shutting off my own air supply, wasn't I?"

"*Ja.*"

"I should have come up, huh?"

"*Ja.*"

"But I could hardly breathe," he said.

"That would be the reason to come to the surface."

He shook his head. "Jeez. I'm an idiot. Thank you for helping me."

What he'd tried to do was completely wrong, but not untypical for people who get certified and only dive once every year or two. Their training isn't habit, it's a class they took forever ago, and equipment failures are rare, so emergency skills aren't tested often.

"*Ja.*"

I looked over, and Thomas was standing at the stern of AJ's boat. He nodded to me, so I knew he'd watch the guy from here. I re-stowed my octopus and let the air out of my own BCD.

"Be careful," I told the man, and popped my reg in as I dropped below once more.

Another accident, I thought as I descended to the wreck. It was turning into a remarkably unlucky week on the island.

10

MY KID KICKED YOUR KID'S ARSE

After the incident with the unfortunate diver, everything went smoothly, and I enjoyed the two dives. From the wreck, we moved closer to shore and dived a shallower reef which was tranquil and beautiful. Once we were back on the boat and heading to shore, the lack of sleep began catching up with me, and was looking forward to taking a nap when I got home. Meanwhile, I was consumed with my new dive computer, putting in all my personal information, and setting the various parameters and alarms to suit my needs.

When we reached the dock, I helped tie in the boat and assisted the customers disembarking with their gear. We borrowed a hose from Reg's crew who'd arrived before us, and Thomas and I washed down the boat and the gear while AJ dealt with her clients. It was by chance that I was near my gym bag when my phone rang.

"Hey," I answered.

"You called me," Rabbit said.

"I did?" I replied, and then my sleep-deprived brain caught up. "*Ja*, I did. I have someone you should talk to about the scammer case."

"Why?" she replied.

I laughed. That would probably be my response too.

"He's a computer geek like you, and he had a good idea."

"Then he can figure it out," Rabbit replied.

"It'll be better if you do it together," I said, knowing that wouldn't be very persuasive to someone who liked working alone. "And he'll be a useful person for you to know down the road."

"Why?"

"Because he's a lot like you, except he's nicer. But you might be able to use him on your projects."

"I don't farm out my work," she responded. "My clients hire me because I do the work."

I wasn't making any progress and my brain was operating at half its usual pace, which was frustrating.

"Just talk to him, okay? He's a great kid, and he's super smart. Plus, you already know him, you just don't know you know him."

"How?"

"How do you talk to him? Or how do you know him?" I wondered.

"How do I know him?"

"He's a gamer like you."

"Who says I do online gaming?"

"El Conejo."

The line went quiet, and I wished I'd asked Robbie what his handle was.

"Better not be Skywalker Five-O," she finally said.

"No, it's not. I'm texting you his number now. Just call him for me. He has an idea how to find this scammer if he's on the island."

"Okay," she said, and hung up.

I texted her Robbie's number, unsure whether *okay* meant she'd call, or *okay*, I'm getting off the phone now.

"I need a nap," I said to anyone who happened to be around, which was only Thomas.

"Nappin' is an underrated pastime which shouldn't be over-looked," he said with a big smile.

"*Takk*," I said, and trudged up the pier to the little hut.

"Thanks for the trip and the computer," I said to AJ, who was finishing up her paperwork. "I'm going to sleep."

"You're welcome. It's good to see you," AJ replied, then stuck her head out of the hut as I walked away. "Aren't you supposed to be at Jazzy's school?"

"*Dritt!*" I muttered, looking at the time on my shiny new dive watch.

It was 4:25pm.

Fourteen kilometres was just under nine miles. That's how far it was to Jazzy's school. But at rush hour on a Thursday evening, it would take me at least half an hour. I ran to the Jeep and skipped the usual engine warm-up which my boyfriend had always insisted upon with the rebuilt engine. When he was still alive. I figured he'd forgive me this once. I wished I had one of those magnetic stick-on police lights I'd seen in movies, but I would have to settle for driving like a lunatic instead.

Traffic moved along the bypass through the first part of the Seven Mile Corridor, then backed up for the roundabouts at Camana Bay. That's where I looked for devious means of making progress, but without an emergency lane to use, I was out of luck. We all inched along frustratingly slowly until everything flowed once more after the second roundabout, then crawled again by the airport junction. I tried Jazzy's mobile, but it went to voicemail. I kept telling myself it would have been rude to jump off the boat and run, but underneath, I knew AJ and Thomas wouldn't have minded one bit. And that wasn't the issue.

I'd forgotten about Jazzy's first athletic meet. There were plenty of excuses I could make about lack of sleep, the diving incident, and who knows what, but the point was, she'd confided in me that she'd put herself out there to be on the team, and I'd simply forgotten. My only hope now was that her event would be later in the program.

It was 5:03pm by the time I finally found a place to park in the Truman Bodden Sports Complex car park, opposite the school. I ran, still in flip-flops, tank top, and damp dive leggings, to the field where it looked like most of the events were happening. Some parents stood beside the running track encircling the field, while others took shade in the impressive grandstands at the facility which hosted the Cayman Islands football team international games as well as various track and field competitions.

I'd never been to anything like this before and didn't really know what to do. Over the loudspeaker, the announcer said something about the girls' 200 metres event being about to begin, and I saw kids gathering at what appeared to be the staggered start line at the end of the back straight opposite to me. That meant the finish was at the far end of the front straight, so I ran behind the crowd, trying not to fall over in my flip-flops. I heard the gun go off and cheers went up as the race began.

"Excuse me," I muttered, gouging my way through a few people to get next to the track and look for a mop of crazy hair hurtling towards me.

It took me a second to pick Jazzy out of the group as they made their way off the end turn and ran towards us. Sensibly, she'd tied her hair back into a bushy ponytail, which bobbled from side to side as she sprinted my way. Her eyes were laser-locked on the far end of the track and she flew by where I stood, easily ahead of the field.

"First place, Jasmine Holder," the announcer enthused, and then he said whoever came next, but I didn't listen.

I ran the rest of the way to beyond the finish line where my little foster kid was catching her breath. Most of the other girls came by and gave her a hug or a high five, and I wasn't sure what I was allowed to do, so I waited by the side amongst the other parents. Getting her disqualified for something I did would pretty much suck. After a few moments, Jazzy looked over and scanned the crowd. She smiled when she saw me.

"You won," I said, as I wasn't sure what I was supposed to say.

I tried to recall what my parents said to me after my swim or sailing races, but I couldn't remember. I was more interested in talking to my coach about how to improve.

"I did," she said, and beamed. "But that was just the semi."

"Did I miss the 100 metres?" I asked. "I'm sorry I'm a little late."

"That's okay. 100 is next," she said. "No big deal. This is just a school invitational. Us against the prep school."

The prep school was where most of the foreign kids paid to go just down the street.

"There's a lot of people here," I commented, looking around.

"Yeah," she replied, clearly taking it all in her stride. "I gotta go down to the start for the 100."

"*Ja*. Good luck," I said, and stepped out of the way as she jogged away.

Figuring the 100 metres finish line would be nearby, I stayed close to make sure I didn't miss it. Around me, parents encouraged, congratulated and consoled their children depending on how their afternoon was going. It seemed like there was an abundance of bullshit being fed to a lot of kids who didn't stand a chance in their chosen sports. I wondered what I'd say if Jazzy sucked at something, but fortunately it didn't look like I'd face that dilemma at this level.

"Nora, is Jasmine competing?" came a voice I recognised from behind me.

I turned to see Detective Whittaker and his wife, Rosie.

"Hello, sir. Mrs Whittaker. She's in the 100 and 200 metres."

"I didn't know she was doing track and field," Whittaker replied. "That's great."

"Neither did I."

"Our niece is in those two as well," Rosie said.

"Okay," I replied, hoping the race would start soon.

I could talk police cases all day with the detective, but I couldn't do regular world chit-chat. And had no interest in trying. Fortunately, when the announcer got done talking about a jumping event of some sort – I didn't pay attention to know whether it was long or high – he called the 100 metres competitors to the start line.

"What lane is Jasmine in?" Whittaker asked.

"One of them," I said, looking at the track next to us.

I supposed these were things parents and uncles were supposed to know.

Rosie laughed. "I get muddled up when Jada-Kai is in several events. I think it's lane two for this one."

To my relief, someone else they knew said hello and began chatting with them, so I stood by the edge of the running track, claiming my vantage point. After a few minutes of cheers and shouts of encouragement for other events, I heard over the loudspeakers that the 100 metres final was about to start. I thought it was going to be another semi-final and realised I had missed several events, although Jazzy had played it down. I leaned forward to see down the line of people crowding along the side of the track and watched the runners bolt out of their blocks as the gun went off.

This time, I picked Jazzy out of the group right away. She was in lane three next to a tall, slim girl with long legs, who I assumed was Jada-Kai. By half distance, they were the only two contending, and I couldn't see how Jazzy would be able to beat the long stride of Whittaker's niece. But in the last 20 metres, she somehow found a little more, and eased ahead to take the win. It was really cool to watch. I actually found it quite exciting.

Somebody squeezed my arm. I turned and Whittaker was smiling.

"Congratulations. Jasmine ran a great race."

"My kid kicked your kid's arse," I said, and grinned.

The detective laughed. "Not by much, but yes, she did."

We walked past the finish line to where the kids were catching their breath and once more the other girls were congratulating Jazzy. Jada-Kai gave her a hug, but her expression was sullen.

"Your niece doesn't look happy about it."

Whittaker leaned closer. "She's never been beaten before."

Jazzy came over, and while she still had her game face on and wasn't smiling, I could tell by the glint in her eyes she was pleased with herself.

"I need longer legs," she said quietly.

"Maybe you'll have a growth spurt," I offered. "How tall was your mum?"

"Not very tall," she replied. "And I've no idea about my father."

Her drug-addicted mother went missing after Jazzy had been taken away from her at age nine. She'd never met her father or even knew his name.

"Is Jada-Kai in the 200 final?"

Jazzy nodded. "How do you know her name?"

"I know things," I replied, which we both knew was bullshit.

Jazzy looked over at Roy and Rosie Whittaker speaking with their niece and grinned.

"I gotta go get ready for the 200."

"Hey," I said, putting a hand on her shoulder. "She knows you have an extra push now."

"Yeah," Jazzy said, biting her lip. "But she doesn't know I was cruising the first 50."

I almost laughed. Maybe it was pride I was feeling, watching the kid jog away, but I wasn't sure. I'd never had much to feel proud about before.

Whittaker walked over to me once Jada-Kai had left and was about to say something when his mobile rang.

"Whittaker."

I couldn't hear the other side of the call, but by the detective's brow creasing, I could tell it wasn't good news.

"Where?" he asked, then looked at his watch.

"No, no," he continued after a few moments. "I'm not far away. Give me fifteen minutes and I'll be there."

Hanging up, he turned to his wife. "Duty calls, I'm afraid."

"Oh," she replied. "I guess I'll have to come with you as we drove together."

"What is it?" I asked out of curiosity.

"Sounds like an unfortunate domestic accident, but I feel like I should take a look. A man died. I'm meeting the coroner at the house."

"I'll drive you," I immediately offered.

"That's okay," he replied. "We can figure something out. I'm sure you planned to take Jasmine home after this."

"She has her bike. I should come with you."

Whittaker looked at me quizzically. "It's a domestic accident, Nora. There's no need."

"It's the third fatality in as many days, sir," I replied. "It's either incredibly bad luck, or something else is going on."

He raised an eyebrow. "That does sound rather odd."

The announcer called the runners to the start for the 200 metres final.

Whittaker looked at his watch again. "But we can wait a few minutes."

He probably wished he hadn't when Jazzy kicked his niece's arse in the 200 metres race too. Or perhaps that was just the way I looked at things.

11

LEAVE IT TO THE PROFESSIONALS

Rosie promised to take pictures at the prize-giving, which I hadn't even thought about until she brought it up. It was a reminder that amongst the growing list of foster parent things I was screwing up, cataloguing the kid's life in pictures was another one of my failings. I simply didn't think of such things. Having spent too many years of my life requiring anonymity, I instinctively avoided having my image recorded. Perhaps that's why social media was so unappealing to me. That, plus I had no interest in seeing the dumb shit people deemed worthy of sharing with the rest of the planet.

Detective Whittaker looked rather out of place riding next to me in my topless, lifted old Jeep. Of course, I was about to look out of place at the scene of a domestic accident wearing flip-flops, Mermaid Divers leggings, and a tank top over a sports bra. The house was on Newport Avenue, a small residential street halfway between the school and downtown. An ambulance, patrol car, and several others were parked out front, and a few neighbours gathered to see what was going on. I parked the Jeep, and we approached the house, drawing puzzled stares from the audience.

I noticed the EMTs were sitting in their ambulance, waiting. I recognised one of them. It was the same man who'd been at Zara

Parsons' house with Jacob's cousin. I didn't know the woman with him. They both looked thoroughly bored.

The coroner, Gareth Davies, met us at the door, giving me a disapproving look before addressing Whittaker.

"Hello, Roy. Thanks for coming. Appears to be a simple case, but I thought you'd like to be aware."

"Electrocution, you said on the phone?" Whittaker replied. "Let's have a look."

Davies led us through the home to a hallway between the kitchen and the living room. A man's body lay neatly positioned on the floor. His shoes had been removed. I assumed he'd been left that way after resuscitation efforts ceased. Above him, on the wall, the electrical breaker box panel was open, and I realised there were no lights on in the home and it was hot and humid inside.

"Victim's name, Gareth?" Whittaker asked.

"Jerald Dilbert. Appears he was messing with the breakers and electrocuted himself," Davies said, pointing to a few tools and electrical parts scattered on the tiled floor.

"Who found him?" Whittaker asked.

"His wife. She's a nurse. Came home to find him lying on the floor. She tried CPR and called 9-1-1. EMTs called me."

"Have you called an electrician?" I asked.

"Hasn't been my top priority," Davies replied, frowning at me.

"You want to know how he died, don't you?" I said.

"I know how he died, Constable. He was electrocuted. See the burns on his fingertips and soles of his feet?"

"Obviously," I rebutted. "But how was he electrocuted? The breaker should have kicked before it killed him."

"I have a guy I can call," Whittaker interjected before the coroner could say anything more.

While he made the phone call, I walked into the kitchen to look around. The house was an older single-storey block home which was tidy, but hadn't been updated in a long time. The cabinets had seen years of use, and the grout between the tiles on the floor bore the stains of decades of spills and traffic. Someone had opened the back door to let the breeze in, and the backyard was small but well maintained. A high wooden fence divided the property from the neighbours on either side, and a low fence in the same style marked the rear of the lot. Beyond, dense woods and shrubs came close, but I could see they'd been kept at bay with a strimmer or mower of some sort.

My mobile buzzed, and I checked the message. It was from a number I hadn't saved, but it must have been Rosie as the attachment was several pictures of Jazzy on the top step of a podium. Jada-Kai stood next to her as they all held up the medals hanging around their necks on brightly coloured ribbons. Jazzy looked like she was tolerating the attention rather than enjoying it. Jada-Kai appeared to be putting on the best smile she could produce after taking her first two losses. The third girl beamed from ear to ear. I guessed she had lower expectations of her own performance.

I then did something I'd never done before. I saved one of the pictures as the home screen on my phone, replacing the stock graphic.

"Electrician is on his way," Whittaker said, joining me in the backyard. "I caught him on his way home for the day, so he said he could drop by. He'll be here in ten or fifteen minutes."

"This is just like the others," I commented.

"How so?" Whittaker asked.

"There's no evidence to suggest it was anything but an accident."

"Except?" he queried.

"Except this is three in a row, and the odds are strongly against three freak accidents of this nature happening within a ten-kilometre radius of each other in the same week."

The detective thought for a moment. "It's certainly strange, but as you said, there's nothing suspicious about this scene, and you were present for the other two. I assume they were the same."

I nodded. "They were. But they all have a few common elements."

"Okay," he replied, inviting me to continue.

"Each victim was home alone and would not be discovered until sometime later in the day. But they would be discovered."

"Here, his wife would come home after her shift," Whittaker followed along. "That would be predictable. What about the others?"

"The first had a cleaner scheduled, and the second was outside where a neighbour was likely to notice when they came home from work."

"Potentially a pattern, but not a strong indicator of wrongdoing," he commented. "What else?"

"Each location is a single-family home which backs up to open space," I explained. "Odds are that one of these accidents would have taken place in a condo or apartment and been in a denser neighbourhood. An assailant had access with reasonable cover to each location."

"I agree the odds are stacking up, but three samples aren't many to form a reliable trend."

"Then we can see who has an accident over the next couple of days," I said.

Whittaker gave me a strange look. "Or hope no one does."

I was about to tell him I didn't think us hoping would make any difference to the number of bodies in the morgue, but I realised what he meant.

"Of course," I said instead. "But I think we should explore the possibilities of more similarities and treat this crime scene as a suspected murder. We've already lost that opportunity with the first two."

The detective thought it over, so I stepped back into the house. The coroner was sitting at a breakfast table, filling out paperwork on a clipboard.

"Where's the wife, sir?" I asked.

"In the bedroom with an officer," he replied without looking up.

I started towards the hallway.

"Where are you going?" Davies asked sternly.

"To speak with her," I said, pausing.

"Are you on duty?" he asked.

He knew the answer to that question from my outfit. I wasn't sure if he disliked me in particular, or was just so caught up in procedures and protocol that he couldn't help himself.

"I'd like to speak with the victim's wife," Whittaker said, coming in from the backyard. "Constable Sommer can come with me."

Davies returned to filling out his paperwork, and I followed Whittaker through the house. We found the woman, understandably distraught, sitting on the side of her bed.

"Sir," the uniformed officer greeted the detective, then looked at me with a puzzled expression.

"Give us a few minutes," Whittaker instructed, and the officer stepped out of the room, giving me another bemused glance.

"Mrs Dilbert, my name is Detective Whittaker, and this is Constable Sommer. We're very sorry for your loss, ma'am. I know this is a difficult time, but would you mind if we asked a few questions?"

The woman looked up. I guessed her to be mid-thirties with long, dark hair, and a light ebony skin tone. Her eyes were puffy, red, and wet with tears. She nodded her assent.

"Thank you, I'll try to be brief. Were you aware of the electrical problems your husband was working on?"

She shook her head.

"He didn't call or text you about an issue?"

"No," she replied, shaking her head again. "The house is older, so we've had a few issues with various things over the past few years, but I don't know what was going on today."

"Was your husband a bit of a handyman when it came to fixing things around the house, Mrs Dilbert?" Whittaker asked.

The detective had an amazing knack for dealing with people in all situations. Here, his voice was reassuring and sympathetic, but he always spoke with an authoritative tone, which made it clear he was a man who would do something about the situation. It wasn't a talent I possessed or felt I was likely to grasp.

"Not really," she replied. "I mean, he could do the basic stuff, you know? But he wasn't about to renovate a bathroom or anything like that."

"Are you surprised he was trying to fix something in the electrical box?"

She nodded and sniffled, trying to keep herself from crying. "He knew how to check the breakers, but I'm surprised he was trying to change one." She looked at the floor. "I wish he hadn't. He should have called someone."

"What did your husband do for a living?" Whittaker asked.

"He worked for a tour company," she replied, wiping her eyes and pulling herself together. "Thursday was his day off, as he worked most weekends."

Whittaker glanced over at me before asking his next question. I figured his look was suggesting we should wrap things up with the poor woman, so if I had a question, I should have it ready.

"And when was the last time you spoke with your husband, ma'am?" he asked.

"When I left this morning," she said, her voice breaking. "We had breakfast before I went to work."

The detective looked my way again, and I shook my head. I couldn't think of anything constructive to ask. *Can you think of anyone who'd like to murder your husband and make it look like an accident* didn't seem appropriate.

"Thank you, and again, ma'am, we're very sorry for your loss," Whittaker said, before we left the room.

I waited until we were out of earshot. "I need to check on CCTV around the three locations. My guess is there's none close by."

"It would be worth a look, I agree, Nora, but we're still a long way from starting a case here. Gareth hasn't suggested he's seen anything suspicious about any of the three accidents."

I stopped myself before I said something inappropriate about the coroner. Which, some might say, was progress on my part. Although it didn't feel like progress to me. More like muting the obvious.

"I don't doubt they all died of exactly what they appeared to die from," I said instead. "It's the frequency which is suspicious."

Whittaker stood in the hallway with his hands on his hips, looking at Jerald Dilbert's body. After a few moments, he carefully stepped past the corpse and I followed him to the kitchen.

"Gareth, would you mind doing me a favour?"

The coroner looked up from his paperwork. "Sure, Roy. What do you need?"

"Did you plan to autopsy the other two bodies from the past couple of days?"

"Didn't see a reason," he replied. "In fact, the female from Tuesday has been released to the family."

"But you still have the woman who drowned in her pool?" Whittaker asked.

"I do. Planned to release her body tomorrow morning. They have services arranged, I believe."

Whittaker scratched his brow. "Could you take another look at her? And check for any other signs of trauma with this fellow?"

Davies frowned, looking at me and then back to the detective. "I suppose so, but I don't see why."

"I'm just talking fingernails and checking for signs of struggle. Foreign hair, that sort of thing."

"And a tox screen," I added, which won me another glare.

"Thanks, Gareth," Whittaker quickly added. "I appreciate it."

"Detective Whittaker," a constable called out from the front door. "Someone is here for you, sir."

"Ah, that'll be the electrician. Nora, would you please show him in and explain what we need? Make sure he wears gloves."

I nodded, and as I left the kitchen, I heard Whittaker address the coroner again.

"I'm going to have CSIU drop by and dust for prints, Gareth, so I'm afraid we'll be a bit longer before you can take Mr Dilbert with you."

12

DON'T RULE OUT THE CAT

I had breakfast with Jazzy before she left for school, then sat on the porch with coffee and lettuce, hoping Edvard would show his ugly face. At one point I heard rustling in the undergrowth by the woods, but if it was him, he must have turned around, as I never saw the stupid lizard. It was my day off, and if I was smart like Jacob, I'd be doing something fun, but Whittaker had given me permission to rack up a few hours of overtime, so I planned to revisit the scenes of the first two accidents.

Sitting in the shade from the morning sun and looking out to the peaceful Caribbean Sea, my unease over the string of accidents was beginning to feel foolish. Gareth Davies might be a cantankerous old goat, but he wasn't an idiot, and he wasn't lazy. He also went by evidence, details, and facts, so if he couldn't see a pattern or any trace of wrongdoing, then maybe I was barking up the wrong wall. *Talking to the wrong wall?* That didn't sound right, either. The English language was a pain in the arse to begin with, but when you added idioms, phrases, and slang, it was incredibly confusing.

I went inside, made another coffee to take with me in my travel mug, and changed into my uniform. After four straight days on shift, nothing was clean, so I picked out the least stinky selection. As I was about to leave the bedroom, which was really just the rear part of the living space, I noticed Jazzy's medals on her bedside table. I picked them up and looked them over. They were probably mass produced in China and kids throughout the world had the same raised image of a winged running shoe surrounded by stars, but I knew they meant something to her.

Before I'd run away from Norway, I had dozens of similar medals for swimming, which hung on the corner of my headboard. My parents had turned my old room into a guest bedroom, and I wondered where the medals were now. Safely stored in a box somewhere, knowing my dad. Once upon a time, those medals had meant something to me too. Until my life turned upside down and they became of little significance compared to the shitstorm I surrounded myself with. I hung Jazzy's medals on either side of the only picture on the walls of the house. It belonged to Archie Winters, the man who used to own the shack and gifted it to me before he left the island. The medals deserved to be on display. I hoped she'd be able to enjoy hers for longer than I did mine.

I chose the second accident scene first, as I knew I could get access to the backyard and the pool. I walked through the side gate and paused to look around. The pool covering had been straightened up and reset with the weighted bags holding it in place. The tall white fence ran down the sides and across the back with a flower bed at the base. I remembered noticing the shrubs and plants were well maintained. The rest of the backyard was concrete, with the pool taking up half of the area. I walked to the rear, where a paving stone bridged the flower bed to a gate. Donning a nitrile glove, I opened the latch and let the gate swing outwards.

Behind the lot, a short stretch of scrub land led to a wooded area, too dense for me to see what was beyond. Zara Parsons' and Joseph Taylor's homes were considerably smaller than the extravagant houses farther down the street. Shorelink Drive was the first road inside The Shores, an upmarket gated community where many of the homes stood alongside canals which led to the North Sound. They must have bought the cheapest two lots in the project. Or least expensive, to be more accurate.

I would drive around and check when I left, but I was pretty sure the woods provided a natural boundary without additional fences or security. Someone could easily approach unseen from the rear of Zara's property. The ground was bone dry across the scrub land, so not much chance of an individual footprint, and besides, the grass was also well trodden down, so probably a neighbour-hood dog walking trail.

Checking the outside of the gate, I noted it didn't have a latch, but it wouldn't have been hard for someone to reach over and open the inside latch if they brought something to stand on. I scoured the ground for signs of an indent, and thought I could see what may have been square imprints from the feet of a stepladder, but I had no way of being certain. I took a photo with my phone, but the marks were too subtle to see in the picture.

Back inside the lot, I tried to replay what could have happened. If someone came through the back gate, they'd need to reach the house without being seen. From where I stood, I was looking at the kitchen and dining room windows on the ground floor, then what I assumed to be two bedroom windows upstairs. Turning back to the gate, the gaps on either side of the posts were certainly wide enough to look through with one eye. An assailant could watch until the coast appeared clear, then duck inside, and by moving along the fence line to my left, approach the house, remaining mostly unseen by the neighbour. Of course, the side gate had been unlatched according to Joseph, so it was possible the back gate wasn't even a factor.

Joseph also told me he'd left early, so if someone approached the house from the backyard, they could well have done so after he'd left, and when it was still dark. If, if, if. I could understand why a killer might want to make a murder look like an accident, but I had no clue why anyone would want to see Zara dead in the first place. Or the other two. Unless the reason was simply getting away with it. The adrenaline rush of not only the kill, but evading detection.

I spent another twenty minutes looking around the pool area for anything which could have been left behind, disturbed, or cleaned to cover up wrongdoing, but didn't find a thing. When I left, I turned right along the side of the woods, which brought me to a large property at the end of a driveway, several hundred yards as a bird flies from Zara Parsons' house. Bringing up a satellite map on my phone, I could see the layout, and the woods made for a perfect entry and exit. All someone had to do was stay close to the edge of the woods and follow it around to reach the road I'd driven down. I hadn't seen a single CCTV or private security camera except for one at the unmanned gate into The Shores, and that was pointed to cover the entrance. Which an assailant had no need to use in reaching Zara's house on foot.

It only took me ten minutes to zigzag across West Bay to North West Point Road, where Heather Lawson had died on Tuesday. A CSUI van was parked outside, and I went in to find Rasha, the head of the department, wrapping up.

"Hello, Nora, I didn't know you were on this case," she greeted me. "If there actually is a case."

Rasha was an efficient, hard-working lady, who ran a department which was always stretched thin. She had a polite English manner, but ran a tight ship in her group, and I could understand why she was wondering what required her attention at the site of an accident.

"Whittaker asked me to follow up on a few details," I said, which was within sight of the truth. "There's been an odd series of household accidents, so he wanted to make sure there wasn't something else going on."

"Well, we've taken prints, and checked entry points into the house for signs of forced entry, but there's not much else we can do this late in the day. I'm sure a lot of the prints will be from police and EMTs."

"Did the coroner or the EMTs take pictures for the file?" I asked, not having checked myself yet.

Rasha lifted the lid of a laptop on the counter and logged in. "There are a few," she said, navigating to a folder on the police server and opening a picture.

Heather Lawson lay on her tiled floor with a small pool of blood around her head. Rasha opened several more shots, taken from different angles. I moved her laptop to the end of the counter where the unfortunate victim had hit her head. I then lay on the floor and tried to set myself in the same position Heather had landed.

"That about right?" I asked.

Rasha reached down and pulled, slid and shoved me around until finally she stood up straight and looked back and forth between her screen and me a few times.

"That's pretty close. You're just a lot taller than the vic."

"Can you outline me?" I asked.

"What? Like a tape outline?"

"Ja."

Rasha slid her Tyvek suit sleeve up and looked at her watch. "Seriously, Nora? I really don't have the time."

"You don't have to do the whole thing, just key points."

She sighed, but unzipped a bag she had packed ready to leave, and produced a roll of tape. I lay still while she marked my position on the floor. When she was done, I stood and took the tape from her. Checking the pictures one more time, I kneeled on the tile and marked out the puddle from the spilt water dish.

"She slips in the water and hits the right rear corner of her head," I said, finding a picture of the woman's wound, which had clearly cracked open her skull.

"Heads don't have corners, Nora," Rasha pointed out.

I ignored her and continued. She knew what I meant.

"Her fall line is directly in line with the kitchen counter, agreed?"

"Agreed," Rasha said, although I knew she was only humouring me to get this over with. At the moment.

I stood with my back to the counter, took one step forward, then swung a leg in the air.

"So she slipped like this."

"Looks that way," Rasha replied.

"Who stands with their back to the end of a kitchen counter?" I asked.

"Apparently, Heather Lawson did."

I raised an eyebrow at Rasha.

"I see what you mean," she conceded. "But maybe she was coming from one side or the other at an acute angle but fell in line with the counter. She slipped on a wet floor. She probably wind-milled her arms, and could easily have twisted, with her feet slipping several times before she hit the counter, then the ground."

I went back to the laptop and searched through the pictures until I found the one I was after.

"Look. Her shoes had rubber soles."

Heather Lawson's work shoes were incredibly sensible and comfortable-looking black slip-ons by a company called Skechers.

"Doesn't mean she couldn't slip on wet tile," Rasha responded.

"Agreed, as obviously she did," I said. "But look where the water puddle was. If her feet slipped out from under her, she'd rotate around the axis of her hips. Her feet would slide away forward, and the weight of her head would rotate her upper body backwards."

"Like table footie," Rasha said with a chuckle.

"Huh?"

"You know, the game with the poles through the players that you spin and kick the little ball. I think they call it foosball in America."

"Yes, like that. Imagine she has a pole shoved through her hips."

Rasha winced.

"A theoretical one," I added. "So for her to hit her head on the counter, she had to lose her footing and pivot like a foosball player, which meant she slipped from about here," I said, placing a strip of tape across the hips of my outline on the floor. "But if she scrambled and thrashed, then the foosball pivot theory goes to shit, because she'd crumple to the floor more than rotate on the way down. So she'd have to be much closer to the counter, and wouldn't have ended up laid out like that," I finished, pointing to the outline.

"That all sounds plausible, but I have two problems you haven't addressed."

"I can guess one. What's the other?" I asked.

"Well, I have no idea which one you think you're guessing, but my first issue is how would you ever prove any of what you just said?"

"That's the one I guessed. So what else?"

"If she was murdered, how was someone else involved?" Rasha asked.

I thought for a second as Rasha began peeling tape from the floor.

"And why," I finally responded, and shook my head.

Because while I was busy coming up with ways an assailant could have reached the victims undetected, and potentially committed the crimes without leaving any trace, I didn't have a clue as to *why* they'd go to all this trouble. It was beginning to feel like the more I found ways for an attacker to be present, the less likely it seemed.

"Maybe this one *was* the cat," I muttered as Rasha repacked her bag.

13

MISSING DOLPHIN

Rasha and her team left, but I stuck around a little longer. I was second-guessing myself over the whole slip on the tile part, but I was here, so I figured I'd look at access. If someone else was involved, they had to get into the house, and there were only two ways in. The front door and a side door into a coat room, or mud room, or whatever it was called where you kept outdoor clothing and footwear. Like many on the island, the home didn't have a garage as it was raised off the ground on pillars to escape flooding in big storms.

Concrete steps led from the side door down to the pad on which the house stood, poured over the ironshore making up this part of the coastline. A pathway ran to the oceanfront where I could see the chrome handles of a swim ladder into the water. It was certainly possible for someone to arrive in a small rigid inflatable boat which could be tied to the ladder. Or walk here from the road under the cover of night. There were streetlamps along the road, but they were spaced quite far apart on the power poles, with low output bulbs. I'd noticed Heather's home didn't have security cameras, but I made a mental note to check for others when I left.

I was standing on the landing, examining the lock, when my phone rang.

"Nora, it's Detective Whittaker."

"Morning, sir."

"Are you anywhere near the station?"

"I'm in West Bay at the first victim's house. Rasha just left."

"Find anything of interest?" he asked.

I hesitated in answering. I wanted to say yes, as I wasn't ready to let this go just yet, but in all honesty, I didn't have anything worth reporting.

"We'll see if we get a hit from the prints," I replied.

"Okay. Well, I heard from my electrician this morning," Whittaker continued. "He said the wiring was typical of an older home."

"What does that mean?" I asked, wondering if the place was charged by lightning storms or a treadmill generator.

"The wiring is original to the house, so 1970s, and the breaker panel had been updated, but likely after Hurricane Ivan back in 2004," he explained. "Things were chaotic back then, and temporary fixes had a habit of becoming the permanent solution. He said the master breaker for the house should have tripped, but didn't."

"Had it been tampered with?" I asked.

"I asked the same question. The electrician told me it was possible, but the box was a fried mess, so hard to tell. In his opinion, based on the burn marks on the screwdriver and the body, Mr Dilbert inadvertently bridged the connections either side of the slot from which he'd removed the breaker. Even that would have been fine, but from the burn on his finger, he must have inadvertently been touching the metal of the screwdriver blade. As the master breaker didn't trip, he received a prolonged shock which killed him. If the master had done its job, he likely would have taken a painful jolt, but survived."

"Okay," I mumbled, trying to picture the electrical box and figure out the circuitry. I had more experience with boat wiring than houses, but I had a grasp of the concepts.

"Autopsies will be on Monday for Dilbert and the teacher,"

Whittaker said. "But I doubt we'll see a report on either until later in the week. Where are you heading next?"

"Looking for CCTV or security cameras nearby," I replied. "Here and Dilbert's house. I've been to Zara Parsons' already."

There was a brief pause, and I guessed what was coming next.

"If we don't have anything more concrete suggesting foul play, Nora, I can't authorise more overtime. You can take four hours today, but after that, we'll need to wait until we have forensic and autopsy results before deciding how to proceed."

"Unless I find something more convincing," I emphasised.

"Certainly."

"Or another weird accident happens."

"Let's hope that doesn't happen," he replied.

"Then I'd better get on, sir."

"I'll talk to you later, Nora," he said, and ended the call.

I went back inside, making sure I locked the side door. Taking one last look around the kitchen, I noticed a few photographs pinned to a corkboard by the door to the coat room. There were three. One was of the victim and another woman huddled together for the picture. They both had rosy cheeks, and the background appeared to be a bar somewhere. The next was of Heather standing with several other bank employees. They were all smiling. The final photograph was at the beach with the same woman from the first picture sitting beside Heather on beach towels. Heather was farther away from the camera, and from her slightly awkward posture hiding behind her friend, I sensed she was uncomfortable having her picture taken in a bathing suit. Apparently, she felt positive enough about it to put it on the wall. Or their friendship meant more to her than overcoming her self-image.

A silver chain around her neck contrasted with her tanned skin, holding a small dolphin charm at the top of her cleavage. I looked at the other two photographs. She was wearing the charm in every one.

"*Dritt*," I muttered and strode to the bedroom.

On the dresser sat a small jewellery box. I opened the lid and looked inside. An unemployed wedding band kept two other fashion rings company, but no necklace. I checked the closet, bathroom, and bedside table. No other jewellery. I called Rasha's mobile phone.

"Yes?" she answered, sounding a little annoyed.

"Check the photos of the victim," I said. "See if she was wearing a silver necklace."

"Hold on a moment. I'm just walking into my office."

"It would be on the personal effects list too," I pointed out.

"Yes, yes, give a minute."

While I waited for Rasha to get situated, I walked back to the kitchen and kneeled down, looking under the refrigerator. Using the torch function on my phone, I shined the light underneath. I could see several cat toys and what looked like a coin, but no necklace. Sitting back, I looked around for any other gaps or spaces into which a flying piece of jewellery could be launched during a fall close by. I couldn't see any.

"Nora?" I heard from the phone.

"I'm here," I said, putting the call on speaker so I could still use the torch.

"Nothing around her neck in the pictures, but she's wearing a watch."

"Okay, thank you," I said, and hung up.

There could be a dozen explanations as to why Heather didn't have her necklace on when we found her, from having lost it recently, to dropping it off to be repaired. But there was also the possibility that it had been taken. A trophy. It was another unproven theoretical which many would argue I was making fit my narrative, but it was enough to keep me looking. For now, at least. Or for another hour or so, according to my overtime restriction.

I'd planned to go to Dilbert's next, but I left via the front door and jogged to the Jeep with a different destination in mind. First, I turned left on North West Point Road, and slowly drove along, looking for cameras. I didn't see any until I reached the Cayman Turtle Centre, which was half a kilometre away. With several side roads in between. At a pinch, I could come back and check their footage from Tuesday morning, but I doubted the footage would reward me with anything useful. Turning around, I drove in the opposite direction, and a hundred metres beyond Heather's house was Lighthouse Point Residences, which I knew had a camera facing the road. But I kept going.

The bank branch where Heather Lawson worked was in the Centennial Towers building just beyond the four-way stop in West Bay. Towers was a generous term for a three-storey building, and the four-way stop was one of probably a hundred in West Bay. But that's what the locals called the one where West Bay Road intersected South Church Street, and it had become a navigational landmark.

I parked and walked inside, nodding to the security guard by the entrance.

"I need to talk with the manager," I told him, and he led me past the line of customers to an office door.

He swiped a pass key over a sensor, waited a moment to hear the lock mechanism disengage, then opened the door for me.

"Ask for Nia Thompson," he said, and closed the door after I'd entered.

The woman must have heard her name mentioned, as she appeared from an office on my left.

"May I help you?"

"Did Heather Lawson work here, ma'am?"

"Yes, she did. Please come in. I'm Nia, the branch manager."

I stepped inside and took the seat she offered me.

"Terrible tragedy," she said, taking her chair behind the desk. "We're all in shock."

"I have a few standard questions we have to ask after a fatality," I said, which was pretty much bullshit. "This will only take a minute."

"Anything I can do to help," she replied. "But I thought Heather's accident was just that, an accident."

"Certainly seems to be," I replied. "Like I said, we just have to tick a few boxes."

Nia didn't look convinced, but I pushed on. "How did Heather seem in the days leading up to her dea…" I began, but quickly checked myself. "Leading up to her accident?"

"Normal, as best as I knew," Nia replied. "Heather was quiet but a great employee, and everybody adored her."

That was usually everyone's respectful response after an employee died, but I hadn't seen any reason to contradict the statement as yet.

"Heather wore a necklace. A silver dolphin charm. Do you recall seeing it?"

"She loved the ocean and living here in Grand Cayman," Nia replied. "I never saw her without that necklace."

I didn't bother pointing out that dolphins weren't native to the island, and the only ones found here were penned up for tourists to pet and swim with in exchange for money.

"Was she working on Monday?" I asked.

"Yes, she had a standard schedule, Monday through Friday."

"Did you happen to notice if she was wearing the pendant on Monday?"

Nia frowned. "I didn't notice she wasn't, but I suppose I couldn't be sure."

"Can we look at CCTV for the end of the day Monday?" I asked.

She paused, looking at me with a puzzled expression. "We can, but why all the interest in a necklace? I don't think it had significant monetary value."

"Last footage you have showing Heather from Monday afternoon please," I replied, deliberately avoiding her question.

Nia took a moment, deciding whether or not to push the issue. Apparently, she chose to help me without asking anything more, as she busied herself at the keyboard. After a minute or so, she beckoned me around to her side of the desk.

"This is at 5:20pm. The tellers have balanced their registers and removed their trays for overnight storage in the vault. That's Heather walking out."

The camera angle was from above the front door, so she walked towards us alongside another woman.

"Back it up a bit and pause, please," I requested.

Nia did so, and I studied the screen. The camera was higher resolution than most security video, and I could clearly make out the chain around Heather's neck. The pendant was hidden below her blouse, which was buttoned conservatively high. I could see the watch on her wrist, and her left hand, which was the only one in view, was void of rings. She was wearing the black Skechers on her feet.

"Thank you," I said, and took a picture of the screen with my phone.

"I can send you this footage if you'd like?" Nia offered.

"Will it be erased?"

"No, we keep security footage for six months, I believe."

"Then I'll let you know if we need it. Thanks again."

Before Nia could quiz me any more, I let myself out and walked across the car park to the Jeep. I contemplated calling Whittaker, but I really didn't have anything more to report beyond the missing dolphin. And I was out of the time he'd allotted me. I jumped in and started the engine, letting it run for a minute while I thought about my next move.

One thing that didn't motivate me at all in this world was money. For me, it was a necessary tool with which to live, and as long as I could feed myself and the kid, and keep a roof over our heads, I didn't worry about getting more of it. Of course, I also had a fallback nest egg tucked away in case of emergencies, which helped keep any monetary stress at bay.

But it meant I didn't care whether I was getting paid for a few extra hours on the job, if it was something I was interested in. And although I sensed I was still barking up the wrong house, I was intrigued to continue investigating. Somehow, that phrase still didn't sound right, but I pulled out of the car park and headed for George Town.

14

ISLAND TIME

I stopped briefly at the Marquee Plaza halfway along Seven Mile Beach and grabbed a coffee and a veggie wrap from Cafe del Sol. Eating lunch on the fly never bothered me. When we were on patrol, Jacob preferred to sit down somewhere and eat lunch, whether that was in a restaurant or taking food to a place we could enjoy the view. He was good at stopping and smelling the trees, as the saying goes. I think. Maybe it was because I had the good fortune of living somewhere with a wonderful view, but I preferred to get on and eat as we drove. Most of the time, that meant just that. Driving around. But the bad guys tended not to come running up to us, so if we wanted to do something useful, we had to drive around.

Sitting in front of a computer at the central office in George Town, I ate the wrap, and opened the file on the second accident victim of the week, Zara Parsons. It was thin. The coroner's report, my notes from the scene, and the neighbour's statement. Next of kin was listed as her parents, Terrence and Marlene Seymour, Parsons being her married name. I called the number listed.

"Hello," a subdued female voice answered after four or five rings. She had a light local accent.

"Is this Marlene Seymour?"

"Yes."

"This is Constable Sommer, ma'am. I have a question for you."

The line was quiet for a few moments.

"A question?" she echoed, sounding perplexed.

It dawned on me that I'd called because I needed answers, but I hadn't given any thought to the mother's state of mind. I thought of Whittaker and how he approached Jerald Dilbert's wife. But I was terrible at all of that, so I pressed on, figuring the sooner I got off the phone, the sooner she could go back to feeling like shit about losing her daughter, and I could carry on finding out what happened to her.

"Did you receive your daughter's personal effects?"

"Err, yes," she stumbled. "Was there something missing?"

"That's why I was calling, ma'am."

"There *was* something missing?"

"Was there?" I asked.

Silence.

"Was there, ma'am?" I repeated.

"I thought that's what you were calling to tell me," she said.

Now I went quiet. Something had gone wrong with this conversation, but I wasn't altogether sure what had happened.

"Constable?"

"I was calling you to ask if you'd noticed if any of your daughter's personal effects you'd expected to see were not included in the items returned to you, ma'am," I said slowly, using far more words than I deemed necessary or desirable.

"Oh," she said. "I can't say."

"Why?" I asked, a little annoyed she wouldn't tell me.

"Because I haven't looked yet."

"Oh. Can you?"

"I dare say," Marlene replied. "Truth be told, I was avoiding looking. It was one more thing that I knew would upset me."

Dritt. Now I felt like an arse for asking her, but I needed to know.

"Hold on a moment, Constable," she said, so I waited and hoped she was looking without me having to press her more.

I could hear muted conversation and shuffling about in the background, but after a couple of minutes, Marlene came back on the line.

"Constable?"

"I'm here," I replied.

"I looked, and I recognise everything here as being hers."

"That's good," I replied, thinking Whittaker might be proud of my reaction when I really wanted to say, *that's not what I asked!* "But is there anything missing from what you expected? A piece of jewellery, perhaps, that your daughter always wore?"

I gave Marlene a moment to think.

"Her class ring, I suppose. But I guess she wasn't wearing it."

"Would that be strange?"

"Her not wearing it?"

"Yes."

"Sure. She always wore that ring."

I'm not sure if I was feeling more excited or surprised. Maybe I was on to something after all.

"One more question, Mrs Seymour. What's a class ring?"

"Where are you from?" she asked.

"Norway."

"Oh my. You are a long way from home, girl."

"This is my home now."

"Oh, I see. They not have class rings in Norway?"

"Not that I know of," I replied, thinking that was a silly question as I'd just asked her what one was. But maybe people in grief didn't think straight. Come to think of it, I didn't when my boyfriend was murdered.

"You can get a ring from your school when you graduate," Marlene explained. "Apparently it's a thing in America, but maybe not so much other places."

"What school was your daughter's?" I asked.

"Barry University in Florida. She was proud of her education."

"I have one more thing to ask, Mrs Seymour. I need to see if that ring is in Zara's house. Can you let me in?"

I heard a sigh. "What's this all about?" she asked. "Seems like you're going to a lot of trouble getting me back her things. Which I appreciate, don't get me wrong, but I'm guessing you're up to something else."

"It's probably absolutely nothing, Mrs Seymour, and finding that ring will put our concerns to rest."

I waited, hoping she wouldn't push the issue, as *we* really meant *me* rather than *our* at this stage. According to Detective Whittaker's guidelines, I was supposed to be out of uniform by now.

"When you need to get in there?" she asked.

"As soon as possible."

"That's another thing I've been avoiding doing, but I guess I gotta go there sometime," she replied, letting out another long sigh. "Can you be there at three?"

"Thank you, ma'am. I'll see you at three."

I hung up and sat back in the chair. A niggling feeling in my gut had been pushing me along despite my brain telling me I was turning unfortunate events into something they weren't. But maybe my niggle was right after all. I had two hours before meeting Marlene, and what I needed now was to know if anything was missing from Jerald Dilbert's body, and to find a connection between the victims. The only way to predict the next victim would be to figure out why these seemingly innocent people were being systematically murdered.

But sitting forward in my seat, ready to push on, I stopped for a moment. I was getting way ahead of myself again. If we found Zara's class ring sitting on her bedside table, then none of what I was piecing together made sense again, and I was wasting police time and stirring up family members over nothing. Maybe I'd hold off making a similar call to Dilbert's wife until after I'd been to Zara's house. But I could still search for a connection without disturbing or upsetting anyone.

Opening up an internet browser, I went to the website which

stored the most information about everyone all over the world. Their social media of preference.

I hated everything to do with social media, but AJ had set up an account for me under the name Cayman Viking, which she thought was hilarious. It was made with a throwaway Gmail account, had a picture of a sandy beach across the top, and not a single photo or piece of information about me. But it was how I could access the site and look at other people's profiles for just such situations.

With a bit of searching and matching profile pictures to less flattering photographs of the victims' dead faces, I found all three. Heather Lawson, the bank clerk, had 753 friends, which seemed like a ridiculously large number of people to call 'friends'. I wondered how many of them she'd ever shared a meal with or even met in person. Zara Parsons was more particular with 131, and Jerald Dilbert's feed was full of work pictures, so I assumed he became online friends with half the tourists whom he met in the office. He had 1,928. I wasn't certain I'd spoken a single word to that many people in the past five years.

Finding something in common was time consuming and incredibly monotonous. I scrolled down each of their timelines, looking for an event or activity they might have in common, and found nothing. Next I checked Zara Parson's 131 friends from her friends list against those of the other two. It took a while. There was no way to export the lists to sort and compare, which meant manually scrolling and comparing. Fortunately, the site had friends listed in alphabetical order, so with three windows open on the screen, I could somewhat expedite the process.

By 2:30pm, when I needed to leave, I had two names which appeared on all three profiles. One was a young local film director and writer who'd been in the press a lot over the past year for helping bring two Hollywood movie projects to the island for filming. It appeared he'd kept a personal profile going along with his shiny business page. He struck me as an unlikely suspect, mainly because his posts from the previous five days were all from Los Angeles, California. The second friend all three had in common was a man named Moses Dilbert, Jerald's cousin, as best I could tell. The last post on his profile was from a year ago when he changed his picture to one showing him staring menacingly at the camera with his arms folded.

Rushing out of the building, I hopped in the Jeep, and drove north, swearing at the tourists cruising slowly along, admiring the island. I reached Zara Parsons' house five minutes late, to find an older minivan parked in the driveway. I rang the front doorbell and waited. After a few moments, it swung open, and a short, dark-skinned woman in her fifties frowned at me.

"You look like you're from Norway, so I guess you're Constable Sommer."

"*Ja*," I replied. "Sorry I'm late."

"Honey, it's the Cayman Islands," she said, stepping aside to let me in. "Nobody's on time here."

I walked into the house, thinking what a strange statement that was coming from a woman who had been on time. Marlene Seymour spoke with a very light, local accent, no doubt softening it further for my benefit.

"Did you come alone?" I asked, surprised she wouldn't have somebody with her.

"Husband's working," she replied, closing the door. "He doesn't know what to do with himself since... you know."

Marlene's eyes were puffy and red, and I realised she'd probably come here early and spent some time crying over her daughter. I'm sure she needed a few words of comfort, but I was pretty sure I'd screw it up if I tried to offer any, so I moved things along.

"Have you looked for the ring?"

She shook her head. "I figured you'd want to see for yourself, as it seemed important to you. But I can show you around if you like?"

"Okay," I replied.

Marlene struck me as a lovely woman. I'd never met her daughter at the school as I'd managed to miss two parent-teacher event things I was supposed to attend. AJ had gone in my place both times. Following Zara's mother up the stairs, I guessed she'd never missed one of her daughter's school events. They'd obviously helped Zara go to university in Florida, which wouldn't have been cheap either. The thought of Jazzy being raised in a loving, sensible, normal home like I presumed Marlene and Terrence Seymour's to be made me feel like I was falling more than a little short. But even I knew asking the woman if she'd like to adopt a fifteen-year-old to replace her dead daughter was poor timing and tactless. Besides, I was becoming somewhat possessive of the kid. It was up to me to do a better job.

"Zara wasn't big on fancy jewellery," Marlene was saying, and I realised she was in the walk-in closet, pointing to a tray on a shelf.

Behind it, several fashionable necklaces of coloured beads hung from hooks. In the tray were a few jangly bracelets and a couple of rings, but none of them were the school ring we were looking for. We spent another thirty minutes searching the house without any luck.

After thanking Marlene and fending off more questions about the significance of the ring being missing, I left the house and climbed in the Jeep. If something personal had been taken from Jerald Dilbert, then I'd have a pattern worth presenting to Whittaker, to go with the other similarities. Home alone at a predictable time, easy access from behind the homes, and knowledge they'd be discovered later in the day. I was about to start the Jeep when my mobile rang.

"Hey," I answered, seeing it was Robbie, who was one of the few names saved in my phone.

"Nora, we've been working on your scammer."

"We?" I questioned.

"Yeah. Rabbit is pretty cool."

My head was buried in the accidental death case, and I'd forgotten I'd attempted to get Robbie and Rabbit together.

"Can you come by?" he asked.

"Can't you just tell me?"

I didn't mind going by, but I was still hoping to see Mrs Dilbert today. It felt like she now held the key to the investigation moving forward. Plus, I wanted to ask her about the cousin.

"You should come by," he persisted. "It's better to show you than explain."

"Fine. Ten minutes."

"Can you bring me a coffee-flavoured energy drink?" he asked.

"Are you supposed to drink that *dritt*?"

"No."

"Your mum home?"

"No."

"Okay. I'll be fifteen minutes."

I liked those tasty, caffeine-filled drinks too.

15

DEVIOUSLY BRILLIANT

Robbie sucked on the straw while I held the can in front of him.

"If this kills you, I'm covering up the evidence," I warned him.

He chuckled and dribbled the drink down his chin. I wiped it away with my sleeve.

"Thanks," he said, took one more, long sip, then moved his head to the side, letting me know to take the can away. "Let me show you what we have," he added.

"You worked on this with Rabbit?" I asked.

"Yeah," Robbie replied. "She came up with an idea, then we figured it out together."

Robbie moved various windows around on his monitor and I noticed one which looked like a dashboard for online gaming.

"We set up a challenge through the community forum on Steam then challenged players to a treasure hunt with a prize."

"What's the prize?" I asked.

"You can't offer money, so the winner gets plus-rep from all the other players, and entry is only open to players of a certain level and rep status."

I looked at the kid. "I've no idea what you just said."

"Sorry. +Rep is a Steam thing that's supposed to show your reliability and trustworthiness for performing trades and other stuff."

"Okay. So what's Steam?"

"You don't know anything about gaming, do you?"

"Why would I?" I rebutted.

"Because it's fun, and would be handy for you to know right about now," Robbie replied, grinning at me.

"I have you."

"And Rabbit."

"True. Now what's Steam?"

"Steam is the largest online gaming site for playing, discussing, and creating games. It has something like 28 million members and often there are six to ten million people online at any time."

"*Fy faen,*" I muttered. "Maybe I should have heard of it."

"That's what I'm saying," Robbie replied, his smile widening.

"How do you figure out who's on the island from 28 million users?"

"That's what I'm trying to show you. We set up a treasure hunt competition, with clues here in Grand Cayman."

"You set up clues around the island in the last twenty-four hours?"

"No, silly. It's all online. A treasure hunt like this uses clues to answers you can find through Google Maps."

I took a long swig of my energy drink. I needed my brain to work faster.

"And you've set up clues specific to Grand Cayman?" I asked.

"Welcome to the show, Constable Sommer," Robbie said, between chuckles and subsequent hiccups caused by his amusement at me.

I thought for a moment. "Hey, I was wondering. What's your handle?"

"Woof on Wheels," Robbie replied, looking pleased with himself.

"I get the wheels, but why woof?"

"My last name..." he said, as though it was the most obvious thing in the world.

"Barker," I thought out loud.

He stared at me with his mouth slightly open.

"Oh, barker, like a dog that barks, so woof like a dog," I figured out.

"It's not as funny when you have to spell it out."

"Give me a break. English is my second language." I said defensively, then realised I was the one wasting time now. "Okay, so how did you set a treasure hunt up so quickly?"

"That was pretty cool. First, Rabbit created a theme through..."

"Stop," I said firmly. "Forget I asked. I don't care how you did it, I only want to know who you found."

"You don't want to see this awesome treasure hunt we put together?"

Robbie sounded like I'd just shot his barker. I held up his can and pressed the straw between his lips.

"No," I replied, knowing he couldn't complain with the straw in his mouth.

But he tried, spluttered, and then I had to wipe his chin again. Which of course made me feel bad.

"It's not that I don't want to see it, Robbie, and I'm very impressed, but I have another case I'm officially working on... well, somewhat officially working on, and I should be in George Town already. So, if you can stick to the basics, then you can show me your clever programming later when I have time."

He looked up at me, and a smile crept over his face. "That was a lot of words for you."

"Too many," I agreed.

"I feel special."

"You are special, Robbie, but it doesn't mean I won't taser you somewhere you'll feel it if you don't get to the point."

His shoulders shook as he laughed, until he abruptly stopped when we both heard the groan of the automatic garage door opening.

"Trouble," he blurted, and I looked at the can sitting next to me.

"Throw the straw away, then pretend you drank them both," he added.

I tossed the straw in a rubbish bin under his desk, then picked up both cans.

"*Dritt*. They're both half full."

"Finish one, quick."

His had less in it, so I went to guzzle it down, but paused. "You don't have some kind of gross teenage mouth fungus, do you?"

He laughed again. "I don't think my problems are contagious, Nora. Just drink it or she'll be mad at both of us."

I swigged the remaining contents of the can and tossed it in the bin, trying not to belch. I couldn't believe I was hiding an energy drink from a parent like we'd been caught with a bottle of vodka. The door from the garage opened, and Robbie's mother came in, carrying several shopping bags of groceries.

"Hello, Nora. How are you?" she asked.

I liked Robbie's mum. She'd been kind to me in the past and appreciated me making her son feel important by helping the police out.

"*Hallo*. Robbie's been reinstated as an honorary constable for a few days."

"Wonderful," she said, placing the bags on the kitchen counter. "He needs something to take his mind off what's going on."

"What's going on?" I asked, looking at the kid.

"Mum!" Robbie snapped.

"I'm sorry, Robbie. I thought you would have said something to Nora. She's your friend," she said, cringing at her mistake.

"Robbie?" I asked, crouching down to be at eye level with him. "What's going on? I wouldn't have bothered you with this if I knew you had shit going on."

"I always want to help with anything I can do," he replied. "And it's no big deal. I'm just having another procedure next week in Miami."

From the look on his mother's face and the way she'd mentioned it, I knew it was far from *no big deal*. I felt like shit. I hadn't asked him how he was doing. Well, I had, but it was the standard "How are things?" I'd greeted him with when I'd arrived. My role with him had always been distracting him from the fact that he spent his life between a wheelchair and a bed. I provided something exciting and fun. Today, my head was caught up in cases, and both times I'd been by, he'd seemed the same as always. I felt incredibly selfish.

"Don't go all droopy eyed and *poor Robbie* on me, or I'll borrow your Taser and zap you with it," he said, looking at me sternly.

"Fry my skinny arse all you want, but I won't stop caring about your bony arse," I replied, and winked.

He grinned in return. "I'll call you next week when I get back and let you know how it went, okay? Now, can we get back to work?"

I stood. "I'm still waiting for you to give me names."

"You're getting ahead of yourself, Nora. We don't have names yet."

"Then why did you call me over?" I rebutted, glancing over at his mother.

She smiled, clearly pleased we'd moved on, and I nodded in return.

"Because the next part isn't standard police procedure," Robbie said.

"You mean it's illegal?"

"Technically."

"*Dritt*. Means I can't use it to get a warrant. And if it comes to light that we used a method like that to track the guy, the case will be thrown out of court."

"So we shouldn't go ahead?" Robbie asked.

"How illegal is it? Will the scammer know?

Robbie shook his head. "No. It's how they get people's info for doxing and swatting, except we just retrieve their IP address, location and name, then give it to you instead of having them raided by the police. Well, I guess we do get them raided, but not by an anonymous tip to the police swat team."

"That's called swatting?"

"Yeah. It's a thing. Unfortunately, it usually gets used to mess with online gamers who are doing really well."

"That sucks. It wastes police time and is probably a big pain in the arse for the gamer."

"It is," he agreed.

"But you're not going to do this to everyone who enters your treasure hunt, right?" I asked.

"No. Only the people we think are on the island."

"And you'll figure that out by who solves the clues?"

"Just one of the clues."

"You've rigged one?"

"Clue five."

"What's clue five?" I asked, hoping I didn't regret asking.

"From Google Maps Street View you can see a portion of the sign needed to solve the clue. The only way to get the complete answer is to go by and look," he explained with a broad smile.

"That's pretty clever."

"Are you kidding me?" he retorted. "It's deviously brilliant."

"*Ja*, it's deviously brilliant," I admitted. "So get me the names and I'll figure out a way to use the information."

Outside Robbie's, I sat in the Jeep and called the number I had for Mrs Dilbert. It went to voicemail. I couldn't blame her for screening calls from unknown numbers. I texted instead, asking if I could speak to her for a few minutes. Not wanting to loiter outside the Barkers' home, I began driving south towards George Town, hoping for the best. Halfway along West Bay Drive, my mobile rang.

"Constable Sommer?"

"*Ja.*"

"This is Marva Dilbert. You need to see me? About what?"

"Thank you for calling back. Are you home? I can come by."

"What's this about?" she asked again. "I have family over."

I could imagine her house full of aunts, uncles, cousins, parents, and assorted other branches of the family tree. The Cayman Islanders were like many cultures who pulled together in times of crisis. It was all hands on deck with food, support, more food, and a plan to never leave the bereaved alone. Not the environment I'd choose to walk into, but I didn't have much choice.

"It'll only take a couple of minutes," I urged. "There's a detail I need to verify."

I heard a quiet groan. "Okay. Come by."

"Thank you," I replied, and hung up, picking up my speed.

It was almost 6:00pm when I reached the house, parked, and knocked on the front door. Cars were parked haphazardly all around the driveway and along the kerb, and from the sound of voices inside, she had half the island for company. A woman I didn't know answered the door.

"Constable Sommer for Mrs Dilbert," I said, and she looked me over suspiciously.

I was glad I hadn't had time to change out of uniform, as at least my visit appeared official.

"Wait here," the lady told me, pushing the door to.

After a minute, Marva Dilbert appeared. "Would you like to come inside?"

"Probably quieter for you to step outside for a moment, ma'am."

Marva looked over her shoulder and we could both hear a hundred conversations going on inside the home. She nodded and pulled the door closed behind her.

"Mrs Dilbert, have you received your husband's personal effects yet?"

She shook her head. "They said I'd get them after the autopsy was done."

I thought about my next question for a moment. I knew what I wanted to ask, but my delay was considering how to ask it. Maybe Whittaker's mentoring was slowly wearing off on me.

"I know this is probably difficult to think about, Mrs Dilbert, but when you found your husband, did you notice any personal items missing from his body?"

She stared at me, her brow furrowed. "All I've tried to do since yesterday afternoon is *not* see my husband lying dead on our hallway floor, Constable. Now you want me to think about it again?"

Dritt. Apparently, I needed more mentoring.

"I'm sorry to put you through that, Mrs Dilbert, but it is quite important."

She ran a hand through her hair and sighed. "I can't say I noticed anything. To be honest, I was too busy trying to resuscitate him."

"Did your husband wear any jewellery?"

"Just his wedding ring, and a thin gold chain around his neck."

"But you didn't notice if he had them on?"

Marva shook her head, then thought for a moment. "Wait here. I'll be right back."

Before I could ask why, she'd bolted back inside, so I stood on the front pathway with a few of the neighbours staring down the street at me. It took Marva a minute to check on whatever she'd thought of before she reappeared.

"They're here," she announced, and opened her hand to show me a wedding band and a gold chain, coiled in her palm. "He'd take them off when he did work around the house. They were on the dresser in our room."

"Did he wear a watch?" I asked, trying to think of something we may have overlooked.

"Yes. I forget the brand. It was nice looking, but not an expensive one."

"And he didn't leave that inside?" I asked.

"I didn't see it, but he usually left his watch on until he went to bed."

That would be an easy check with the coroner's office, although I'd probably have to deal with Gareth Davies. Which was like a trip to the dentist.

"I appreciate your help, Mrs Dilbert, and once again, I'm sorry for your loss," I said, ready to leave.

"Why is any of this important, Constable?" she asked.

I stopped and took my time turning around. "Just buttoning up details," I said, unwilling to start the shitstorm that would accompany the real reason.

"Oh, I almost forgot," I blurted, suddenly remembering the second question I needed answered. "Your husband has a cousin, I believe. Moses Dilbert?"

Marva rolled her eyes. "What do you need to know about that deadbeat?"

That answered part of my question. They obviously didn't get along, but the next query would be tricky without getting Marva suspicious of my motives.

"Did your husband ever spend time with his cousin?"

"Hell, no. We wouldn't let him near our house."

"May I ask why, Mrs Dilbert?"

"'Cos he stole and lied enough times that we couldn't have any part of that man anymore."

Her answer made me wonder why on earth the other two victims would be friends with Moses Dilbert if the guy was such an arse. But there again, Jerald was still friends with him on social media despite their feud. I really didn't understand that whole thing.

"Do you have an address or phone number for Moses?" I asked.

Marva shook her head. "No idea. That man changes numbers all the time to keep people he owes money from hounding him. If he hasn't got himself fired, you can find him at CUC. He works maintenance for them."

"The electric company?" I asked. "He's an electrician?"

Marva scoffed. "He ain't that smart. He's building maintenance."

Which meant he had to have a general knowledge of just about everything to do with how a commercial building ran, I considered as I walked to my Jeep.

16

CYBERCRIMES, PATTERNS, AND LAUNDRY

I sat in my Jeep and looked at the phone in my hand. It was now 6:30pm on Friday night. Not the ideal time to call Detective Whittaker with an update on the not yet official case he told me not to rack up any more overtime pursuing until Monday. I could tell him I wouldn't put in my hours for this afternoon's work, but I knew he wouldn't accept that. I was doing police work in uniform, therefore it needed to be on the books. There were so many rules, protocols, and budget restrictions to be considered when trying to catch bad people who live by no rules at all. It drove me crazy, but I'd fought the system too many times already, and I was out of free passes. I called Whittaker.

"Evening, Nora," he answered.

"Sorry to call you on a Friday evening, sir."

"That's okay. I'm still at the office. What can I help you with?"

"Will you be there for a few more minutes?" I asked.

"A few more, but I was hoping to leave in fifteen or twenty minutes."

"I'm close by," I said. "I won't keep you long."

I hung up before he could protest. Although he'd see I was still in uniform, I always found it better to talk to him in person, so I sped through Friday evening traffic to the station. Which actually meant I crawled the 1.2 kilometres from Newport Avenue to Elgin Avenue in eight minutes.

Which became eleven minutes by the time I'd parked, run inside, gone upstairs, and stood in front of Whittaker.

"You're still in uniform," he opened with.

"Yes sir, I haven't been home yet, but I've only been working on the accidental death case for part of the afternoon."

"Opposed to stopping at midday and picking it up again when you're back on duty Monday," he spelt out for me.

"I may have found something more to the case," I replied, choosing to get to the point. "The first two victims both had an article of jewellery missing. If their accidents had outside help, sir, the perp may have taken trophies."

Whittaker now took a little more interest. "What was taken? Well, missing. It's possible the items were misplaced, correct?"

"A class ring and a pendant, sir. And I've searched both premises without finding either item. Plus, I have CCTV from the bank showing Heather Lawson leaving the evening before with the dolphin pendant she apparently wore every day."

"Hmm," Whittaker grunted. "What about the fellow who electrocuted himself?"

"His wife found his ring and gold chain in their bedroom," I explained. "She said he took them off when he worked on stuff, but I have to check with the coroner's office, as he should have been wearing a watch."

"It sounds like you have worked all day on this, Nora," he commented, eyeing me suspiciously.

"No, sir, I spent some of the afternoon working on another case."

"Which Sergeant Redburn at West Bay station no doubt approved?"

Dritt. I walked right in to that one.

"Off the clock, sir. Some arse scammed Jacob's grandmother and we think he's here on the island. I've been helping out."

"If you're in uniform, you're either on the clock or travelling between work and home, Constable," he pointed out.

I couldn't wait until I made detective and was allowed to wear regular clothes and not have to punch a damn clock. Although I wasn't sure what the dress code was for female detectives. To my knowledge, there weren't any currently on the force.

"Sounds like a case for cybercrimes," he added.

"They're swamped, and this is Jacob's grandmother, sir."

Whittaker nodded. "Fair enough. Make sure you log the hours and I'll sign off on them," he said begrudgingly.

"I also have a suspect, sir."

"In which case?"

"The accident case, sir."

"Really? You honestly think someone is killing people and staging it to look like accidents? You know what that means, don't you?"

"He's clever," I suggested.

"And we're talking about a serial killer, Nora," he said and ran his hand through his neatly trimmed salt and pepper hair. "To my knowledge, we've never had a serial killer on the island, and I'd hoped we never would."

"We're not there yet, sir, but I've linked one man to all three victims."

"Who?"

"His name is Moses Dilbert. He's Jerald's cousin, but according to Jerald's wife, Moses is a deadbeat and they don't get along. Moses is social media friends with all three."

"Is that it?" Whittaker questioned.

"Yes, sir. I'm aware it's thin, but a place to start."

The detective thought for a few moments while he tidied his desk, which already looked pretty tidy to me.

"Find out if the watch is missing. If it is, then we have enough evidence to keep pursuing the theory. We'll also see what the autopsies give us. If neither bear fruit, then I'd say we're barking up the wrong tree."

Tree. I knew *wall* didn't sound right. Or house.

"Okay," I relented. For now. "I'll check on the watch."

Whittaker stood and began gathering his things.

"And we should keep an eye out for any other strange accidents, sir."

He paused and looked at me. "Accidents are often just that, Nora."

"Of course, but when has a string of fatalities ever happened in a week like this?"

"An accident spree?" he replied, allowing himself the slightest of grins. "I can't say I can recall this many since Hurricane Ivan. Which, of course, was extenuating circumstances."

"How many people died, sir?"

"Two," he replied, taking his sport coat off the hook and picking up his briefcase. "So, yes, Nora, this is unprecedented."

"Then this should be easy," I said, walking with him out of his office.

"How so?" he asked.

"If there's another fatal accident, then they're not accidents," I replied.

He paused at the top of the stairs. "In that case, I'm going to say it again. For every reason I can think of, I hope we don't see another unfortunate accident anytime soon."

We walked down the stairs and across the reception area in silence, before saying goodbye once we exited the building. I could tell Whittaker was shaken by the idea we had a serial killer on the island, but I was surprised he wouldn't want to push an investigation a little harder in case we did. There'd be no harm if they were indeed an odd string of accidents.

I stopped before I reached the Jeep and turned around. It was Friday night. The coroner's office would be closed even if Gareth Davies was still working, so they wouldn't answer their phone and I didn't have Davies' mobile number. If I'd thought of it, I could have got it from Whittaker. I went back inside, hoping Davies had updated the case file. I really didn't want to call Whittaker again, although, based on the way Davies and I didn't get along, the detective might not be keen to offer up the man's number. And by the way Whittaker had been keen to get home, I presumed he had plans for the evening.

Firing up one of the communal computers, I impatiently tapped a toe while the system booted. I logged in and found the Dilbert case on the server. There wouldn't be an autopsy report until next week, but I found a document entering the body into the system and cataloguing Jerald Dilbert's personal possessions. I leaned forward in the seat and read the details. Each article of clothing was listed, including the shoes which had been removed at the scene. A package of chewing gum from his trouser pocket, a Sharpie marker pen, and that was it. No watch.

I left the station with mixed feelings. On one hand, it appeared my gut might be right, but it was hard to feel good about that, and on the other, we could be looking at an incredibly stealthy murderer who'd left no evidence at the scenes. We had three corpses and nothing to work from except a slim common denominator through social media. I was about to text Whittaker before leaving the car park, when my mobile buzzed. It was Jazzy.

"Where are you?"

Normally, I would text back as I hated being called instead of texted in return. The medium had been chosen. If I wanted to talk to you, I'd have called in the first place. But I had to drive, and I was in uniform, so the last thing I needed was some Goody Two-Feet snapping a picture of me texting and driving. The Jeep had a hands-free system for calls, but it wasn't easy to hear over the wind and tyre noise.

"Hey, I'm driving," I explained before she gave me shit for calling. "I'm on my way home now."

"Where are you?" she asked again, verbally this time.

"Just left Central Station."

"Ugh," she groaned. "That'll take you forever in Friday traffic."

I scrambled to recall what I must have forgotten. I couldn't come up with anything, so I gave up.

"What am I missing?"

"It's Friday night," Jazzy replied, as though the world knew exactly what took place on a Friday evening in West Bay, Grand Cayman.

"It is," I agreed, refusing to be baited.

"And what do we do at least one Friday evening every month?"

The penny finally dropped. It must be the night Reg's wife, Pearl, played at the local pub. I had forgotten. She usually played on one or two Friday evenings, depending on whatever special events or holidays were going on. Jazzy didn't care so much about the music, but she liked the food and the company. It had been the first place I'd taken her for a real meal after she reluctantly let me approach her when she'd been living on the streets. It also explained why Whittaker had been keen to leave. He and his wife, Rosie, rarely missed Pearl's performances. No point texting him if I was about to see him at the pub.

"I figured we'd skip it this month," I teased.

"Okay," Jazzy replied without missing a beat. "I'll ride my bike over if you're not going."

"Oh yeah? And you've got money for your own dinner, do you?"

"AJ will buy me dinner," she replied cheerily. "Or Reg."

I laughed. I was only messing with the kid, but she was right. Any one of about six people that would be there tonight would gladly buy Jazzy dinner. Without trying, she'd built herself a family of unrelated people who cared about her very much.

"Bring me something to wear and I'll text when I'm five minutes away. Meet me on the road."

"Okay, see ya," she said, and hung up.

A little over twenty minutes later, I picked her up by the side of Conch Point Road, then backtracked to North West Point Road and the Fox and Hare pub. The gravel car park was full, so I created a spot at the end of a row, leaving just about enough room for cars to get by. I stood behind the Jeep, stripped off my shirt, and slipped on the red and black summer dress Jazzy had chosen. Dressier than I would have picked, but I didn't have a choice at this point.

"Really?" I asked, shaking my head. "You couldn't have picked shorts and a T-shirt?"

"Everything's in the laundry hamper," she claimed, and probably had a point.

I laundered based on necessity rather than schedule.

"Besides, you look good in that dress, so maybe you'll get lucky," she said, laughing at her own joke.

"I'm not looking to get lucky, and you better hope I don't, or you'll be out on the porch for the night."

"Ewwww," Jazzy responded in disgust, which I was happy to hear.

I hoped it meant she wasn't ready to get intimate with boys just yet, although I knew that time couldn't be far away. She was fifteen, and advanced for her age in many ways, yet behind in others from the convoluted way she'd grown up in a mixture of foster homes, on her own, and now with me.

Stepping out of my uniform trousers, I stuffed everything, including my utility belt and boots, into a lockbox chained in the back. My flip-flops felt good after another long day on my feet, and we trudged into the pub to find our friends.

Pearl was already playing, and the packed crowd was buzzing as her powerful voice boomed from the little stage. AJ spotted us and Jazzy pushed through the people to give her a big hug. Reg stood and pointed to a pair of chairs they'd saved us around the table. He reached over with his big bear claw hand and softly squeezed my shoulder.

"Alright, love?" he asked, his deep voice audible over his wife's amplifier.

I smiled and nodded, taking my seat. Because I was alright. Sometimes, it didn't always feel that way, but when I pushed the bullshit aside, I was actually more content than I could ever remember.

17

SPRINTS AND LADDERS

Jazzy could be a con artist when she wanted to be. I'd been sold on taking my morning run with her through West Bay. This was a first. The kid was incredibly fit from fending for herself on the streets for years, and being an active teenager, but she'd never wanted to go for a run with me before. Two and half kilometres in, I found out why today was different. We arrived at the primary school off Hell Road, where they happened to have a nice running track encircling their football pitch.

"Hey, look," Jazzy announced, pointing to the school field where several people were exercising and a few kids were knocking about a football. "I could do a few sprints. I need to work on getting up to speed faster."

I had to admit, it was a well-planned ruse. A decent warm-up jog, and now she was ready to work on her sprinting. As we would have to run home afterwards, I figured it wasn't a total loss for me, and I could run laps of the track while she practised.

"I brought a stopwatch with me," she added, handing it to me.

So much for my exercise needs.

"You don't have starting blocks," I pointed out.

"I know," she replied. "Coach says I should jog to a starting point and practise accelerating up to full speed."

So apparently, I'd been caught up in a conspiracy. A plot devised before today. We jogged around the fenced field and through the school's entrance to reach the track.

"When do I start and stop the watch?" I asked.

"At the line over there," she said, pointing, "until where you'll be standing, 30 metres down the track."

"So you want me to stand in the same place for however long you practise?"

Jazzy frowned. Looked like she hadn't counted on her timing system having a say in the event.

"How about I put a marker by the side of the track so I can return to the same spot?" I suggested.

She shrugged her shoulders. "That's fine."

While Jazzy walked beyond the line she'd pointed out, I found a white limestone rock by the fence, and placed it across the track at what I guessed to be 30 metres from her start. It all seemed fairly inaccurate to me, but I played along as I wanted to encourage her new-found interest in athletics. Being involved in both swimming and sailing had taught me, and tested me, in my commitment, willingness to sacrifice, and work ethic. Qualities I'd been able to put to good use in the past few years.

"Ready?" she shouted, and I gave her an okay sign.

She jogged towards the line, then accelerated into a sprint as she crossed the stripe. I started the watch at what I judged from my angle to be the right moment and stopped it when she broke the plane between me and my rock. Jazzy ambled back to me and I showed the watch.

"Okay. That's my baseline. I have to do better than that."

Seemed like a reasonable goal, but I couldn't get over how flawed the testing method seemed to me.

"But how can you be sure you're crossing the line at the same pace every time? And look, I'm having to judge when to start the watch from here, where I'm looking almost straight at you."

Jazzy glared at me as though I'd cancelled Christmas, her birthday, and all Friday nights at the Fox and Hare.

"You could buy me a set of starting blocks," she shot back.

"How much are they?"

"Couple of hundred dollars plus shipping to the island," she said without pause. "No one has them in the sports shops here."

That didn't seem too horribly expensive, although shipping anything to the island was costly and took a while. Starting from blocks would help the manual timing, but it still wouldn't be accurate to the resolution she needed to see changes over such a short distance.

"A timing system is anywhere from 200 dollars for a shitty one up to thousands for the good ones," she continued as though she'd read my mind.

"Oh," I muttered.

It appeared she'd done her research before setting me up to be her stopwatch operator.

"Don't swear," I added, remembering I was supposed to be in charge of some things between us.

"Okay," she replied, not sounding in the least bit remorseful. "Now, how about you do your best with what we have to work with until you spring for the cool stuff?"

"Sounds good," I relented, making sure I didn't allow myself to grin in front of her.

But inside, I was laughing my arse off. She trotted back to her start and raised a hand when she was ready. I indicated I was paying attention, and she tried sprinting again. When she walked over, catching her breath, I held up the stopwatch and showed her the time.

"What was the baseline?" she asked.

"I don't know," I admitted. "I gave it to you."

Jazzy threw her hands up and rolled her eyes. "One job. You have one job to do."

"Technically, that would be two jobs if I'm to store the information as well as time you."

"I'm doing the hard part," she complained.

"And I'm doing the part of thousands of dollars' worth of equipment."

"Well, write them down or something."

"I have a better idea," I replied, letting the stopwatch drop on its cord around my neck. "I'll use the stopwatch on my mobile. It remembers the numbers."

"Yours has that?" she asked, rolling her eyes again.

"*Ja.*"

"Mine doesn't."

"That's because you have the cheapest phone I could find."

Most teenagers would instantly complain about how poorly they had it with a cheap phone, but Jazzy didn't. She didn't care that other kids at school had the latest $1,500 devices, and in fact, laughed about how ridiculous it was. Which she may have got from me. I hoped she'd be able to keep her sensible and balanced view of life with all the crazy possession and fad-orientated influences flooding everyone's worlds.

As Jazzy jogged to her starting spot, I found the timing app on my mobile, and jumped when it rang. It was Whittaker.

"Nora, are you busy?"

I looked at Jazzy, who was now staring back at me with her hands on her hips.

"I'm with the kid, but what's up?"

"Then I don't want to interfere with your time together on your days off, Nora," he responded. "We can pick it up Monday."

"What's happened, sir?" I asked, knowing I wouldn't be able to shake the curiosity from my mind.

"An accident has been reported at a home off Batabano Road. I'm heading over to take a look," Whittaker explained.

"Can you pick me up in West Bay?" I replied immediately, unable to stop myself.

"You don't have to, Nora. I can let you know if it seems related in any way. I'm told the woman is alive, but unconscious."

A survivor of the attacks would be a goldmine for the investigation, and I realised I was thinking of it that way now. An investigation.

"I'd really like to be there, sir. I'm at the primary school if you wouldn't mind picking me up."

The line was quiet for a moment and I hoped he didn't piece together the fact that I'd said "me" despite having Jazzy with me.

"Okay. I'm on my way. I'll be there in ten minutes."

He hung up, and I looked at Jazzy.

"Are you ready, or what?" she shouted.

"Waiting on you to go," I called back, quickly switching back to the stopwatch app.

Jazzy did another sprint, and when she jogged over, I showed her the time.

"That was a little faster," I commented, having made sure I remembered the prior time.

She nodded. "What's the deal?"

"It looked like you kept your upper body lower for longer getting up to full speed," I replied.

"Not that – with your phone call."

It was hard to slip anything past this kid.

"I've got about ten minutes, and then I have to go. It's a work thing."

"Home?" she asked.

"No. Whittaker is picking me up."

"You. Or us?"

I guess I hadn't thought that part through. This foster parent thing bites me in the arse at every turn. I really didn't want Jazzy running through the back roads of West Bay on her own. Which sounded ridiculous in my own head. She'd lived alone on the streets for several years, but now it was different. I was responsible.

"I'll ask him to drop you home."

"I can run home when I'm done," she retorted firmly, and started walking away.

Dritt. How could I argue with that when my reasons sounded unreasonable to me?

"Come with us. It won't take long, and he can drop us back here. You can practise some more, then we'll run home."

I wished I'd asked Whittaker where on Batabano we were going, as we probably could have run there in ten minutes. Jazzy got ready for another sprint, but I could see her mind was whirring, and I knew it wasn't about running. I'd ruined her practice session she'd conned me into helping her with. I started the watch on my phone as she ran once more and stopped it as she crossed my imaginary line to the rock I'd placed. This one was unsurprisingly slower. I held up the screen, and she scowled.

"Why didn't you just tell me you wanted to practise?" I asked.

She shrugged her shoulders. "I came up with the idea when I saw the track."

"BS. You had this planned before we left the house."

She scowled again, this time at me instead of the times.

"Just say next time," I said, hearing a vehicle turning off of Hell Road.

I turned and saw Whittaker in his Range Rover. He was here faster than advertised.

"Let's go," I said. "We'll come back."

"You're always doing stuff," Jazzy blurted as we walked across the track towards the school entrance. "I didn't know if you'd have time."

"I'll make time," I replied.

"Ummm…" she said, and looked at me with wide eyes.

"I had no way of knowing this would come up," I responded, a little more defensively than I intended. "And, if you'd asked me this morning if I'd help you practise, I would have said yes."

"And we still would have been interrupted," she pointed out as we reached the SUV.

"Yeah," I agreed. "But shit happens. I'm a copper, remember," I continued, stopping and putting a hand on her skinny shoulder. "I'll support you and help as best I can. Just ask next time, okay?"

"Fine," she replied, but not in a dismissive way, so I think she heard me.

I opened the back door, and she climbed in, then I took the front passenger seat.

"I brought backup," I said, looking at Detective Whittaker, who couldn't really protest now the kid was in the car.

"I see that. Hello, Jasmine," he said, looking over his shoulder. "Congratulations on your wins Thursday night."

"Hello, sir," she replied, putting her seatbelt on. "And thank you." I saw a frown tense her forehead. "But I'd appreciate it if you didn't tell Jada-Kai I'm doing extra practice. She's tough enough to beat already."

Whittaker laughed. "Your secret's safe with me."

He turned the SUV around and pulled up to the main road.

"So what happened at this one?" I asked, shivering as the cool air conditioning hit the perspiration on my skin.

I realised we were both leaving sweaty patches on the fancy seats, but Whittaker didn't seem to notice as he headed east.

"A lady fell off a ladder behind her house," he replied.

"And she's alive?"

"She was when the ambulance took her, but I haven't heard an update. Apparently, she suffered a nasty head wound and was unconscious."

"Hmm," I murmured.

"What are you thinking?" Whittaker asked, looking over at me.

"Let's take a look," was all I replied, but I was already pretty sure this accident was unrelated.

The killer, if we were indeed chasing a killer, was too good to leave a victim alive.

18

GUTTERS, LUNCH, AND SWAMP

The home was close to where West Church Street changed its name to Batabano Road for no obvious reason. Two other roads intersected in a staggered fashion from either side of three houses on the south side of the street, the victim's being the centre residence. Detective Whittaker double checked the address he'd been given, as the driveway was empty, with not a soul in sight.

We got out of the Range Rover, leaving Jazzy unimpressed when we told her to stay in the car, but she didn't protest in front of Whittaker. As we approached the house, a neighbour appeared, no doubt confused by a neatly dressed man in a suit with a young blonde in running gear showing up.

"Help you?" the woman asked with a strong local accent.

Whittaker held up his badge. "Police, ma'am. We're checking on a reported accident at this address."

"Bit late, I'd say," she responded. "Dey taken Mary to da hospital. Ain't nobody home."

"Okay, thank you, ma'am," Whittaker replied, and I took the path around the side of the building.

The backyard had a concrete patio extending from the house to where shrubs lined a patchy garden of grass. It took a lot of water and usually imported soil to keep a decent lawn on the island. The stony limestone base wasn't particularly fertile. On the patio lay a ladder and a scattering of leaves and grimy clumps of dirt.

"Cleaning the gutters," Whittaker commented as he joined me.

"How old is the victim?" I asked.

"I didn't ask," Whittaker admitted.

I tried the back door, but it was locked, so I peeked through the window. The furnishings were floral patterns and I could see picture frames perched on every available surface. The room was too dim and the sunshine too bright for me to make out who was in the pictures, but I'd have bet money on them being grandchildren.

"I feel bad for bothering you now," Whittaker said. "There's not much we can learn here at the moment."

"I'm glad you did," I replied. "I think we learnt enough."

I looked at the concrete patio. It was old and stained from years of weather and use, but a small patch of freshly dried blood was still easy to spot.

"Any reason why I can't pick the ladder up?" I asked.

Whittaker shook his head. "Should probably use gloves in case we need to dust for prints, but otherwise, no. I doubt it's exactly where it fell anyway. They probably moved it to attend to the victim."

I slipped on the nitrile gloves he handed me, which were always a pain in the arse to get over your fingers in the island humidity. Picking up the ladder, I propped it against the metal gutter running along the edge of the roof. I climbed up and studied its brown paint or coating. It didn't take long to see a set of scratches to my right. Looking farther, I had a clear view into the neighbour's backyard, and turning, I could see the other side as well.

I scrambled down and moved the ladder to line up with the beginning of the scrapes. They corresponded perfectly to the rails.

"That looks like the spot," Whittaker commented, observing me closely.

I climbed back up and went a step higher to look into the gutter. To my left, it had been cleared of debris, but just more than an arm's length to my right, leaves and dirt filled the trough. I looked down at Whittaker.

"Stand back a bit, sir."

"What are you doing?" he asked, but reversed a few paces towards the lawn.

I reached over and stretched to just touch the mess in the gutter, then leaned my body farther and farther that way until the ladder began to tip.

"Nora!" Whittaker shouted, as the ladder, with me along for the ride, toppled over.

I jumped clear and landed on my feet as the ladder clattered to the concrete. A metre or so to my right was the blood stain. Apparently, the victim hadn't been nimble enough to react in time. Not surprising if she was indeed a grandmother.

"Good Lord, Nora," Whittaker complained. "You scared me to death. How about you warn me before you pull stunts like that?"

"I don't think this fits the pattern at all, sir," I said, ignoring his concerns.

He let out a long breath. "I'd agree with that, but give me your reasons."

"She's alive," I began, while heading for the path beside the house. "And it would have been easy for the killer to check."

"If we're chasing a killer and not just a string of bizarre accidents," Whittaker reminded me again, as he followed.

"Of course," I conceded. "But access to the house is too open and activity in the backyard can be seen from either neighbour, at least one of whom appears to be home."

"Okay," the detective responded. "Carry on."

"Weekends are unpredictable," I continued. "People are less inclined to have routines which tend not to vary during the week. Our killer, if he exists, seems to plan and observe his victims. He knows their routines and those of the people close by. He won't kill again until next week."

"That's a bold prediction, Nora. I truly hope you're wrong."

"I'm not making a prediction, sir. I'm just saying he's more likely to kill during the week."

When I turned the corner to the driveway, I saw Jazzy leaning on the low wall dividing the property from the neighbour's, chatting with the woman we'd spoken to earlier. I walked closer.

"How old is Mary?" I asked.

The woman, who was probably in her sixties, eyed me up and down. "She turned fifty-five a few weeks back."

"Does she live alone?"

"No. Her husband was out doin' someting dis mornin' so she decide to climb up that ladder herself. I'd o' helped if only she'd asked."

"Miss Powery didn't see Miss Mary fall off the ladder, but she heard the noise and came out to see," Jazzy announced, looking back and forth between me and Whittaker. "She was the one who called 9-1-1. She didn't see any strangers nearby and just yesterday Miss Mary was complaining about her husband not cleaning the gutters like they'd talked about."

"He's a good man," Miss Powery added. "I ain't speakin' ill o' him. Just sayin', Mary been on him about dem gutters."

"Thank you, Miss Powery," Whittaker said, ushering me and Jazzy towards the Range Rover. "We appreciate the information and hope Mary has a swift recovery."

"Bye now," she responded, giving Jazzy a wave.

As we drove away, I turned to Jazzy in the back seat.

"What happened to stay in the car?"

"I figured I'd save us time if I interviewed Miss Powery while you were looking around. She's a nice lady."

I sensed Whittaker shifting in his seat and was sure he'd regretted picking us up.

"But I asked you to stay in the car for a reason, Jazzy," I said firmly. "There are procedures we have to follow at a crime scene."

"Was it a crime scene?" she retorted.

"No, but you didn't know that."

"Are you interested in becoming a police officer, Jasmine?" Whittaker asked.

Jazzy thought for a moment. "Perhaps. But seems to me, you never get to not be working. I don't think I'd like that."

Whittaker laughed. "Not everyone on the force works long hours. Most have more regular schedules."

"But not you two," Jazzy replied.

"Detective Whittaker is one of the bosses," I pointed out. "Bosses have to handle anything that comes up, whenever it comes up."

"What about you, then?" she asked. "You're not in charge of anyone, and you still work all the time."

I was becoming good at walking straight into these verbal traps.

"Nora is working towards becoming a detective, so she puts in extra time towards that goal," Whittaker offered, and it sounded good to hear him say something positive about my future.

I'd given him plenty of reasons to cap my career at constable. Or boot me off the force.

"Then maybe I'll consider it," Jazzy announced. "After college."

I wasn't sure what to say about that. College was news to me. One more notch in the *I'm a shitty foster parent belt.*

"Well, I'd strongly advise you to pursue a higher education at college, Jasmine," Whittaker said as we arrived at the primary school. "But after that, if you'd consider a career in law enforcement, I think we'd be lucky to have you."

"I'll give it more thought," she responded before getting out of the Range Rover.

"She's a keeper," Whittaker said quietly to me.

"It seems I'm stuck with her now, so that's a good thing."

He laughed.

"Where are we regarding these accidents, sir?"

"Hard to know, exactly," he replied. "You put forward a good theory, but in all honesty, it lacks anything substantial to move forward with."

I couldn't argue his point. It wasn't like I was completely

convinced, but the itch in my gut hadn't gone away, so I still wasn't ready to drop it.

"Dilbert's cousin is about all we have to go on, sir."

Whittaker nodded. "Maybe the pawn shops," he suggested. "There are only a few on the island. Perhaps the missing jewellery will show up."

"If there's a killer staging these accidents, sir, he's keeping his trophies."

He nodded again. "True," he said softly and thought for a moment. "I don't see how it would hurt to speak with the cousin."

I opened the door. "Jazzy! Get back in."

"I wasn't saying now, Nora," Whittaker blurted. "I was thinking on Monday."

"When the window opens for him to attack again, sir?" I pointed out.

This time, he shook his head. "*If* there's a *him*."

Jazzy got back in and buckled her belt, letting out a huff of displeasure.

"If you'd drop me by home, I'd be happy to go myself, sir," I replied. "But I should put my uniform on."

Whittaker looked at his watch. "What's the address?"

"He works for CUC in maintenance, but I pulled his home address from DMV records. It's on Brinkley Drive in George Town. We can take the bus back to West Bay, sir."

"Brinkley Drive?" Whittaker echoed. "Is that off Eastern?"

I put the address into my maps app and zoomed in. "Yeah. It's in Swamp."

Whittaker groaned. Swamp was the nickname given to an unsavoury district on the edge of George Town. Not *The* Swamp, just Swamp, as though it were a normal name like Oslo or London. I'd never been through there after heavy rains, but I guessed it earned its name from being extra low-lying land. There weren't too many dodgy areas in the Cayman Islands, but the few acres within which Moses Dilbert supposedly resided was one of them. Run-down homes were tightly packed into a neighbourhood of narrow streets. It was no place for a shiny Range Rover.

"Call central. Have a patrol car meet us at the petrol station at Eastern and Godfrey Nixon. We'll have them drive us in."

"I get to ride in the patrol car?" Jazzy asked, and I looked over at Whittaker, who stared back at me.

"You'll be in charge of keeping my Range Rover safe. If I can depend on you for that task, Jasmine?"

"Sure," she replied, but I could tell she'd rather be in the patrol car when it drove through Swamp.

Our presence would certainly draw a mixture of interest and figures scattering out of sight. Whittaker pulled out of the school and headed back the way we'd just come towards the bypass into town.

"Is lunch part of this police business?" Jazzy asked.

It was gone eleven, so by the time we were done with this little episode, it would be midday at least.

"We'll get something to eat before we take the bus home. Okay?"

"Not before?" she urged.

"It's still early," I replied. "This won't take long."

"Hmm," Jazzy muttered from the back seat. "I've heard that before."

I ignored her comment, but glanced over at Whittaker. He was trying his best not to show his amusement.

19

NEVER LEAVE THE KEYS IN THE CAR

I didn't know the two constables who met us at the petrol station, and they gave me odd looks despite Whittaker introducing me as a fellow police officer. But I was getting a lot of strange looks today. More than usual. Probably due to the fact I was wearing Lycra shorts, a tank top over a sports bra, and bringing a teenager in similar gear along.

We moved the vehicles to the car park of a paint shop along Godfrey Nixon Way, where the Range Rover and Jazzy would be safe, then took the patrol car into the neighbourhood. In one short block, the surroundings immediately and dramatically changed. Every home appeared to be held together with patches of plywood on the walls and tin on the roofs. Weeds grew wild everywhere, and old vehicles and household appliances lay abandoned around the tatty houses. Faces pressed noses to windows as we drove by.

Brinkley Drive was the first right turn and the house number we were looking for was on the corner. Except the lot contained three small shack-like homes, all painted a different shade of turquoise blue, with old, rusty cars parked at all angles in the short driveway.

"Was there a unit number on the address?" Whittaker asked.

"No, sir," I replied, staring at the tall chain-link fence surrounding the small compound-like cluster of buildings.

"Circle around and park on Grackle Street," Whittaker ordered the driver. "Keep the patrol car out of sight, then watch the side and back as best you can."

"Sir," the driver acknowledged, turning the corner at the end of Brinkley, which brought us to a dead end.

"I guess we'll have to double back," Whittaker said. "I was hoping not to drive past again before we could knock on the door."

"We could walk," I suggested. "Then the car can follow afterwards."

I went to open the door but forgot I was in the back of a police vehicle.

"Okay," Whittaker agreed. "Let us out, please."

The two constables upfront got out and opened the back doors for us. The guy on my side gave me a good look over as I climbed out. As I walked by him, I unlatched the safety strap for his Taser, pulled it from its holster, and handed it to him before he'd realised what was happening.

"Keep your eyes out for trouble, Constable," I told him. "Not on my chest."

"What was that about?" Whittaker asked once we were far enough away that they couldn't hear.

"Just making sure our backup is prepared," I replied.

I could tell Whittaker knew there was something more and wanted to ask, but we turned the corner and watched several people step back into their homes from their front porches. We both needed to stay alert. The patrol car had served up a warning and now we were easily spotted as not belonging in the neighbourhood.

We walked through the open gates to the property and around the first few vehicles.

"That's Dilbert's," I pointed out, checking the licence plates. "Expired registration, sir."

I'd seen that on the DMV check, which gave us a reason to talk with him. Not that we needed an excuse to knock on a door.

"Take the place on the left," Whittaker said. "I'll take this one."

I liked the idea of splitting up. Word got around fast in a neighbourhood like this, and dividing gave us a two out of three chance of getting the right home. I knocked loudly on the front door and immediately heard movement inside, picking out voices despite the rap music playing. The door opened, and an older dark-skinned man with a cigarette hanging from his lips stared at me through the smoke venting from his nostrils. His eyes widened at the sight of a blonde woman in workout clothes on his step.

"Moses Dilbert live here?" I asked.

"No," the old man said in a scratchy voice. "But you can come in if you want."

From the building behind me, I heard hinges of a door complaining, and I swung around to see a man sneaking out the back of Whittaker's building.

"Police!" I shouted. "Hold it right there."

The man, who looked to be in his thirties and a good match for the DMV picture I'd seen of Dilbert, glanced over his shoulder in surprise, then bolted.

"Runner!" I shouted, and took off after him.

For the first time since Whittaker called me earlier in the day, my outfit became an asset. Except for the fact that I was completely unarmed. Dilbert ran behind the third structure, which was even more decrepit than the other two. I could see the chain-link fence wrapping around behind the shack and wondered where he thought he could go. The fence was six feet high, so neither of us could leap over it. When I rounded the corner, I found out.

Crashing down in a heap was a stack of wooden crates, now partially blocking a gate which rattled open on its hinges. Beyond, a narrow path led between thick trees and shrubs to what appeared to be a dead end. I pulled a few crates aside and sped off after Dilbert, who reached the end of the path and turned hard right without pausing. Sprinting as fast as I could, I found the gap led into someone else's debris and junk-ridden backyard.

In the distance behind me, I heard Whittaker calling over his radio, shouting directions to the constables as he tried to figure out where Dilbert was heading. I was wondering the same thing as the man deftly dodged obstructions like he'd practised his exit route. Meanwhile, I was catching my feet on all kinds of rubbish hidden under the weeds. He ran around the side of the house, and if I had it figured right, he'd be hitting Grackle Road where I hoped the constables had staged themselves. A dog barked loudly and bashed against a screen door as I turned the corner, and I hoped it couldn't break out and attack me.

The back of a storage building on our right blocked my view of where Dilbert was heading as he veered that way after shoving through the gate at the front of the yard. I could see I was gaining when we both ran down the pavement, which was good, as the constables were nowhere in sight. Dilbert turned left again, this time along the far side of the storage, and I heard a woman yell in surprise. By the time I reached the turn, something came flying out of the pathway, just missing me. It was Dilbert riding a bicycle. A woman sat on the ground surrounded by groceries spilt from her bags.

"He stole my bike!" she shouted at me, but I'd already figured that part out, and cursed myself for not bowling him off the thing when I'd had the chance.

Dilbert furiously pedalled down Grackle Road towards Godfrey Nixon Way, so I did the only thing I could do, which was run after him. The bicycle looked like a single-speed cruiser with a basket on the front, so he wasn't going a lot faster than me, but he was still pulling away. He turned left, cutting across the corner of the paint shop car park.

I saw Whittaker's Range Rover parked where we'd left it, and considered chasing with the car, but I had no idea if he'd left the keys inside, so I ran on past. Godfrey Nixon Way didn't have a pavement, but it did have a white line urging the cars to stay to the right and leave room for pedestrians and cyclists. Which was helping Dilbert more than me. He was steadily stretching away and I couldn't keep up my full-out pace much longer.

Just as I wondered in annoyance where the patrol car and the two constables who were supposed to be our backup had got to, I heard a car slow just behind me and honk. I eased up and turned to see Whittaker's Range Rover on my heels. But it wasn't the detective behind the wheel. Jazzy waved at me from the driver's seat as we both came to a stop.

I swung the passenger door open. "You can't drive!"

"Can too," she shouted back. "Get in. He's getting away."

I jumped in and the SUV lurched away, slamming the door closed beside me, before I really took in what was happening. I'd just become the passenger of a 15-year-old kid illegally driving my boss's SUV.

"Jazzy, you have to pull over so I can drive!"

"No way, we'll lose him!" she assured me. "I got this."

"When did you learn to drive?"

"From the car park to here," she replied, perched on the front of the seat, peering over the steering wheel while seatbelt alarms beeped at us. "It ain't that hard. I've watched everyone else do it enough."

I had to admit she was staying in our lane and we were quickly catching Dilbert without her having to go too fast. Although, it was amusing that she hadn't managed to accomplish the one thing she had done plenty of times in a car before. Adjust the seat position.

Dilbert had ridden past several opportunities to make turns, but I knew he wouldn't stay on Godfrey Nixon for much longer. The road led into the large airport roundabout, which was busy with three lanes of traffic going in all directions.

"He's going to turn left soon," I warned Jazzy as we gained to within 20 metres of him. "Get ready. You'll need to indicate and brake before you turn."

I was barely done speaking when Dilbert cut hard left into the car park of an urgent care centre, which I hoped we wouldn't need.

"Put your indicator on!" I ordered, and Jazzy hit one of the stalks.

The windscreen wipers squeaked back and forth across the bone-dry glass.

"*Fy faen*, just brake a bit, then turn," I told her, settling for making the corner.

Jazzy stabbed the brake once, then turned the wheel, and the tyres squealed as we hurtled into the car park. The noise made Dilbert turn and look, so he now knew we were in pursuit. He thrashed on the pedals and rode on while Jazzy punched the throttle and shot between the parked cars. Her calm driving down the main road had been thrown out the window, and she was getting manic behind the controls. This was escalating into a bad situation.

"Slow down a bit, Jazzy, and breathe. We're going to catch him, so be gentle with the controls."

"Okay," she muttered, focused on her target up ahead.

We bounced out of the car park onto a narrow road twisting around a small industrial estate adjacent to Swamp. Dilbert followed the road to the right, and I could see up ahead we'd quickly meet a T-junction. We had just about enough time to catch him before then.

"Get alongside, but please don't run him over, Jazzy."

I powered the passenger window down and hung on as she accelerated again, throwing me back into my seat.

"Easy!" I shouted, trying to pull myself up so I could lean out of the window. I made it just in time to take a swing and smack Dilbert in the side of the head as we swept by.

"Brake!" I yelled, as we hurtled towards the junction.

Jazzy braked. Hard, as instructed. I smashed into the dashboard as the SUV shuddered with the ABS braking system fully engaged. From the corner of my eye, I saw Dilbert tumbling over a parked car after I'd redirected him straight into the front bumper.

When the SUV came to a stop, I scrambled out and ran over to where the man lay moaning on the ground. His limbs all appeared to have the appropriate number of joints and I couldn't see any red leaks, so maybe we'd get away with our unorthodox apprehension.

I looked up when I heard a car coming around the corner, and held my breath when I realised it was the constables in their patrol car, with Whittaker in the back seat.

I was about to shout at Jazzy, but she was a step ahead of me. She was sitting in the passenger seat, leaning through the open window with a big grin. She'd even thought to leave the driver's door open to make sure it looked like I'd come from there. I grinned back.

"Moses Dilbert, we just wanted to chat with you, but now you're under arrest for stealing a bicycle."

"You done tried to kill me," he moaned.

"That's my personal car, Nora," Whittaker said as he walked up.

"I didn't think you'd mind if I borrowed it, sir. You did leave the keys."

"The last time you drove my car, you dented the tailgate," he pointed out.

"Not a scratch on her this time, sir."

"Yet you still managed to wreck something," Whittaker commented, wincing as he walked around and looked at a series of dents on the bonnet and roof of the parked car.

"That was all him, sir," I replied, pointing at Dilbert. "He owes that poor lady a bike too," I added, pointing at the bicycle lying on its side with a pair of buckled wheels. The basket was nowhere to be seen.

20

COFFEE AND NEW BICYCLES

Moses Dilbert was fine. He'd have a few bruises and aches and pains, but nothing over-the-counter pain pills couldn't handle. But of course he insisted on being taken to the hospital to be checked over, whining and complaining about police brutality. When I pointed out a 15-year-old girl was in the passenger seat of the Range Rover, he decided the side mirror must have been responsible for hitting him in the ear, rather than a fist. I was fortunate that he hadn't figured out the seating arrangements in the SUV when he'd turned around and seen us. Regardless, with his story jumping around and changing, and neither Jazzy nor me recalling any part of the vehicle contacting the suspect in our statements, his claims were falling on deaf ears.

But it all took forever to get sorted. Long enough that I was able to get a ride home, have a late lunch with Jazzy, where we made a pact to never speak of the actual turn of events again, and drive back to the station in uniform. Whittaker had scuttled his lunch and afternoon plans, so he was in the doghouse with his wife, which meant he was keen to get the interview started and was in no mood for Dilbert's games.

A public defender sat next to Moses, who I figured was about to be surprised at where our line of questioning was heading. I'd run across Marlon Rankin before. In his fifties, he was a portly, dark-skinned local who seemed like a nice man who had a sensible approach to his line of work. He knew the law, and defended his clients, but didn't put up ridiculous defences just to stall for time. Once Detective Whittaker had given the usual spiel about recording and rights, the detective kicked off the interview.

"Let's start with why you ran from us this morning, Mr Dilbert?"

"Didn't know what it were about," he answered. "Strange man in a suit showin' up at da door."

I knew from his DMV record that Moses Dilbert was 35 years old, and he spoke with a local accent, but not as heavy as I'd expected. He had a decent job at CUC, the local electricity company who supplied power to the island, so it was curious to me why he was living in Swamp and running from the police. His life appeared to be a mixture of success and failure. He didn't have a police record.

"If you'd answered the door instead of running away, I could have told you," Whittaker pointed out.

Dilbert just shrugged his shoulders.

"You then assaulted a lady, stole her bike, and continued trying to evade us," Whittaker continued.

"I didn't know she was police," he replied, pointing at me.

"Did you announce you were police, Constable Sommer?" Whittaker asked me.

"Yes, sir. Loudly."

"I didn't hear nuttin'."

"I did," Whittaker responded. "I heard the constable clearly announce she was police and order you to stop."

Moses shrugged his shoulders again. "She didn't look like no police I ever seen before. Anyone can say dat dey police."

"You usually run away from women who ask you to stop?" I asked. "Guilty people run, Mr Dilbert. Innocent people don't. They ask why someone is looking for them."

"I don't think we're contesting that Mr Dilbert made an error in judgement when he ran from you this morning," Marlon interjected. "He's prepared to claim no contest to a misdemeanour of taking the bicycle."

It was a smart move. Usually, in these situations, a resolution could be negotiated, providing the woman was unharmed. It would save time and money all around without further burdening the island's legal system, which struggled to keep up with its workload of petty crimes. But Marlon was yet to ask the more important question.

"Mr Dilbert, how did you get along with your cousin, Jerald?" Whittaker asked, and the two faces across the table both looked up in surprise.

The running from police, bicycle theft, and subsequent ride over the top of a parked car had them both forgetting we were there for a reason in the first place.

"Jerald?" Moses echoed. "He died just da udder day."

"We're aware," Whittaker responded. "And I'd like to know about your relationship with your cousin."

"May I inquire why you're asking my client about his cousin, Roy?" Marlon said, holding a hand in front of Moses before he said anything. "Didn't the poor fellow electrocute himself?"

"He did indeed die from electrocution, Marlon, but we haven't ruled the incident as purely accidental just yet," Whittaker replied. "We'd like to know a little background from a family member."

Marlon thought for a moment. "May I have a moment of privacy to confer with Mr Dilbert? I'll admit, it's for my benefit, more than his. I'm a step behind on anything to do with his cousin."

"Certainly," Whittaker replied. "We'll grab a coffee. Ten minutes enough?"

"That'll be plenty. Thanks, Roy," Marlon replied.

"Interview paused for a short break," Whittaker said for the benefit of the recording, hitting pause before we left the room.

It was now late afternoon and the coffee supply downstairs

looked like it had been on the warmer since lunchtime, so we walked upstairs to Whittaker's office. He had one of those single-serve machines.

"Just so I'm clear, Nora, our connection here is the fact that he's related to Jerald, and he works for the electricity company, but not as an electrician," Whittaker asked as he set about making two coffees. "Is that about right?"

"And he's social media friends with the other two accident victims from this week, sir."

"Oh, that's right," he said, waiting for the first cup to brew. "Tenuous enough to be discussed on his doorstep if he hadn't insisted on breaking the law in front of us."

"Quite handy, as it turns out," I replied, but he frowned at me.

"Only if you didn't have plans for your Saturday afternoon."

I shut up and listened to the machine gurgle and hiss.

After the allotted ten minutes, we sat back down in the interview room, and Whittaker began the recording once more.

"Okay, may we ask you about your cousin, Mr Dilbert?"

He nodded. "You asked how we were, right?"

"That's a start, yes," Whittaker confirmed.

"We got along fine," Moses continued. "Didn't see dat much of each other."

"His widow didn't describe it that way," I said.

"You didn't ask me about her," Moses snapped back. "She's a piece of work, that one."

"Mrs Dilbert told me you and her husband weren't on good terms at all," I continued.

"Like I say, she don't like me none."

"Because you owe them money?"

"She say dat?"

"Yes."

"She show you a note, or some kinda paperwork?"

"No, but I didn't ask to see any."

"Den go back and ask if she got some, but I tell you what she say, den," Moses ranted. "She say she ain't got nuttin'. Cos there ain't nuttin' to be had."

"So you're saying your cousin's wife doesn't get along with you, but you were fine with Jerald?" I challenged, turning to Whittaker. "How does your wife feel if you're mates with someone she doesn't like, sir?"

"I can't say I'd have the nerve to test that situation," Whittaker said, playing along.

Although, having met Rosie, who was a lovely lady, I still wouldn't want to land on her bad side, so he was probably speaking the truth.

"When was the last time you saw your cousin?" Whittaker continued.

"Been a few weeks, I'd say," Moses replied.

"And what is it you do for CUC?" I asked, figuring we'd bounce the questions around and try to catch him off balance.

"Fix stuff. I do maintenance."

"Electrical maintenance?" Whittaker asked.

"Are you suggesting Moses had something to do with his cousin's demise?" Marlon interrupted. "He's already told you he hasn't seen the man in weeks."

"We haven't suggested anything at this point, Marlon," Whittaker responded. "But Moses has shown up in several lines of inquiry during our investigations this week."

"So, electrical maintenance, Mr Dilbert?" I asked when Whittaker paused, giving me the opening.

"Sometimes, but simple stuff," he replied. "You can't be thinkin' I had anyting to do wit Jerald fryin' his own ass? That's crazy, man. She put you up to dis? His wife?"

"I assure you, no one put us up to anything, Mr Dilbert," Whittaker responded curtly while I sipped coffee. "Simple electrical work such as household wiring, then?"

Moses shook his head. "I don't believe dis shit, man."

"How well do you know Zara Parsons?" I asked.

"Who?"

"You're friends with her on social media. Are you saying you don't know that name?"

"I guess not, maybe she friend request me sometime, I don't know."

"What about Heather Lawson?" I asked. "She friend request you as well?"

Marlon held up a hand again. "Isn't that the schoolteacher who died last week? What does my client and his cousin have to do with Miss Lawson, or the other woman you mentioned?"

"He's friends online with all of them," I replied. "And they're all dead."

"Good Lord," Marlon muttered. "None of them were actually accidents?"

I found it funny that the solicitor was now more fascinated, or at least distracted, by the possibility of a series of murders, and appeared to have forgotten he was representing Moses.

"They most likely were," Whittaker quickly interjected.

I'm sure he was getting concerned about rumours of a serial killer starting on the island. A story like that would certainly cause a big fuss. Or wide-scale panic.

"We are simply doing our due diligence and thoroughly investigating each incident," Whittaker clarified. "And as I said, Mr Dilbert has a connection with all of them."

"Friends online hardly constitutes evidence of a real connection," Marlon complained. "We live on an island. Everybody is friends here."

That was a bit of an exaggeration, but he'd sensed we were light on evidence. As in, we didn't really have shit to go on. There were probably a thousand people with the same or better electrical know-how than Moses Dilbert.

"I think Moses has answered enough questions, Roy," Marlon continued. "Let's figure out something on this bicycle business, and move on with our weekends."

Whittaker let out a sigh. "The lady was generous in suggesting that if you replaced her bicycle with a nicer one, she wouldn't press charges."

"How nice?" Moses snapped back. "Dat ting was a piece of crap."

"A new bike, with a basket on the front," Whittaker replied firmly. "She uses it to carry her shopping and laundry."

Moses shook his head and glared at me. I glared back.

"Fine, I'll buy her a bike, but gotta wait till next Friday when I get paid."

"Didn't you just get paid this Friday?" I asked. "What happened to that money?"

"Dat had places to be," he muttered in reply. "I'll get her stupid bicycle next Friday."

"Okay," Whittaker responded with an air of finality. "I held off submitting the paperwork, charging Mr Dilbert," he continued, looking at Marlon. "If that nice lady doesn't have a new bicycle to her satisfaction by 4:00pm Friday, then I'll be charging your client with theft and assault. Okay, Marlon?"

The public defender looked at his client, who shook his head again, before switching to a brief nod in agreement.

"Say it for the recording, Mr Dilbert," Whittaker ordered.

"Fine, she'll have her damn bicycle."

We all stood, and Whittaker leaned over to stop the recording. I nudged his leg, and he paused.

"With the purchase receipt, Mr Dilbert," I said.

He glared at me again, and this time I grinned. Without that addition, the poor lady would have been the recipient of a stolen bike next Friday. She might still, but at least he'd have to go to the trouble of forging some kind of receipt. Which would be a stretch for this guy.

"Wit a receipt," he said through gritted teeth.

"Think he's involved?" Whittaker asked me when they'd left, and we walked out to the reception.

"No. He's not smart enough."

"Some people are more cagey or intelligent than their demeanour suggests, Nora."

"True, sir, but he's not. If there *is* a killer involved, he's *really* smart."

The detective ran his hand over his closely cropped hair. "Agreed. Which means we're still a very long way from connecting these accidents together. With nothing more than the missing items to suggest there's foul play."

"I know," I admitted. "Maybe the autopsies will turn up something."

"Gareth told me he was doing both of them first thing on Monday," Whittaker explained. "If he turns up anything suspicious, we'll continue investigating. But if he doesn't, we'll need to drop this and move on, Nora."

I thought it over for a few moments. He was right, of course. We couldn't keep hammering away trying to find evidence of wrongdoing if there wasn't any to be found, but my itch was still there.

"Can I attend the autopsies, sir?"

Whittaker frowned. "I know you're a tough young lady, but autopsies aren't much fun to witness, Nora. Are you sure?"

"*Ja.* I want to see for myself."

In truth, I wasn't certain at all that I wanted to see what went on, and I definitely wasn't looking forward to hanging out with Mr Sunshine, Gareth Davies. But unless I was there when he confirmed there was no evidence of foul play, I wasn't sure my stomach would unknot. My stomach might react in other ways when the scalpels and bone saws came out, but I knew I needed to be there.

"Okay," Whittaker replied. "I'll let Gareth know to expect you Monday morning."

"Thank you, sir," I said, although there was every chance by Monday I'd wish he denied my request.

21

GRINDING GEARS AND TROPHIES

Shortly after daybreak on Sunday morning, I went for a swim and freedive on the reef a few hundred yards out from my shack. Nothing cleared my mind more than spending time underwater, alone in a vastly different world. When I focused on nothing except my breath hold and the vibrant life around me, all the madness in my life above the surface usually found some kind of order. By the time I stripped out of my bathing suit and washed away the salt water under the outdoor shower beside the shack, I felt at ease with both cases.

The biggest thing for me to get straight in my mind was that I could only do so much. With Jacob's grandmother's scammer, it was still most likely that the person was overseas, which meant we'd have zero chance of getting her money back. If Robbie and Rabbit came up with names, we'd knock on doors, but I didn't hold out too much hope we'd accomplish anything except scare the wits out of a few innocent online gamers.

With the accident case, it would be what it would be. I still had this nagging feeling inside, but I'd second guessed myself so much, I couldn't tell if it was real or a touch of ego refusing to admit my instincts were wrong. Both women had ex-husbands who'd be obvious suspects if my whole theory wasn't based around the incidents being related. And if they appeared to be anything but accidents. With the missing items as the only common element, everything rested on the autopsies on Monday, highlighting a nugget of evidence that suggested foul play. We'd missed the opportunity with Heather Lawson, but perhaps the other two bodies would give us something to keep the investigation alive. Or the case would be put to bed as the unfortunate string of accidents they probably were.

I dried off, wrapped the towel around me, hung my bathing suit over the porch railing, and went inside for coffee. Jazzy was awake, so I poured us both a cup. She'd decided lately that coffee wasn't disgusting anymore, but she preferred the type AJ bought her at the shops with fancy names and lots of sugar. I let her put milk in it at home, but no sugar. If she wanted to drink coffee, that was fine with me, but turning it into dessert wasn't drinking coffee.

We sat out on the porch, and I took a piece of lettuce for Edvard, who still hadn't shown his wrinkly face since we'd come home from Norway. It was strange how it sounded right to say we had returned home. Norway was the place where I was born and raised, but Grand Cayman had become my home, despite the island holding a mixture of good and bad memories.

"Do you think he's okay?" Jazzy asked, her legs curled up in the chair as she clutched her coffee cup.

"The lizard?" I responded, her question snapping me out of my wandering thoughts. "There's a reason the blue iguanas are on the endangered list, and it's not because they're too clever."

Jazzy shook her head. "You love him. You're just as worried as I am."

"I'd hate to think he's gone," I admitted. "If we'd plumped him up a little more, he would have made a cool pair of shoes."

Jazzy gasped, but knew I wasn't serious and couldn't help giggling.

My mobile buzzed on the little table between us, and I looked at the caller ID. It was Robbie.

I answered the call. "*Ja?*"

"We have three names," he replied proudly.

"That was quick."

"We set a short timeline on it. That's not unusual for a challenge like this. In theory, all they have to do is follow clues and look up stuff on Google Maps."

"Okay, who do you have and where are they?"

"I just sent the details to your mobile," Robbie replied. "Put me on speaker and take a look."

As he was speaking, my phone vibrated with the incoming message. I put the call on speaker as he'd said, and looked at the information he'd sent me.

"Are these addresses current?" I asked.

"You should check your police or DMV records," Robbie replied. "They're all coming through VPNs, so I'm not a hundred percent sure whether the IPs we have are the final destinations or a bounce location. But all three showed they were here on the island."

"Want more?" Jazzy asked, getting up and pointing to my coffee cup.

I nodded and handed it to her.

"Hi Jazzy," Robbie said over the speaker. "Congratulations."

"Hey," Jazzy replied, frowning at me, no doubt wondering who this was. "For what?"

"Your two wins in the track and field event," Robbie explained.

"Oh, thank you. Who is this?"

"I'm Robbie."

"Do we go to school together?" she asked, probably figuring out his age by the tone of his voice.

Robbie laughed.

"Robbie helps out the police from time to time," I explained. "He's in college."

"Oh," Jazzy repeated. "Well, nice to meet you."

She frowned at me again, then went inside. I'd have to explain to her who he was after I was done with the call.

"If the addresses are accurate, we have one in West Bay, one in George Town, and one in East End," I thought aloud as I read down the list he'd sent.

"I've come across JunkDog00 several times, and he seems pretty cool online," Robbie said. "But I don't know the other two."

I looked at the notes. JunkDog00 was the one in West Bay. None of the names looked to be obviously South Asian, but that didn't necessarily mean anything. The person could be adopted, living under a false identity, or Grandma could have been mistaken.

"Being nice online is how the scammer gets old ladies to open up their computers to him," I pointed out.

"Yeah, I guess so," Robbie replied sullenly. "I suppose you have to check them all out."

"Thanks for all this, Robbie. I'll let you know what we find."

"It was Rabbit as well," he was quick to point out. "She's helped every step of the way."

"Okay. I'm glad you've met. Maybe she can use you for work stuff in the future."

"We talked a little about that," Robbie said, and I could tell he was feeling proud about that too.

"*Vi snakkes*," I said and hung up.

"This Robbie guy speaks Norwegian?" Jazzy asked, coming back out of the house with our coffee.

"Huh?" I said, still studying the names and locations. I hadn't realised I'd slipped into my native tongue. "No. Well, he knows a few words. He'll look that up and know it next time."

"He works for the police?"

"Not officially, but he's consulted for us. He's a cool guy. You'd like him."

"He must be cool," Jazzy said, standing at the wooden railing and staring into the woods, trying to spot Edvard.

"Why? Because he knew you'd won medals?"

Jazzy laughed. "No. That was a little weird. Like he was stalking me."

"Believe me, he's safe. You don't have to worry about Robbie."

Jazzy turned and sat down. "I meant he must be cool because you actually saved his number," she said, and grinned. "You don't save anyone's number."

I smiled absentmindedly as my thoughts were elsewhere. I'd just explained to Robbie how we had to look at everyone as a suspect, yet I'd never considered him and I'd ruled out Rabbit because I thought I knew her well enough. In truth, I shouldn't be ruling either of them out. They both had the skills, and now they were in control of the information I was using to find the scammer. The thought made me hate my job, and the way I had to look at everybody. Including the few people I considered friends. The idea made my stomach knot in a different way.

"I need to take care of something," I grumbled, standing up.

"What?" Jazzy asked.

"A work thing."

"Oh," she muttered, and stared out across the ocean.

I started to go inside, then stopped with my hand on the door.

"Why?" I asked.

"Why what?" she responded, without looking at me.

"Why are you asking me what?"

Now she turned and frowned at me. It wasn't her pretending-to-be-annoyed frown either. "'Cos you asked me why."

"Yes. Because I want to know why you asked me the first what you asked."

"Huh?" she said, shaking her head.

"Ugh," I groaned. "Did you have something you wanted to do?"

She shrugged her shoulders.

"We don't do that teenager BS. Just tell me what it is," I said impatiently.

"I *am* a teenager," Jazzy complained.

"But you don't normally act like one, and you don't need to act like one now."

She let out an aggravated sigh. "We didn't get to finish at the school."

Dritt. We didn't, and I hadn't offered to make up for it.

"Get changed. We'll make a stop on the way, then go to the school."

She looked at me defiantly. "You forgot all about it."

"*Ja.* I'm sorry. Now, do you want to go or not?"

"Can I drive?" she asked, trying to maintain her stern expression.

"No. The Jeep is a manual transmission."

"I gotta learn to shift sometime."

"I can't afford a new gearbox. Now get your arse in gear or I'm leaving without you."

Fifteen minutes later, I let the Jeep warm up as we wiped the overnight moisture from the seats, and then I let her make a few tries at pulling away. She finally kangaroo'd for 50 metres but got it rolling down Conch Point Road and tried a shift up to second. By the grinding sounds from the gearbox, I was sure the shafts and gears were about to fly out from underneath my CJ-7, but somehow it all held together and we made it another hundred metres until I had her brake to a stop. Which was enough for my poor Jeep, and my nerves.

I'd put my uniform trousers and shirt over leggings and a sports bra, so I could change at the school when we got there. But first, I parked off Mount Pleasant Road, on Jade Drive. Ahead, a smaller lane led back north, parallel to Mount Pleasant, where a newer, earth tone stucco home filled the corner. It was the address of Christopher Ellington, who went by JunkDog00 online. According to Robbie's notes, the kid was seventeen, so I assumed this rather nice-looking house belonged to his parents.

"Stay in the Jeep," I told Jazzy, and gave her my best *I'm not screwing around* look.

"Okay," she replied.

I took the keys with me.

A TV blasted the announcers' voices of a sports game, so I knew someone was home. The door opened not long after I rang the doorbell, and a woman appeared surprised to see me on her doorstep.

"What's happened?" she asked in an English accent.

"Sorry to disturb you at the weekend, ma'am. There's nothing to be alarmed about, but I need to speak with Christopher Ellington."

"Chris? Really? What for?"

The lady seemed ready to launch into full panic mode.

"I'm hoping he can assist us with an inquiry, ma'am," I said, hoping I sounded like he wasn't in trouble.

Although I didn't want to actually say he wasn't, in case he was.

"Come inside," she said more calmly, then turned and yelled into the house. "Turn that down, Trent!"

I closed the door behind me and looked down the short hallway, where I could see a man on the sofa waving his arms at the television.

"Sorry," the woman I guessed to be Mrs Ellington said. "My husband's a Manchester City fan. They're playing this morning."

He hadn't turned the volume down, and from what I could see, had no interest in any visitors at the moment.

"Let me get Chris. He's in his room," she added, and left me standing in the foyer with the coats and shoes.

Framed pictures lined the hallway, but I could only see the first photo on each side from where I stood. The one on my left appeared to be the mother on stage, acting in a play or some kind of production. On the right, the picture was of a couple and a young boy in front of a large stadium.

A few minutes later, she returned behind a kid, who if I didn't know was seventeen, I would have guessed to be fourteen or fifteen. She was herding her reluctant child down the hall. He looked terrified, but he certainly didn't look South Asian.

"Christopher, I'm Constable Sommer. I'd like to ask you a few questions, if you don't mind?"

He nodded, shakily. I took his positive response to mean he didn't mind, despite my question requiring a negative answer.

Sometimes the English weren't very good at following their own language rules.

"Are you known as JunkDog00 online?"

He nodded.

"Have you been playing a challenge online which required you to find information from signs and locations around the island?" I asked, wishing I'd asked Robbie what their game thing was called.

"Is that what you had me drive you around for yesterday?" his mother asked, and Christopher nodded again.

"I d-d-d-didn't think I was d-d-d-doing anything wrong," he said with a pronounced stutter.

He also had a pre-pubescent high voice. There was no way it was this kid. He wasn't scared about being in trouble for scamming old ladies; he was just plain scared.

"Do you know a lady by the name of Beatrice Rivers?" I asked and watched his face.

His brow creased in thought while he slowly shook his head. "N-n-n-no."

The man cheered loudly from the living room, then finally muted the television.

"What's all this about, then?" he called out in what I thought was a Manchester accent, somewhat guided by his team of choice.

He strode our way.

"The constable had questions for Chris about something he was doing online," the mother replied.

Trent put his hands on his kid's shoulders. "What he do? Hack into the government or something?"

"Nothing like that, sir," I replied. "I have what I need. Thank you."

I hurried out the door, leaving the father asking his wife and son more questions. Halfway to the Jeep, my phone rang. I didn't recognise the number.

"Ja."

"Is dis Nora?" a female voice asked. She sounded slightly familiar.

"*Ja.*"

"Dis is Maya Tibbetts. Jacob's cousin."

I stopped next to the Jeep.

"Is Jacob okay?" I immediately asked.

"Yes, yes. I was calling about someting else."

"Oh, okay. What's up?"

"I spoke wit Jacob, and he asked I call you too. Said you'd wanna know. We found a watch in da ambulance dis morning. Tink it may belong to dat man who electrocuted himself. Musta come off when we was takin' him to da morgue. Da strap was broken."

"*Dritt,*" I muttered.

So much for my trophy theory.

22

BONE SAWS AND CROISSANTS

My four days off had evaporated quickly, and I couldn't say I felt rested as I drove into George Town on Monday morning. Jacob would pass out at the thought of attending an autopsy, so Sergeant Redburn had arranged for another constable to join my partner on patrol for the morning. He'd join me later, and we had permission to visit the second name we'd been given in the scam case.

Autopsies took place at George Town hospital, so after fighting the morning traffic and dropping Jazzy off at school, I parked and walked into the building a little after 7:00am.

"You're late," Gareth Davies greeted me once I'd found his office.

I was all about getting to the point and regularly accused of being blunt, but the coroner had me beat, arms down. *Or was it arms up? Or hands something?* Anyway, he was an arse.

"Ready to get started?" I responded, refusing to be baited.

"This way," he ordered, and I followed him down a hallway which smelled of disinfectant and some kind of air freshener.

The combination confused my senses and didn't make anything more pleasurable. They should stick with the bleach.

He opened a door and the odour of air freshener quickly disappeared, leaving an even stronger, acrid smell of disinfectant. So, maybe it wasn't better after all. A corpse lay on a stainless-steel table, covered by a white sheet.

"Usually, a coroner orders a post-mortem examination to be performed by a pathologist, or in cases where foul play is suspected or known, a forensic pathologist," Davies announced, as he scrubbed in like a surgeon would. "But here, in the Cayman Islands, I must assume all three roles."

I was happy to forgo the self-adulation speech and get on with things, but I had to admit the man carried a lot of responsibility on his shoulders. A woman dressed as though ready to assist in surgery handed me a plastic bag containing a Tyvek suit, booties, and nitrile gloves, which I opened and began slipping over my clothes.

"Adele is an anatomic pathology technologist," Davies explained. "She'll be assisting me today."

I wondered if that was how Adele chose to announce herself or if she went with nurse when asked, to keep from explaining her role. "I help doctors cut up corpses" didn't seem like a great opening line for first dates. Anyway, she seemed adept and efficient as she quietly went about her business.

When we were all prepared, we stood around the table, and Adele pulled the sheet from the body. I'd last seen Zara Parsons lying on the patio next to her pool after I'd attempted chest compressions before the EMTs had arrived. I could now see the irregular profile of a couple of her ribs just below her breasts where I'd broken them in my attempts. Her brown skin had an odd pallor, taking on a greyish hue, and I reminded myself I was looking at the host formerly used by the person I knew as one of Jazzy's teachers.

"First step is to confirm the identity, which has been done prior to this examination, and as coroner, I was the one to do this, so I can verify we are examining the body of Zara Clare Parsons."

As Davies spoke, Adele checked off or made notes on a computer tablet mounted on a stand. From the small microphone hanging over the table, I presumed the session was also being recorded. I hoped the tape wouldn't be marred by me retching at any point.

"We'll begin with an external examination," Davies continued, and described the body which lay before us, while he and Adele measured Zara's height and noted her weight, which apparently the table handled through load sensors.

When he was done with the basic details, he began at the top of her head and moved down, explaining everything he saw, whether it was normal or not. He paused at the ribs.

"Two distinctive rib fractures of T4 on both sides, consistent with chest compressions performed at the scene."

"I did that," I admitted from behind my mask.

Davies ignored me, continuing down her body. When he reached the woman's fingertips, he paused for a moment and looked at me.

"Scrapings from under the fingernails were already sent to the lab, but I can tell you there wasn't much there."

"Had they been cleaned?" I asked, wondering whether Heather Lawson's had been. But of course we'd never know.

"Recently, I'd say, but that's not uncommon," Davies responded before quickly moving on.

I supposed he was right. Women had manicures or took care of their own nails. I thought about mine, hidden beneath the pale blue gloves I wore. They were short and unpainted. I clipped them that way and only ever filed them if I'd done a shitty job with the little clippers and an edge was catching on the sheets or something. Maybe that made me unfeminine, but I simply didn't care. My hands were functional tools that I didn't want compromised by long nails.

"...several scratches around the wrists and fingers," Davies was saying as I tuned back in.

He held up a hand and Adele took several pictures, as she had been doing throughout the autopsy, with a small camera attached by a cord to the computer.

"Could they be defensive wounds?" I asked.

"They're not typical of such, but I would imagine she would have flailed her arms and grabbed at anything she could find to pull herself out of the water," Davies replied.

"Then shouldn't her nails be damaged?" I pointed out.

"Hmm," he grumbled, and continued. "Slight perimortem bruising of the wrists, again consistent with flailing arms."

The pathologist continued down Zara's pale body, remarking how nothing appeared abnormal, including her feet, which didn't have any bruising or scrapes. No doubt because she'd been wearing shoes. He and Adele then turned the body over to examine the other side, and I immediately pointed to patches of faint darkening in her lower back.

"Is that bruising?"

"We start at the head and work down, Constable Sommer," Davies informed me curtly, and continued talking about all the normal things I didn't care about.

Finally, he reached her lower back, and rather than address my concerns, he continued his monologue, describing the darker patches as perimortem bruising, before moving on again.

"Wait," I said, not ready to move on from the part that interested me, and in my opinion should interest him. "What would cause that?"

His shoulders sagged as though I'd ruined his life, and he slowly turned to me.

"I've no idea, Constable. That would be your job to bring me evidence of what may have caused the bruising if you think this was anything but an accident, as I ruled at the scene."

Now we were getting to the root of the problem. His nose was out of joint because he'd already ruled this an accident.

"In your professional opinion, sir, what are the likely causes of bruises such as these, and how close to her death would they have been made?"

"The same way most bruises are caused," he replied impatiently. "The woman bumped against something or something bumped into her."

"But they're consistent on both sides," I said, pointing to the bruises. "More like something wrapped around her."

"Then bring me an item or show me a location consistent with the bruising, and a reason why they would have been involved in causing this woman's untimely demise."

This guy was really starting to annoy me.

"Timeline on the bruising?"

"The water immersion plays havoc with determining timing, but I'd say within an hour or less. The bruises had barely formed before her heart stopped pumping fresh blood to the vessels which had broken in the area."

"So these would have been significant bruises if she'd lived?" I pushed.

"Potentially," was all he'd give me.

He continued with the visual external examination until he was done, then rolled the body again. Adele brought over a tray of instruments and an ominous-looking device which reminded me of something I'd seen in an automotive garage.

"We'll now begin the internal examination," Davies announced as though he'd just decided to have a tea break, before he took a scalpel and drew it from her shoulder to the middle of her chest.

When he'd completed the traditional Y-shaped incision, he sliced back the woman's flesh and revealed her internals. The smell which permeated the room was overwhelming. I could handle the slicing, but the odour was far more powerful than I'd expected. I sensed Davies keeping an eye on me as I tried my best to not show a reaction as my stomach heaved and churned. There was no way I was giving him the pleasure of seeing me lose my dinner. I'd deliberately skipped breakfast.

Breathing through my mouth, I struggled to hold it together while Davies eagerly continued, picking up what I'd suspected was the bone saw. To my surprise, the blade wasn't completely circular, and oscillated rather than spun. I could now see the two ribs I'd broken as the pathologist removed the chest plate and each rib using the saw, placing the bones on a tray Adele provided. Without noticing the transition, my fascination in the process distracted me from the increasingly awful smell, as one by one Davies removed Zara's internal organs.

He worked with precision and care. Either he or Adele weighed and measured everything he removed, and Davies narrated his observations for the recording. Apart from her lungs being full of water, Zara died an otherwise healthy woman from what I could glean from the commentary. The process took over an hour, and when complete, Davies returned the organs into the empty cavity and took his time, making sure the puzzle went back together in the way it had been.

Finally, when Zara was stitched back together and her corpse re-covered with the sheet, Adele began cleaning up the equipment, and Davies removed his face mask and gloves.

"Anything that surprised you?" I asked after removing my own mask and gloves.

"Not really," Davies replied flatly. "She drowned."

As much as it seemed he was simply being obstinate, I had to remind myself that he also wasn't wrong. We had zero physical evidence of wrongdoing, and with the watch showing up, my theory was holding less and less water.

"Did you notice any bruising on Heather Lawson?" I asked, taking a different tack.

"Not around the lumbar region, no, but of course, we didn't perform a full autopsy."

"Any other scratches or bruising?"

Davies shook his head and sighed. "Here, come to my office. You can look at the photographs yourself."

I was pretty sure Adele was hiding a smile as I followed the coroner out of the examination room and down the hall to his office. After a few clicks, he vacated the chair and pointed at the screen.

"Far fewer pictures, as I only made a brief, visual examination, but here they are."

I sat down and expected Davies to leave me to it, but he

lingered. He probably didn't trust me to be left alone with his computer. I scrolled through what he had, which showed Lawson stripped and placed on the examination table. Naturally, the photographs mainly focused on her head wound, but I double checked her lower back, where I verified she had no obvious bruising. In fact, I couldn't see any strange markings, scratches, or bruising on her arms, hands, or upper body. The last few pictures were of her legs and feet.

"What are those?" I blurted, looking at a photograph of the back of the dead woman's ankles.

Davies came around and leaned over my shoulder. "Those marks?" he said, pointing to what had caught my attention.

"Ja. What would cause that?"

"Shoes, Constable Sommer. Shoes can create those marks at the base of the ankle just above the foot. Especially women's shoes."

We both peered a little closer. I could see faint, but noticeable red marks and the beginning of bruising across both ankles.

"This bruising looks fresh, right? From what you told me earlier. The bruising was just forming shortly before death."

"Possibly," he replied, studying the picture but remaining non-committal. "The backs of her shoes could easily have dug into her ankles when she fell."

I scrolled through the pictures to where three shots showed her clothing spread out over a table.

"Those super comfy Skechers with their soft material made those marks?" I asked, without hiding my doubt.

"Hmm," Davies grumbled, and stood up straight. "Do you have physical evidence which contradicts my ruling of accidental death?"

"Email me those pictures, sir," I said, as I stood. "And the bruises from Zara Parsons."

I didn't have anything, and we both knew it. I also had absolutely no idea what could have caused the marks on either woman, so I had no clue where to start looking.

"Thanks for allowing me to observe," I forced myself to say as I walked towards the door and left.

He didn't ask if I wanted to attend Dilbert's autopsy next, and I didn't bring it up. I'd had all I could take of Davies, and I'd be tempted to test out his bone saw on him if I'd stuck around. The pictures from the second examination would be in the case file by the end of the day. I didn't think the coroner and pathologist were covering up anything, but he was certainly resisting the idea that something more could have been involved in the deaths.

I texted Jacob, who happened to already be on his way, and after ten minutes pacing around outside the hospital, he pulled up.

"I brought you coffee and a croissant," he said, handing me a large cup and a paper bag as I got into the patrol car. "How did it go?"

I looked over at my squeamish partner. "You really want to know?"

He looked at the half-eaten pastry he held in his hand. "Let me say dat a different way. Did you learn anyting new about da accidents?"

"Maybe," I answered. "But too soon to tell."

23

THE UNIVERSAL LANGUAGE OF POINTING

The address Robbie had given me in George Town was just around the corner from the hospital on Walkers Road. It was also not very far from Rabbit's apartment, and more importantly, within a kilometre of where the cruise ships anchored outside of the harbour. A distance over which I was certain the noise of their horns honking could carry.

The house was a small, single-storey block home, typical of the island, painted yellow and brown. We parked by the side of the road, and Jacob called a friend in the East End police department, giving him the address of the third person who'd responded to Robbie and Rabbit's scheme. It wasn't out of the question that Charise Wong had an accomplice who spoke with targets over the phone, but we felt we'd be pushing our luck with Sergeant Redburn to ask for permission to drive to the other end of the island. Jacob explained what we were investigating, and his friend promised to let us know what he found after dropping by the address.

We walked to the front door and knocked. It was just after midday, so chances were that nobody was home, so I was surprised when a man in his early thirties opened the door.

"Mr Aung Naing?" I asked, hoping I landed the pronunciation somewhere close.

"Yes," he answered, looking at us with concern.

He was dark skinned and appeared to be South Asian, leaning more towards Asia itself.

"We'd like to speak with you about online activity that we're investigating."

He stepped back. "Please. Inside," he replied in stilted English with a heavy accent.

We followed him into the living room, which more closely resembled a NASA control room than a place to sit and watch the telly. Four large monitors filled one wall and a desk with three more monitors took pride of place in the middle of the room.

"My English, not good," he said. "But I try."

"Online, are you known as 3Kyarr3?" I asked.

"3Kyarr3," he repeated, although his pronunciation sounded quite different to my attempt. "Yes. Problem?"

"Do you live here alone?"

He looked puzzled. "You," I said, pointing to him. "Alone?" I held up one finger, then brought a second finger alongside, then wiggled my fingertip.

He smiled as he got my crude sign language, and held up one finger and pointed to himself. "One."

Now I wasn't sure if he was telling me he was alone at the moment, or lived here alone, but I had no idea how to make my question any clearer, so I moved on. I pointed to myself. "Norway."

Then to Jacob. "Cayman Islands."

I then pointed to him and held up my hands to show I intended this as a question.

"Myanmar," he replied, and held up six fingers. "Six months," he continued and pointed to the floor.

With a little more pointing, and from him handing me the business card of the man I presumed was his boss, I established the obvious: that he worked as IT support for a local wealth management company. Although I wasn't altogether sure exactly what a wealth management company actually did and figured I'd never need one. I decided I'd test the man.

"We need to take you in for playing naughty games on adult sites you shouldn't be visiting, sir. You need to come with us and you definitely need a lawyer."

Both men looked at me in confusion. Jacob, wondering what I was babbling on about, although he understood the words, and Mr Aung Naing because he only understood a few of the words I said. I carefully watched his eyes, which displayed nothing but concern and bewilderment. If he was faking his lack of English, he was doing a stellar job.

"Sorry?" he responded. "No understand."

"It's possible he has an accomplice who does the talking," I said to Jacob. "But I don't see how this guy could be Grandma's caller."

"Da accent fits," Jacob pointed out.

"There's a couple of billion people in South Asia, Jacob. That's a lot of accents which fit."

"You'd hear dat horn from here," he pointed out.

"Sure, but your grandma would have said if the bloke could barely speak any English. She just told us he had a slight accent."

"I suppose," Jacob admitted. "Okay, I look around?" he asked the man, using hand signals to echo his question.

Aung Naing nodded and swept his hand in front of himself.

"Give us a hundred dollars and we'll leave and forget your name came up," I said, which stopped Jacob in his tracks.

Mr Naing looked at me and didn't register any reaction beyond confusion.

"Look around, but it's not him, Jacob."

My partner nodded and poked his head in the rooms down a hallway. He returned a minute later.

"Only one person lives here," he reported. "Spare bedroom, but nuttin' in dere."

"Thank you, sir," I said, and we walked to the front door.

He rushed around us and politely opened the door for us.

"Thank you," he said, and I smiled as we left.

Once we were in the car, Jacob started the engine and looked at me.

"What now?"

I held up the business card we'd been given. "Let's drop by and find out how they manage to communicate with the guy. They wouldn't have him here on the island if they couldn't tell him what to do."

Jacob drove us around downtown, avoiding the waterfront as a pair of cruise ships were in today. He took Eastern to West Bay Road, where we headed north past the hotels on our left and the shops and restaurants on our right. It was a beautiful day. Spring time was my favourite season on the island. It wasn't quite as crazy with tourists as the summer months, and the humidity was a little less oppressive.

After nearly five years in the Caribbean, I'd become used to the stark contrast from my homeland, and on our recent trip, I'd found the chill of the Norwegian spring tougher to handle than I'd anticipated. Jazzy thought she'd landed in the coldest place on earth and couldn't understand how anyone survived. It cost me a fortune in clothing, as she didn't own anything warmer than a sweatshirt before we left. Despite her protests, I left her new wardrobe with my parents, as there seemed no point in bringing a ski jacket, soft-shell trousers, and woolly socks back to the Cayman Islands.

Mr Naing's employer, named Cayman Star Wealth Management, had their offices in The Grand Pavilion Commercial Centre, about halfway up Seven Mile Beach on the inland side of the West Bay Road. We parked, located their suite from the big board by the entrance, and walked into their reception. It appeared the company had a corner of the building on the ground floor with five or six private offices and a warren of maybe a dozen cubicles. The receptionist forced a concerned smile when we entered.

"Tristan Bennett, please," I said, reading from the card.

"Is Mr Bennett expecting you?"

"I doubt it," I responded.

"Okay, then, may I ask what this is in regard to?"

"No."

"It's a simple matter which Mr Bennett can help us wit, ma'am," Jacob quickly added, so apparently I was being too abrupt again.

But it was none of this woman's business why we were there.

"Oh. One moment please," she replied, and instead of calling him on the phone, she got up and walked back to one of the offices with windows to the outside world.

After a few moments, she reappeared and beckoned us to join her. Escorting us past the cubicles of wealth-managing worker bees, she accompanied us to the office door as though we'd run amok if left to our own devices.

A man stood and smoothed his tie behind a large desk. "I'm Tristan Bennett. How may I help you?" he asked in a BBC English accent.

"Constables Sommer and Tibbetts, sir. Do you employ a man named Aung Naing?"

"Aung?" he echoed. "Yes, he handles our IT and website needs. We don't actually employ him, but we contract with the company he works for. Brilliant fellow."

"How do you tell him what to do?" I asked, eager to get to the point.

Just being in the offices with people in suits made me long for the outdoors.

Bennett laughed. "Yes, it's a bit tricky. Generally, we contact the company and they instruct him, but if he has cause to come by the office here, we point a lot, and use an online translator where we type it in English and it pops up in the Burmese alphabet. Not the most reliable system, but it's worked for us so far and he's got us out of a few computer pickles."

"He's the only one from his company on the island?" I asked.

"To my knowledge, yes," Bennett replied. "Is he in some sort of trouble I should know about?"

"No sir. Thank you," I said, and turned to leave.

"We dropped by to see him, but after talkin' wit him and wit you, I'd say we can rule him outta our investigation, sir," Jacob explained.

"Okay, well, happy to help," Bennett said as we left his office.

I waited until we were outside the building before speaking. "Why did you explain all that and say he was ruled out?"

"Because they were both nice to us, and we don't tink they did nuttin', Nora," Jacob said defensively. "You da one who said dat fella don't even speak good English."

"Right. But he has a bloke at his office who he's in communication with all the time who does."

Jacob's face dropped. "I didn't tink about dat."

I thought it over as we got in the car. "*Nei*, it's not him."

Jacob held up a hand after he started the car. "If it were da man off the da island, how was da cruise ship horn in da background?"

"Exactly," I agreed. "Which means we're nowhere again."

"Well, dat's good in one way."

"How's that?" I asked.

"I kinda liked dat fella, and I feel bad he's got no one on da island to talk to."

I shook my head at Jacob, but in all honesty, I had been thinking the same thing.

He pulled out of the car park and had just started north when my mobile rang. It was Whittaker. I answered through the car's hands-free system.

"Sir. Jacob and I are just heading to patrol," I answered, to let him know he was on speaker.

"Constables," he responded. "Anything show up in the autopsy?"

I thought for a moment before answering, but I couldn't come up with a great way to spin what I'd seen.

"Unexplained bruising on Zara Parsons, and I noticed strange marks on the back of Heather Lawson's ankles, sir, but otherwise, no."

"I thought Lawson's body had been released without an autopsy?" the detective asked.

"Pictures, sir."

"I see. Does Davies think there's something to these bruises and marks?"

"He didn't have a plausible explanation for them, sir."

"What was his conclusion?"

It pained me to answer, but I had no choice. "He saw nothing to sway him from his accidental death finding, sir."

Whittaker didn't immediately respond, so I gave him the other piece of news I'd rather have kept to myself.

"Dilbert's watch showed up, sir. The EMTs found it in the ambulance. It must have fallen off during transport."

"Where does that leave us, Nora?" he asked, to my surprise.

But I realised he was testing me. I had nothing worthy of moving forward with. My uncomfortable feeling wasn't enough.

"We don't have anything to form a case, sir."

"Agreed," he replied. "At the end of today, I'll close these three as unfortunate accidents."

24

SLOTHS AND OLD CASES

We returned to patrol in West Bay, using our coin toss system to decide the route, but my heart wasn't in it. I relished the challenge of solving cases, but when they fell apart or came to nothing, it bothered me more than it should. Maybe it was ego, but I didn't like to think it was. Of course, that could also be my ego covering up the fact that I was wrong in both ways. Egos are scheming little bastards.

Jacob knew I was in a funk when I passed up the chance of pulling over an IDC. The guy was driving a lowered piece-of-crap Toyota with stupid chrome wheels and ridiculously low-profile tyres, cranking his reggae song with all his windows down. The car seemed to shudder with every bass note.

"Which one got you so screwed up that we not gettin' after that guy?" Jacob asked.

"Both," I replied.

We sat at the four-way stop, two cars back, and the thumping finally drove me nuts.

"*Fy faen*," I muttered and flicked the lights and siren on.

"Dat's better," Jacob laughed, pulling around the car in front and following the Toyota north on West Church Street.

The guy pulled over in the car park opposite one of the many churches the street could have been named after.

"Go ahead," Jacob said, gesticulating towards the car where the driver was busy throwing a joint out the window and picking the back of his seat up from the ridiculously laid-back driving position he'd decided was cool.

"I'll just Taser the idiot. You go," I told him.

Jacob shook his head at me, his eyes full of concern, but he left the car without saying anything more.

The accidents bothered me the most. I felt really bad for Jacob's grandma, but we still had the cybercrimes unit who were far better equipped to follow up on her case. Whenever they'd get to it. The accidents were being dropped, and I now felt a sense of unease which bordered on panic.

Motivation was a big problem. Not my own, but if there was a killer staging these deaths, what was his? Short of a sadistic desire to kill innocent people, I couldn't find a strong connection between the victims or their circumstances. The trophy element was the one link I'd been counting on. The two women seemed to fit more than Dilbert, so it was possible that he was an outlier and their similarities a coincidence. All three still had the location and predictability of them being alone, yet later discovered in common. Two were divorced and one was married. Two female, one male. Three different causes of death.

Jacob came back, and I realised I hadn't being paying attention at all. He could have been attacked or needed my help in some way, and I was off in my own world.

"Sorry," I blurted, as he sat in the driver's seat.

"For what?" he replied with a smile as he drove us away.

"For leaving that one to you," I lied, figuring it was easier than explaining my mental absence.

"Worked out best. I know dat kid. He's actually a decent guy from a good family. Works for an uncle of mine at a nursery."

"He works with kids?" I asked in disbelief.

"No!" Jacob laughed. "Da flowers kind o' nursery, not da children kind."

The English language had a word for everything and every version of everything, but they hadn't bothered making a distinction between raising plants and raising children. It made no sense to me. Pursery could be a word.

Jacob's mobile rang, and I used the touchscreen on the dash to answer his phone through the car's hands-free system.

"Did you find anyting out?" he asked, and I assumed it was his friend from East End station, although I'd expected a man.

"Charise Wong is a nice young lady. Seems pretty smart too," the woman explained. "She takin' online college from home. Her father from Hong Kong and da mother Caymanian. Nice house, dey got some money, I tell you. Don't see her being your guy, Jacob."

"Tanks for doin' dat for us. We owe you one."

"You owe me more dan one, Tibbetts. I be keepin' a tab," the woman joked.

"Dat's probably da truth. Tanks again," he said and hung up. "Back to square one," he added, turning to me. "What are we missing here?"

I thought again about Robbie and Rabbit, but my gut couldn't get past the guilt of even considering either of them.

"The only one of the three we've checked who remotely fits the description is Aung Naing, but unless he had an accomplice, there's no way it's him."

"Maybe he's dat good at actin'," Jacob suggested.

"Why would he act like he doesn't speak English at work?" I pointed out. "That would only make his life a lot harder, and Bennett verified they have a language barrier with him."

Jacob had driven us back to the four-way, and was getting ready to turn right.

"I need one of those coffee energy drink things," I said, and woke up the dash mounted laptop in front of me.

He flipped the indicator left and turned south on West Bay Drive, heading for Foster's Market.

"Did you tink o' someting else to try?" he asked, glancing over at me.

"*Ja*," I replied, then realised he was thinking about his grand-mother's case. "With the accidents," I clarified.

"Oh," he murmured, turning into the car park.

Our onboard laptop ran through a built-in cell card but was frustratingly slow. I could access most data available in the police system. If I was patient enough to wait for it to load. Sometimes, it simply wasn't worth the time, and it was faster to drop by the station and use one of the desktops. In this case, we were supposed to be on patrol, and I no longer had an excuse to be researching a case that had been closed. Well, to be accurate, it had never been opened. The accidental death rulings were just delayed.

"Can I help while you get your drink?" Jacob asked, and I thought about telling him what to get me and sending him in, but stopped myself.

He'd do it, but he wasn't my errand boy, and more importantly, he was a smart policeman, and I was starting not to trust my own judgement with these accidents.

"I'm searching old cases, cold cases, and accident rulings from the past twenty-four months," I explained. "Looking for any detail which might connect to the current deaths."

I pivoted the stand around so he could reach from his side. "I put in a series of tags and it's searching now. The connection is as slow as a... *dovendyr*. I don't know the name in English."

"Describe a doven-deer," Jacob replied.

"A weird-looking animal that hangs in trees and moves really slowly."

"A sloth?" he asked.

"If that's what you call one of those animals, then yes. The computer is as slow as a sloth."

He seemed to think that made sense, so I left to get my *not good for me but tasty and wakes me up* coffee-flavoured energy drink.

I used the loo while I had the chance, grabbed my drink, bought Jacob a chocolate bar snack, and made it out in less than ten minutes.

"Find anything?" I asked as I sat down and handed him his treat.

"You're right," he said, without taking his eyes from the screen, which I couldn't see from my side.

"There is a connection?"

"No. Da computer is really slow. It took half da time you bin gone to upload your search."

"Give it back and eat your chocolate," I said, but Jacob didn't move.

He continued scrolling and studying the list.

"Dat's okay. I gotta finish dis now I started."

"How many cases came back?"

"Seventy-four," he replied.

"*Dritt*. That's a lot."

"It is, but I tink most of dese we can rule out," he replied. "Like all da ones witnessed by someone, right?"

"*Ja*. Good point. Can we filter eyewitnesses out?"

"If you wanna wait for dis ting to start da search over," he laughed. "Best just skip dem ones."

I patiently sipped my drink while Jacob diligently searched the list. Which was complete bullshit. I wasn't patient at all. I sat there sipping my drink, but it was driving me crazy that he was seeing all the data and I wasn't. It had nothing to do with trust. I knew Jacob would do just as good a job as me looking through the cases, and if I was somewhere else leaving him to it, I'd be fine. But maybe he'd miss a tiny detail that I would have caught. So, I suppose it was a trust thing. I didn't know what the hell reason it was, but it was driving me nuts sitting in the passenger seat doing nothing while he scrolled and occasionally hemmed and hawed over what I couldn't see.

"We should get back on patrol, Jacob," I said when I couldn't stand it anymore.

"Almost finished," he muttered, intensely focused on the screen.

I got out of the car and walked a lap of the car park. It took about five minutes, and the people's reactions were amusing. About a third looked at me as though I were up to something shifty. A third smiled and said hello, and the other third hurried in the opposite direction. When I returned to our patrol car, Jacob frowned at me.

"Did you just walk around in a circle?"

"*Ja.*"

"Why?"

"Are you done?" I asked instead of answering his question.

"Yes, ma'am," he said proudly, and pivoted the laptop mount my way. "Here are da three cases I'd say worth lookin' at."

I eagerly studied the screen. I couldn't know what he'd discarded, but the three he'd kept looked promising. Serial killers rarely started with a spree. They dipped a toe in the water and when they found the power of taking life intoxicating, it could then escalate. Sometimes taking years between kills, sometimes less.

None of the three were listed as homicides, so none were cold cases. They were all accidental deaths. Two had very little information, as they were immediately ruled that way, but the third took an unusually long time between the accident and the ruling. The file didn't contain much, but it felt like the best chance of having a connection. *To what?* I reminded myself. Three deaths with almost no link to each other or evidence of foul play. But there it was again. That niggle in my gut that something wasn't right.

"Detective Weatherford filed paperwork on this one," I thought aloud. "I can call him."

Weatherford was a good man I'd worked with a few times alongside Whittaker. I liked him, and he was a no-nonsense bloke. He'd tell me if he'd smelled anything fishy about the accident. The other person I could talk to was the coroner, of course, but I knew how that would go.

"Don't say much in da file, but struck me funny how long dey take to close the case as bein' an accident," Jacob commented. "Not to mention, it look like an ugly way to go."

He winced. The man died when the car he was working on in his garage fell off the jack and crushed him. From the report, it was estimated he took several hours to succumb to the injuries. While remaining pinned, alone, under the car.

I thought I had a number for Weatherford, but if I did, it appeared I hadn't saved it. Maybe there was merit to storing a few more numbers. It took a minute over the slow connection, but I finally brought up a registry with official contact information for everyone who had a police-issued phone and called the detective's number. It went to voicemail. Maybe he hadn't saved my number either.

"This is Constable Sommer. I have a question about a case. Call me back. Sir."

We continued on our patrol, and after only a few minutes, a text buzzed and I figured it was Weatherford getting back to me. It wasn't. It was Jazzy. She had another track meet tomorrow evening at the school. She said it was team trials to see who would represent the school for some other, bigger inter-school event, so it was no big deal if I couldn't be there. Perfect. Another opportunity to be a shitty foster parent.

I didn't care what she said. I needed to be there.

25

CHEATER

The rest of our afternoon and evening went without incident, and I'd stayed up later than usual and slept in, preparing for my night shift, which started at 7:00pm. In the morning, Jazzy left quietly, and although I woke up, I was able to go back to sleep. Until my phone buzzed. I kept the ringtone permanently muted, but the vibration on the nightstand still woke me out of my shallow slumber. I scrambled to answer when I saw it was Weatherford.

"*Ja*," I answered sleepily. "*Takk*... I mean, *thank you* for calling back."

"Did I wake you? I'm sorry, Nora."

"It's okay," I said, shuffling out of bed and switching on the coffee maker.

"My kid had a birthday party yesterday, so I had my phone off. I apologise. What is it I can help you with?"

My first thought was to make a note that a good parent shuts off work when they prioritise their kids. I hadn't managed to do that. Ever.

"Do you remember a case involving a man who was crushed under his car in his garage at home?" I asked, moving on. "Guy's name was Philippe Girard."

"Hmm. Yes, I do remember something about that. It wasn't really a case, as it was deemed accidental, but I was the detective who took a look. The coroner asked for a second opinion. That was a year or more ago, wasn't it?"

"Eighteen months," I clarified. "What caused the hesitation?"

"In deciding it was accidental?" he asked.

"*Ja.*"

"Hmm, let me think a minute. You might be better off asking Gareth Davies. I bet he has a better memory than I do. You've met the coroner, right?"

"*Ja.* I was hoping to avoid having to call him," I admitted.

Weatherford laughed. "Yeah, he's an acquired taste."

"If that means he's an arse, then I agree."

He laughed again. "That's pretty much what that means. But he knows what he's doing."

I couldn't disagree, but I didn't say anything more.

"As best I recall, the suspicion was based mainly on the fact that his family and friends all said he never worked under a car without jack stands. The guy was an EMT, I think, but he fixed up cars on the side. From what we could tell, the jack slipped out from under the frame, so the car slammed down on the poor guy."

"It slipped out?" I questioned. "It didn't fail in some way?"

"No, the jack was scooted off to the side of the garage, still pumped up. The jack stands were sitting close by, but hadn't been placed underneath."

"Anything else odd or suspicious about the scene?" I asked.

"Not that I remember. Why the interest, Nora?"

Weatherford worked for Whittaker and they were good friends, but I also felt he could be discreet when trusted with something that didn't need to be brought up.

"We've had a run of strange accidents lately, and none of them are perfectly related, but the odds of three fatalities in the space of a week are slim. I was taking a look to see if I could find any common links, but we've not discovered anything yet. Whittaker decided we should move on, but I was just finishing checks into old and cold cases."

I deliberately omitted details of the timing of the two events and left it sounding like my search was already in progress before the plug was pulled. While he could be discreet, I didn't expect Weatherford to support me going against our boss's wishes.

"Does this accident fit in any way?" he asked.

"Where did it happen?"

"West Bay. At the guy's house."

"Where exactly? Are there other houses close by?"

"Do you know Glidden Lane? It's the first right off Watercourse Road if you're heading north from the coast."

"*Ja.*"

I hadn't known what it was called, but I could picture the narrow lane he was talking about.

"He had a place down there. Smallest house on a good-sized lot. Neighbours sold and now there are bigger homes built, but they're well-spaced apart. No one could see his garage out back and his lungs were crushed, so he couldn't yell. Had friends and family coming by that evening for a barbecue. They found him."

"Woods or vacant land behind the house?" I asked.

"Hmm. You'd have to take a look and see to be sure, but I don't recall anything backed up to the place. I think those new condos are there now, but they would have been being built back then. May not have even broken ground yet."

"Did the family mention anything missing? Like a ring, watch, jewellery of some kind."

"That I don't recall. If it was, I didn't hear about it."

I thought for a moment. It was still the same circumstantial, unprovable connections, but it ticked a few of the boxes.

"I doubt it's anything, but the location and timing are all similar," I said, not wanting to create too much interest in case Weatherford decided to ask our boss about it. "Thanks for filling me in."

"Any time, Nora. Sorry it took me a bit to get back to you."

"That's okay," I replied. "Kids have to come first."

My own words echoed in my head as I hung up the call.

I stood naked in the kitchen. Which made it sound like it was a room unto itself, when in fact it was simply one side of the living area. I looked around my little home and realised it was only a few minutes past 8:00am. If I had any sense, I'd be going back to bed, but I knew I wouldn't sleep. There was far too much crap whirling around inside my brain.

While the coffee brewed, I found a bathing suit to wear, then sat on the porch with my new Shearwater dive computer and played with all the functions some more. Every once in a while I heard rustling from the undergrowth and I looked up, but Edvard never appeared. Once I'd set the computer up, customising all the parameters to how I liked them in freedive mode, and finished my coffee, I headed to the water with fins and mask in hand.

It was 9:30am by the time I came back, showered and towelled myself dry. I felt more centred for having been on the reef, but wide awake with no chance of going back to bed. On Jacob's grandmother's case, I'd come to the conclusion that we were stuck. All we could do now was pass on the little info we'd found to Luke and let cybercrimes take a look whenever they could get around to it. I hated to admit defeat, but I didn't know where to turn to next. I figured I'd call Robbie and Rabbit later this morning to let them know.

With the accidents, I was equally stumped about how to proceed. The old case certainly sounded disturbingly similar in a few ways, but I'm sure I could find a handful of coincidental nuggets between the sinking of the *Titanic* and the assassination of Martin Luther King if I tried hard enough. Anyway, with Whittaker's decision to move on, there wasn't much I could do. But along with the thought of moving on, I felt my stomach slowly twisting into the knot I'd just spent the past hour underwater untying.

Jazzy's track meet was at four, so I had a day to fill, which desperately required sleep at some point, or tonight would be a nightmare. But I knew it would be fruitless to try again now. I walked inside and opened the fridge, looking for something appetising for breakfast. It was bare. I hadn't been to the grocery shop in ages. Doing something felt better than sitting around wishing I was doing something, so I threw on leggings and a T-shirt and headed for the Jeep.

Rolling down Mount Pleasant Road on my way to Foster's, I noticed an ambulance parked outside the McRuss Grocery Store, a small shop I had only been in a few times. Jacob's cousin, Maya, leaned against the driver's door, eating a savoury pastry of some sort that the locals called patties. I turned into the car park and pulled up next to the ambulance. Maya looked over and smiled at me.

"I have a question to ask you," I called over after I turned the engine off.

"Good morning, Nora," she said in reply, reminding me I'd forgotten the usual pleasantries people tended to prefer.

"Hi," I responded, and looked around for her partner.

I noticed it was the man I'd seen her with at Zara Parsons' house. I recalled his name was Jimmy. He was walking around at the edge of the car park, talking on his mobile phone. Glancing our way, he studied me while I watched him. He didn't smile or wave, but there again, I didn't either.

"What you wanna ask me, Nora?"

I returned my attention to Maya. "Do you recall an EMT named Philippe Girard?"

She stopped chewing and looked at me. "Of course. Why?"

I didn't want to share too much, but she was being helpful, so I had to tell her something.

"We were looking at old accidental death cases, and his file stood out."

"Stood out how?" she asked, then took the last bite of her pattie.

Maya should have been a copper instead of an EMT. She was full of pertinent questions.

"What do you remember about the incident?" I asked, hoping I could re-establish our roles.

"It was horrible," she said, shaking her head. "It was too late by the time anyone got to him. Bin pinned for hours, dey reckon."

"Was anything suspicious?"

"What do you mean? Like, someone do dat to Philippe?"

"*Ja.*"

Maya looked taken aback. "He was a great guy. Don't know why anyone would wanna see him hurt," she said, then thought for a moment.

I waited, but she didn't say anything more.

"Did you know him well?"

Maya nodded. "Worked together a bunch."

"Who didn't like him?"

She looked at me with what I took as an annoyed expression. "I told you. He got along wit everyone."

"There's something you're not telling me," I persisted, aware I was pushing my luck with Jacob's cousin.

I didn't need her getting mad at me and giving Jacob an earful about his partner, but I sensed she had more to say. Maya glanced around, her gaze settling on Jimmy for a moment.

"It was just rumour, okay?" she said in a hushed tone. "But word was he was seeing anudder man's wife."

"That would make one person dislike him quite a lot," I pointed out. "Whose wife?"

Maya shrugged her shoulders. "I got no idea."

"Someone from work?"

She shrugged again. "Maybe."

"How many married guys work as EMTs?"

"I dunno. Never counted," she replied, then looked off in the distance while I assumed she was doing the maths in her head. "Four, I guess. No, three. One was already divorced."

"So, which of those three do you think it was?" I pressed.

"Dat, I got no idea," she replied, but her eyes darted towards Jimmy again.

"He one of them?"

Maya gave me another look, but then nodded. I wanted to ask

her for more names, but that was something I could look up rather than make her feel like she was telling on her workmates.

"Thanks," I said, and was about to start the Jeep when the radio came alive in the ambulance.

"EMT Three, this is dispatch, do you copy? EMT Three, this is dispatch."

Maya opened the door and reached inside, grabbing the radio mic. "Dispatch, go for EMT Tree."

"EMT Three, we have a category one. Repeat, category one, at Wild Wood Lane. Copy?"

Maya waved to Jimmy, who ran towards the ambulance while finishing his call.

"Dispatch, this is EMT Tree responding to category one. Over."

I remained parked, so they didn't have to worry about me getting in their way. They both reacted quickly, and were pulling out of the car park within seconds with lights flashing and siren blaring. Category one was the code for a life-threatening incident. Probably a heart attack or a road accident, although Wild Woods Lane must be a small street as I'd never heard of it.

The siren echoed around West Bay as I backed up and prepared to continue my trip to the market. As I put the Jeep in first gear, ready to pull to the exit, my mobile rang. I looked at the caller ID. It was Whittaker.

"Nora, where are you?" he asked without his usual polite greeting.

"West Bay, sir."

"There's been another accident," he said.

"On Wild Woods Lane?" I asked, pulling to the road.

"How did you know?" he asked.

"I'll meet you there," I replied, quickly hanging up, then opening my map app to find Wild Woods Lane.

26

BACKWARD OR FORWARD

Poinciana Lane was a small, dusty but paved road off Watercourse. Wild Woods Lane was an even smaller unpaved track off Poinciana. A couple of homes were well spaced apart on either side, and I found the ambulance parked outside a small two-storey, nestled against a wooded area near the end. The front door was open, and I paused outside. Maya was crouched over a woman at the base of the stairs.

"Is she alive?" I asked.

Maya looked up and shook her head. "Neck's broke, and she got head trauma."

"Witness?"

"Neighbour come by for coffee. She found her," Maya replied. "Jimmy wit her in da kitchen," she added, pointing across the living room.

That was enough information, combined with the location similarities, to make up my mind how we needed to proceed.

"Treat this as a crime scene, Maya. You have booties and gloves in the ambulance?"

"A crime scene? She fall down da stairs, Nora," Maya responded. "She was home alone."

"It's a crime scene," I repeated firmly. "Gloves?"

Maya stood. "Yeah. In da wagon. Just inside da back door on da right."

"Tell the others not to touch anything, and have them come out of the house," I barked before striding over to the ambulance.

I found the supplies and grabbed a set in my size, and a set in Whittaker's. I was closing the back door of the ambulance when I heard a car and saw his SUV approaching. Waiting until he joined me, I handed him the coverings.

"What do we know?" he asked, taking the gloves and booties from me.

"Location matches the others. Woman is dead. Appears to have fallen down her stairs. She was alone. Neighbour found her when she came by for lunch. Too many points fit, sir, so I've asked EMTs to treat it as a crime scene."

Whittaker nodded, and we walked towards the house. "I agree. At this stage, we should preserve the scene unless we can rule out foul play. Any indications of another person present?"

"Haven't been inside yet, sir."

We both donned the booties at the doorstep, then fought our hands into the nitrile gloves.

Whittaker paused. "I still hope you're wrong about all this, Nora."

I wasn't sure whether he expected me to respond or not, but I didn't. Hoping wouldn't make any difference, and we needed to figure out whether someone was involved in this spate of deaths or if the weirdest run of bad luck ever had struck the island. My gut had tweaked when I'd heard the radio call, and twisted again when I'd pulled up and seen the location. Nothing I'd observed since had given it cause to unwind. I wasn't wrong.

"Hello, Detective," Maya greeted us, stepping back from the body. "Jimmy took da neighbour out da back door. She'll wait at home."

I wished he'd brought her through the house and out the already open front door, but that was my fault for not being clear.

"Hello, Maya," Whittaker replied, studying the scene from a few paces back. "Any details you noticed we should know about?"

"Not really," she replied. "But talk to Jimmy. He was first through da door. Da lady was already in da kitchen. Said she couldn't look at her friend all broken like dat."

"Victim's name?" I asked.

"Renae Waybridge, according to da friend. I haven't verified dat as yet."

"Have you called Gareth Davies?" Whittaker asked.

"Yes, sir. I'd done dat shortly after we arrived."

"Great," I groaned to myself. I'd like to get a good look around before the coroner showed up and complicated things.

"Constable Sommer," Whittaker said, getting my attention. "Can you carefully go up the stairs and see if you can identify where the head wound came from?"

"I'm getting outta your way, so shout if you need anyting," Maya said. "I'll be in da wagon."

"Thank you, Maya," Whittaker replied as I stepped over the body and took a look from my new perspective.

Renae Waybridge was probably early forties, dressed casually in jeans and a simple dark blue blouse. Her feet were bare. Her right arm lay outstretched and several fingers were definitely broken. The victim's other arm was partially trapped beneath her body, but the lower part of her forearm was visible and her hand pointed at an unnatural angle, broken at the wrist. Renae had the pale brown skin tone of many of the island's citizens, reflecting Cayman's mixed race history. Her black hair was pulled back in a ponytail, and her eyes stared lifelessly at the wall, with her head resting at a grotesque angle to her torso. The head wound was deep and could well have been fatal without the broken neck.

Whittaker called for our CSI team to attend, while I gingerly placed a foot on the first hardwood step, making sure I wasn't treading on any obvious evidence. Looking up, I quickly saw the offending wood, which may well have caused both injuries. A splotch of blood marked a step approximately halfway down the flight, and a small amount of splatter had reached the next two steps below the point of impact. I walked up, delicately placing my feet to avoid stepping in anything the forensic team would need to collect. Stopping three down from the impact point, I judged the height up to the landing. If someone tripped at the very top of the stairs, without forward momentum, it appeared to be about the right spot they'd land on their head.

"I shouldn't go any farther until Rasha has been here," I called down. "The victim hit her head here," I continued, pointing to the offending step.

I looked down at the woman. Her feet were draped on the lowest step and her body curled in what was close to the foetal position, except her torso was rotated halfway towards facing the ceiling. Turning, I looked up at the landing and pictured her falling forward, hitting her head, then crumbling and rolling down to the ground floor. Something wasn't right.

"She fell backwards," I said, voicing my thought aloud.

Whittaker peered up at me from below. "The wound is on the back of her head," he commented, following my theory.

"And she should be face down if she'd fallen forward," I added.

"Could she have been walking upstairs and slipped somehow?" the detective asked. "Any marks you can see? Scrapes on the wall from a hand thrown out to save herself?"

I studied the sand-coloured wall. A few scuff marks marred one or two spots, but nothing significant or fresh looking. They had the appearance of older damage from moving furniture or larger objects up or down.

"How did she break her fingers and wrist?" I asked, picturing the fall once more. "When people fall backwards, they windmill their arms in the air."

"Perhaps when she hit the floor?" Whittaker suggested.

From outside I heard another vehicle arrive, and a few moments later, Gareth Davies appeared in the doorway, where he stopped to look inside the house.

"Hi, Gareth," Whittaker greeted him.

"Roy," the man responded, then frowned as he saw me halfway up the stairs. "Try not to disturb anything," he said flatly, and disappeared outside once more.

"You'd better come down, Constable," Whittaker instructed me. "We'll let the coroner do his job while we look around."

I tiptoed down the steps and paused for a moment to look at the corpse one more time. It was going to be interesting to see what Davies made of her fall. Crouching down, I checked for jewellery. Protruding behind her torso, behind her back, I could see a gold watch strap on her left wrist. Around her strangely distorted neck was a delicate gold chain. Her broken right wrist was bare. But I did notice a small abrasion across the back of the joint.

"Odd," I commented, and Whittaker leaned over.

"The mark is lateral across the joint," I elaborated.

"Could have smacked her wrist on a step," he responded. "That would have been what broke it."

I stood and stepped over the body to get a better look at her left wrist, but the back of her hand was against the floor.

"Not if this wrist has a similar mark, sir."

"I assume forensics has been called?" Davies asked, reappearing with a Tyvek suit hung over his arm.

"Yes," Whittaker replied. "Probably an hour or so before they get here."

Davies nodded. "Good. That'll give me time to take a look. Any witnesses? Who found the body?"

"A neighbour," the detective replied. "We're going to speak with her in a moment. We'll leave you to it."

The coroner nodded and began suiting up while we walked through the living room to the kitchen. The house was neither old nor modern, inside or out. It was a brick home with functional hurricane windows and an interior layout which probably came from stock plans available online. The decor was practical, functional, yet comfortable looking. A few family pictures adorned shelves, and a pleasant painting of two horses galloping in the edge of the sea took pride of place on the main living room wall. The television was on a stand in the corner and couldn't have been larger than 120 centimetres. Relatively small by modern standards.

We stood in the kitchen and looked around us. A half full coffee cup sat on the counter, and the carafe on the hotplate was one-quarter full. If she was like most coffee drinkers who drank two cups in the morning, she'd only had time for her first cup. I dipped my finger into the mug. It was room temperature.

Whittaker stared out the window across the backyard towards the woods. "Why would someone wish to harm these people?" he asked, although I figured he didn't expect a response.

I wondered where Jimmy the EMT had got to. He never came back through the house, so he could still be next door with the neighbour. After the weird looks he was giving me outside the grocery store, I wanted to speak with him as much as the witness.

"Remind me again. What are the connections you've found with the other cases, Nora?" Whittaker asked, using my first name now we were away from others.

"Location," I replied. "Easy access and escape to and from the house. Victim predictably home alone, but knowledge they'd be discovered later in the day. The missing items, but Dilbert's watch showed up, so I'm not sure on that point, but it's a question to ask."

"Anything else?"

"The strange bruising on the first two victims. I haven't seen the coroner's report on Dilbert yet, so I don't know about him. Oh, and I found an old case which might be a match, sir."

"Really? How old?"

"Year and a half. Weatherford looked into it, sir. I spoke to him. Location and predictable movement matched."

"Did Weatherford think it was suspicious?"

"He said everyone he spoke to told him the guy would never work under a car without jack stands in place, but he was killed by the car dropping off the jack and crushing him."

Whittaker winced. "Any missing item?"

"Haven't got that far, sir. But he was an EMT and Maya told me there was a rumour he'd been screwing another EMT's wife."

"Having relations with, Constable," Whittaker responded.

"No. Pretty sure he was screwing her, sir."

Whittaker shook his head. But I also saw him hiding a grin. I wasn't sure why.

"The terminology we use, Nora, in such circumstances, is *having relations*, not... what you said."

"Oh," I muttered. "Sorry."

"Okay," Whittaker said, moving the conversation along as I examined the back door, looking for signs of forced entry. "But why would a man seeking revenge on his co-worker for *having relations* with his wife now stage a series of accidents?"

I stepped outside to further examine the door frame, which appeared to be in perfect condition.

"Perhaps he got a taste for it, sir."

"Hmm," Whittaker murmured, following me to the backyard.

A patio ran across the back of the house with a grass lawn extending to a boundary marked by a simple, low picket fence. From there, the woods stretched in both directions. A well-worn track led from Renae's backyard, across the scrub land between her property and the next home, which I presumed belonged to her friend who found her.

I checked the patio for muddy tracks, but nothing stood out. The ground was too dry. Facing the woods, I looked to my left. This was the last home in the cul-de-sac and the treeline curved around beyond the side of the lot. Someone could have approached from that direction, coming from the woods, and easily stepped over the fence. Unless her neighbour, off to my right, happened to be standing in her backyard or walking this way, she'd never see the intruder.

Turning, I noticed something blue under a wooden patio chair. "*Dritt*," I muttered, as I walked closer and realised what it was. A blue nitrile glove like the ones we all wore at an incident.

"I told them to treat this as a crime scene," I complained as I picked it up.

That Jimmy character was starting to piss me off.

"Shall we speak with the witness?" Whittaker asked, already walking that way.

I was happy to follow. He could talk to the lady, while I cornered Jimmy, the clumsy EMT. Maybe he'd know something more about the French guy under a car. Or his wife would.

27

THE CAT DIDN'T DO IT THIS TIME

The neighbour, who we learnt was named Jennifer Colbert, leaned against her kitchen counter, sipping a coffee. Jimmy was there with her, but attempted to excuse himself when we arrived.

"Stick around," I told him.

Whittaker looked at me in surprise, but he didn't question my motives. Instead, he addressed the witness.

"Walk us through your morning, please, Miss Colbert."

"Mrs," she corrected, and I detected an English accent. "I worked for a few hours, then went next door as I do most days for a coffee and a chinwag. That's when I found Renae."

The woman's eyes were already red and puffy from crying, and she clutched her forehead, trying to stem more tears from flowing. She was a few years older than the victim, wore the odd combination of sweatpants and a nice white blouse. What makeup she had been wearing was now either streaked or wiped away.

"You work from home?" Whittaker asked.

She nodded. "I do website design and maintenance."

That explained her strange garb. She was dressed for internet video calls.

"Your visits are most days, you said?" Whittaker clarified.

"Yes. I take a break about ten or a bit after, and I go to hers. Gets me out of the office for a few."

"Where's your office?" I asked.

"Upstairs," she replied.

"Okay if I look?"

She frowned at me. "I suppose. What for? I mean, it's a bit of a mess, is all."

"I'll just be a minute," I replied, and left before she quizzed me again.

I heard Whittaker continue with questions and felt Jimmy's eyes on me as I climbed the stairs. From the landing, I had my answer. The door to what was originally intended to be a spare bedroom was open, and she was right. Her office was a mess. It also faced the street, so she wouldn't have seen anyone in Renae's backyard. I quickly checked the master bedroom, which did overlook the rear of the house. Because of the placement angle of the home, I had to press my cheek to the glass to see the bottom of Renae's garden. The only upstairs windows facing the neighbour were both bathrooms with frosted panes.

Hurrying downstairs, I noticed Jimmy watching me again. I caught his eye, and he quickly looked away. Maybe he was just being lecherous, but the guy made me uneasy, and my presence seemed to bother him. Although he appeared quite content to look at my skinny arse.

"So Miss Waybridge leaves her back door unlocked?" Whittaker was asking.

Jennifer nodded.

"When does she unlock it in the mornings?" I interjected.

"I don't really know. She used to have a cat, so she'd unlock the door to let him out in the mornings. But I couldn't tell you now. I know it's always unlocked when I go over."

"Where's the cat?" I asked.

"He died," she replied, and looked at me as though it should be obvious.

I didn't know. She could have given it to a friend or something. But at least we knew the cat didn't do it this time.

"What time did she let him out before he was dead?" I asked, and all three people in the room looked at me strangely.

Perhaps I phrased that oddly, but she answered anyway.

"Around seven, I think. That's when she gets up most mornings."

Whittaker was still looking at me, so I gave him a subtle nod to let him know I was done with questions for now. I guess I had hijacked his interview.

"So you entered the house, Mrs Colbert," the detective continued, "and then what?"

"I thought Renae must be upstairs, so I called out, but she didn't answer. So I walked into the living room and saw her at the base of the stairs."

She clutched her face again, trying her best to keep her emotions in check.

"I know this is difficult, ma'am," Whittaker said softly, "but these initial observations are very important."

Jennifer wiped her eyes and nodded.

"What position was Miss Waybridge in when you found her?"

"On the floor. Sort of on her side," she replied, taking deep breaths between each statement. "Her feet were still on the stairs. I didn't move her. I could tell she was…"

We waited while the woman sobbed for a few moments, turning away from us.

"It's quite alright, ma'am. I know this is very distressing. My apologies for putting you through it."

Jennifer turned around once more, using a paper towel to wipe her face. "Sorry," she mumbled.

"Did you see or hear anyone or anything odd during the morning?" Whittaker continued, pulling the witness away from the image of her dead friend.

She shook her head.

"Do you know if Miss Waybridge was seeing anyone at the moment?" he asked.

Jennifer shook her head again. "No. She was going through a difficult divorce. It's dragged on and was almost, finally done, and now this..."

That was another similarity to the first two, but not Dilbert.

"Was anything missing?" I blurted out, then checked myself. "*Dritt*. Sorry, sir."

"That's okay, Constable," Whittaker replied, although the look he threw my way didn't suggest it was completely okay. "Did you notice anything missing from Miss Waybridge?"

"How do you mean?" she asked.

From the corner of my eye, I watched for Jimmy's reaction. But he looked at me again, so I had to refocus on the witness.

"On her person. Were there any personal items, like jewellery perhaps, that were missing?" Whittaker elaborated.

"I don't think so," Renae replied. "But I was horrified, so I'm not sure I would have noticed."

"What did she regularly wear?" I asked.

"Jewellery wise?"

"Yes."

Jennifer thought for a moment. She touched her throat. "She never took her gold chain off. It belonged to her grandmother. And she usually wore a watch. But that's all I can think of."

"No rings?" I asked.

She shook her head. "Not since the divorce."

I couldn't help but feel a touch disappointed, although the trophy theory had already gone out the window with the ambulance crew finding Dilbert's watch.

"Her pink bracelet, of course," Jennifer added. "But that's not really jewellery, is it?"

"A pink bracelet?" I shot back. "You mean one of those rubbery type bands?"

"Yes. Renae was a breast cancer survivor. She always wore the pink bracelet."

"Right wrist?" I asked.

Jennifer looked at her own wrists. She had a watch on her left, as most people do. "Yes, it would be her right wrist. Opposite her watch."

"Did you notice it when you found her?" I asked.

"I couldn't see anything past my friend with her neck snapped," Jennifer replied, breaking into tears.

Dritt. I'd hear some BS about sensitivity again. I looked at Jimmy, so Whittaker's glare bounced off the back of my head.

"Did you notice a pink bracelet?"

Jimmy shook his head. "Can't say I did."

"Did you move the body?"

"Constable Sommer," Whittaker jumped in. "Why don't we step outside and give Mrs Colbert a little space?"

I walked to the back door and held it open for Jimmy and the detective. It was fine with me. As far as I was concerned, there was no doubt someone was involved in these deaths, and Jennifer Colbert didn't have the answers we needed.

"Did you move the body?" I asked again, the moment we were all outside, and I'd closed the door.

"Wasn't any point," Jimmy replied. "It was obvious she was dead."

I still couldn't place his English accent, but they had so many regional dialects, I didn't know them all.

"What was the body temperature when you arrived?" Whittaker asked.

"We didn't check with a thermometer, but her skin was below normal to the touch. I checked for a pulse by hand and stethoscope."

"She died between seven and eight," I said, announcing my thought.

I noticed I was doing that more lately, and I didn't like it.

"Habitually unlocks the back door at seven, and cool to the touch by a little after ten," Whittaker said, looking at me.

I nodded.

"Are you married, Jimmy?" I asked and he looked stunned.

"Why? You want to ask me out?"

"*I drømmene dine,*" I replied, and by his expression I figured he got the message that asking him out was not my intention. "Married?" I asked again.

He held up his hand and showed me the lack of ring on his finger.

"But you were."

He nodded. "Didn't work out."

"Did you know Philippe Girard?" I asked and watched him carefully.

He noticeably tensed.

"Sure."

"How well?"

Jimmy wrinkled his nose. "Not well. I worked with the guy a few times."

"Let's see how Gareth is coming along," Whittaker suggested and began walking away before I could ask another question.

"I left something in the house," Jimmy mumbled, and headed for Jennifer's back door.

I caught up with Whittaker.

"Why are you hammering questions at the EMT?" he asked as we walked.

"Because our only lead right now on a suspect, sir, is an EMT whose wife was scre… *having relations* with Philippe Girard. And that could be Jimmy."

"Hmm," Whittaker murmured. "Everything about these accidents is a stretch, Nora. If we weren't looking at another unfortunate victim, I still wouldn't believe there's anything sinister about them at all. We need to tread lightly."

I wanted to say that we needed to jump in with jackboots or we'd find another body in a few days, but I knew Whittaker was all too aware of that. His treading lightly meant being polite and careful in the way we were treating people, while investigating as fast as we could. But I didn't like Jimmy, and if he was involved, then me airing my suspicions might make him stop for a while, which would buy us time.

"Are you on shift tonight?" Whittaker asked when we reached Renae Waybridge's house.

"*Ja*."

I hadn't thought about it, but the day was flying by and I had to be at West Bay station by seven. I couldn't see how sleep would fit into the plan.

"Let me call Sergeant Redburn and see if he can spare you tonight. You're ahead of me on this one, and if we have a killer on the loose, this case will take priority over everything else."

I nodded my assent, and he stepped aside to make the call. Redburn would pretend to be mad, but he'd only be really pissed off if he couldn't find someone to cover my shift. But Jacob would feel slighted. I made a mental note to call him later. I had to speak with him about his grandmother's case, anyway.

After a few minutes, Whittaker returned. "You and Jacob are with me this week. Redburn is letting Jacob know."

"Thank you," I said, more for Jacob than for me. He was right. I should be involved. I knew more than he did about these deaths.

Rasha and her forensics team were with Davies when we went inside. One of them, decked out in a Tyvek suit, gave us new booties and gloves to put on.

"Thoughts, Gareth?" Whittaker asked.

The coroner scratched his head, rustling his suit. It was hard to look anything but awkward wearing that gear.

"I've taken a series of location pictures, which I'll use to reconstruct the most likely course of events. It'll take me a few weeks with everything else we have going on."

I swallowed hard. At this rate, we'd have six or seven more corpses by the time he figured out Renae fell down her own stairs backwards.

"Did you look at her wrists?" I asked, trying my best not to sound as infuriated as the man had made me.

"All the pictures will be on the server this afternoon, Roy," he said, never looking my way.

I took a step forward, but Whittaker held out a hand and stopped me.

"We noticed an abrasion on the back of her right wrist, Gareth. Does she have a similar mark on her left?"

"She does," he replied, still refusing to acknowledge my presence. "I'll be able to take a more thorough look when I do the autopsy in the morning."

I wanted to strangle the man. But I resisted and took off across the room instead, heading for the front door.

"Hello, Nora," a Tyvek suit said as I rushed by.

"Hi, Rasha," I replied, recognising her voice.

Reaching the Jeep, I pulled the tool roll out from under the passenger seat and opened the contents. Finding what I needed, I strode back towards the house, but stopped outside the front door. Turning, I saw Maya sitting in the ambulance with the doors open, playing a game or something on her phone. Apparently, they hadn't been called away to another incident.

"Maya," I called out, and she looked at me.

I waved her over.

"We ready now?" she asked as she walked towards me.

"*Nei.* I need your help for a minute."

We went inside the house to where Whittaker was still speaking with the coroner.

"Put your hands behind your back," I said to Maya.

"Say what?"

"Give me your hands," I repeated, and she reluctantly obliged.

Whittaker looked on with interest. Davies scowled from beneath his dorky elasticised hood.

I took the zip tie I'd brought with me, and secured Maya's wrists together, with the backs of her hands facing each other.

"Easy, girl," she muttered.

I turned her around so her bound hands faced the two men.

"He's either getting sloppy, or was rushed. Renae Waybridge

had her hands bound something like this and was pushed backwards down those stairs. Zara Parsons would have been restrained too, but with something softer which didn't mark her."

"That's why you think he was rushed," Whittaker commented.

"He knows we've figured out they're not accidents," I replied.

"You're making a lot of assumptions, Constable," Davies began.

"Are you telling me she didn't fall backwards?" I said, interrupting him. "She hit the back of her head," I continued, tilting Maya back and tapping the back of her head. "Then broke her wrist and fingers when they hit the steps. The zip ties made the marks."

"Don't be demonstrating dat part wit my fingers, blondie," Maya quipped.

Whittaker looked at the coroner, who was still glaring at me.

"Gareth?" Whittaker prompted. "I know we're rushing you, but time is a luxury we may not have if we're right about these so-called accidents."

Davies sighed. "My preliminary, and unofficial, opinion, is that what Constable Sommer just described is indeed plausible."

Hardly glowing support, but still more than I'd expected. It was nice that Davies was finally working with me instead of against me, but more importantly, Whittaker had said *we*. He was onboard, which meant *we* were now looking for a serial killer.

28

NIPPING AT YOUR LEG TYPE PARTS

By the time we left the scene, Whittaker had pulled a little more information from Davies. I made a point of being quiet, so he'd hopefully talk more, which seemed to work. He'd found no bruises or other injuries on Jerald Dilbert during the autopsy, only the damage from a shitload of amps. He did mention the bruising on Heather and Zara, finally conceding that they could be evidence of a yet-to-be-explained outside influence.

I'd also taken Maya aside and pried the names of the EMTs from her. Three who she recalled were married at the time. One of them was still married, and one was separated. The other was Jimmy, who was divorced.

"Let's start with the evidence we have of someone else present at the scenes," Whittaker said, as we walked from our vehicles into Central Station. "You gave me the circumstantial points, but now we have three cases where there are physical marks or bruising we can't explain."

I didn't respond, as he hadn't actually asked me anything, and I was still working on the reasons in my mind.

"Your zip tie theory looks solid, but what about the other two? Those lower back bruises are odd to me."

Dritt. Now he had asked a question. One I wasn't prepared to answer just yet.

"She didn't have wrist marks, but I still think she was restrained," I replied. "She could have stood in the pool if she'd been able to get the cover farther aside. There was also no sign of skin or blood under her fingernails, and she would have been thrashing at anything she could reach while drowning."

"Soft restraints of some description?" Whittaker suggested as we made our way upstairs to his office.

"*Ja*," I agreed.

I needed time to think through how I would go about staging these accidents if I was in the killer's shoes. Which meant setting my boss on a task and freeing myself up.

"Here are the three names from Maya," I said, handing him the piece of paper I'd written them on.

He could have told me to go downstairs and run them on one of the communal computers, but he did as I expected and sat down to do it himself. Rather than stand behind him to look, I stayed seated opposite and began picturing the scenes. The easiest, to me, was the electrocution of Jerald Dilbert. A gun to the head, and most people will do whatever they're told, providing the task offers a better chance of survival than a bullet to the brain. Which offers none.

Threats of harm to family is another persuader, but unless it's a threat in the moment, that can be harder to get someone to do something like electrocute themselves. A gun to the head of a loved one is very persuasive. The threat of harm to someone not present is less so. Either way, with no other physical evidence to suggest there was a struggle, I concluded a gun or deadly weapon was used, and Dilbert probably didn't know the wiring had been rigged to not blow the breaker.

"The first guy, Sanchez, looks like a boy scout," Whittaker said without looking up from his screen. "Not even a parking ticket."

"What about his wife?" I asked.

"Hmmm. Good point," he replied and tapped away on his keyboard.

I didn't have too much interest until he found something alarming.

My thoughts wandered back to Heather Lawson and her kitchen. And her cat. He probably didn't do it, unless it was indeed an accident. In which case, he might be crying over the spilt water.

"Nora?" Whittaker was asking me.

"Sir?"

"What are you grinning at?"

Dritt. I didn't realise I was.

"Sorry, sir, it was unintentional," I replied, not wanting to explain how occasionally I made myself laugh inside. Especially as I thought I had something wrong in the phrase, but I wasn't sure. "Sanchez's wife, sir?"

"Yes. She has a speeding ticket, but nothing more."

I nodded, and as Whittaker returned to his keyboard, I assumed he was moving down the list.

Cat nonsense aside, I thought I had Heather Lawson's demise figured out, so I shifted my thoughts to Zara Parsons. Her death was harder to fathom, but then again, I was a good swimmer, so it was difficult to imagine drowning in water in which I could stand. But she couldn't swim and would have been in full panic. And then a thought hit me, and I knew I could demonstrate how it was done.

"We need to go back to the scenes, sir," I blurted, and Whittaker peered at me from behind his monitor.

"We do?"

"Yes, sir. I can recreate what happened."

"Okay," he said, nodding. "That's good. But a solid suspect would be better."

"Of course, sir," I agreed. "Any luck?"

"Maybe," he replied, and thought for a moment. "But let's revisit the scenes in the morning, and you can show me. I'll ask Gareth Davies to join us."

Whittaker must have read my mind. Or the sour look I undoubtedly had on my face gave me away.

"I know you two aren't loving each other's company, but he's key in this process, Nora. As a detective, you'll deal with him a lot more."

"Of course, sir," I conceded and tried my best to soften my expression, but I was pretty sure my facial muscles wouldn't cave to that bullshit.

"Did you get to James Gates yet, sir?" I asked, ready to move on once more.

"Yes. Jimmy. He doesn't have anything on record either."

"But he divorced not long after the French guy was killed," I pointed out.

Whittaker sat back in his chair. "Which reminds me, to remind us both, we're moving forward on the premise that the Philippe Girard incident is connected. The only reason we're looking at EMTs is because of a rumour that Girard was having relations with a co-worker's wife."

"And his accident matches many of the key points in the new deaths," I pointed out.

"Certainly," Whittaker reacted. "But they're eighteen months apart. I'm not saying we're barking up the wrong tree, but we need to keep an open mind."

"We're looking for a trigger," I thought aloud. Again.

"Possibly," he agreed, thoughtfully. "An event that provoked the man into killing again."

"How about the other EMT who is separated from his wife?" I asked.

"Fairchild. He's a local lad. Married a girl from Hawaii," he said, reading from notes he'd made. "We should interview Gates and Fairchild, then speak to their exes."

"Do we have addresses, sir?" I asked, rising from my seat.

"We do," he replied, looking at his watch. "I'm supposed to be somewhere at four, but I'll have to let my wife know I won't make it."

"Four?" I blurted, checking my own watch. It was 3:55pm. "*Dritt.*"

"Yes, I dare say you're supposed to be at the team trials too, aren't you?"

"I'll text Jazzy and tell her I can't make it," I said, feeling a knot forming in my stomach. I was letting the kid down again.

"Nonsense, Nora," Whittaker insisted. "Go ahead. I'll meet with whoever I can get a hold of. Besides, I planned on starting with the paramedic service they work for. It only needs one of us. You should be at the trials."

I stood there, unsure of what to do. Whichever decision I made left me feeling like I wasn't fulfilling my role correctly.

"I've done this once or twice before, you know?" Whittaker said, and grinned at me.

"Promise you'll call me if one of these leads looks useful, sir?"

"You have my word," he replied. "Now go. You're already late."

I wasn't yet, but unless I could beam myself to the sports field like a sci-fi movie stunt, I was about to be.

By the time I drove the short distance, found a spot to park, and made it to the field, it was 4:14pm. Not too bad for me, but I could have got there sooner if I'd simply run from the station. Second time at a competition, and I felt a bit more at home, but I still had no clue where to find Jazzy before her event. People assembled in clumps around the field, depending on their kid's discipline, but I couldn't figure out where the sprint distance runners gathered. I was also wary of wandering into the wrong spot and being yelled at or receiving a javelin in the head.

After fifteen minutes of walking around like an idiot, I asked someone where I might find the sprinters. As they were telling me, the announcer told us the 100 metres semi-final was about to start, so I hurried off in the opposite direction to the one they told me as I knew where the finish line was. They probably thought I was a weird foreigner, and they were correct. Just not in the way they thought.

The gun sounded, and Jazzy stretched a clear lead by halfway, cruising to an easy win. After the other girls congratulated her, she spotted me and came over. She was barely winded.

"The times don't matter?" I asked.

"Not really," she replied. "Why?"

"Because you could have won by much more."

She grinned. "Maybe I'm saving myself."

"Might as well if the times don't matter," I agreed. "Is Jada-Kai in the other semi?"

Jazzy nodded as we stepped to the side for the next race. The gun sounded again, and Jada-Kai's tall, lean figure was easy to pick out from the other runners. She comfortably won her round as well, easing up for the final 20 metres. Jazzy cheered her on and applauded after she crossed the line.

"Think you have her beat?" I asked.

"This is just our school trials," Jazzy replied. "We'll both make the team as long as we don't get hurt."

My competitive instinct wanted to tell her to beat her rival every time, no matter what. The mental gain was worth it. But I resisted. Jazzy had said she was doing this for fun, so I didn't want to put pressure on her, although it took a lot of restraint to stay quiet.

"You're working tonight, aren't you?" Jazzy asked me.

"No. I've been switched. Day shift tomorrow instead."

"Can we get dinner afterwards?" Jazzy asked.

"Only if you win," I replied, and grinned.

She rolled her eyes, jogged towards the start for the 200 metres event, and I realised I'd already blown my cool, no pressure approach.

Jada-Kai was in the other 200 semi once again, and they both won their rounds without trying too hard. I kept checking my phone for calls or texts from Whittaker, but so far he'd sent me nothing. The longer it went on, the more I wished I'd gone with him, but I kept trying to remind myself that he was probably knocking on unanswered doors. He'd give me an update if he had something to share. And I was where I should be. Standing in a field with the late afternoon sun scorching me as sweat glistened on my skin. But at least I didn't have to run anywhere.

When it came time for the 100 metres final, a bigger crowd gathered at the finish line, and the cheers for the runners echoed around the grounds as they hurtled towards us. Jazzy and Jada-Kai ran neck and neck, and I eagerly watched for my kid's extra kick of speed when the other girls reached their limit. But it never came. The taller girl won by half a stride. Dutifully, I congratulated Jazzy, who seemed unperturbed by her loss to her closest rival. It was my understanding that the two girls were the best on the island in their age group, so although this event was only team trials, it was the same match-up she'd face at bigger competitions.

The heat finally began to abate, although it was still several hours before sunset. The grandstand cast a shadow over the front straight of the running track, which helped. I watched as the 200 metres final began with the crack of the starter's gun. With the staggered start for the curving first part of the race, it was difficult to tell who was ahead with the two favourites several lanes apart. But as they made the front straight, there was nothing between Jada-Kai and Jazzy.

I found myself screaming at the top of my lungs as they pushed for the line, and I may have sworn in Norwegian when the scoreboard placed Jazzy in second position. By the strange looks from the people standing around me, it appeared I did. At least they didn't understand exactly what came out of my mouth, but I think my tone gave them the general idea. Fortunately, by the time Jazzy made it my way, I'd forced some semblance of a smile on my face.

"Well done," I said, almost choking on the words.

The kid looked at me and frowned.

"Are you okay?" she asked.

"Sure. Where do you want to go for dinner?"

"I thought I had to win to get dinner?"

"I didn't mean that."

"You mean, you take it back, as I didn't win," Jazzy replied, now grinning.

"You want dinner or not?" I said in return.

She was being far too happy about finishing second, but I was determined not to be an arse about it.

"Are you sure you're okay?" Jazzy asked me again. "You look like you tasted something bad."

Either she was perceptive – which she'd proven before to be – or I was shit at hiding my feelings – which I also had a solid track record of not achieving.

"You've been training so hard, I was hoping you'd run a personal best," I said, struggling to not say what was on my mind.

"It was hot," Jazzy replied as we walked.

"That's true," I replied, knowing it wasn't any hotter than it was when she trained every day.

"I think there was a bit of a headwind," she added.

"Possibly," I said, knowing that too was a bunch of BS.

"Oh, and I let her win," Jazzy said in a low voice so no one else could hear.

"*Fy faen!* What did you do that for?" I blurted in a not-so-quiet voice.

"Shhh," Jazzy hissed, grabbing my arm. "Because I want Jada-Kai to keep running."

"Why? You should beat her every time, so she thinks she can never defeat you," I replied, managing to stay quieter. "The mind games are all part of it."

"You don't understand, Nora," Jazzy complained. "I'd already done that, and her friend told me she was thinking of quitting."

"Good. Let her quit," I replied.

"But I need her. She makes me better."

I stopped and looked at the kid in wonderment. "What's that supposed to mean? You don't need her to do your best. I've seen what you can do on your own in training."

"But that's because of her," Jazzy insisted. "I'm racing her in my head every time. If she quits, who will push me?"

The kid made me feel dumb sometimes. She had it all figured out. I never would have been brave or smart enough to *allow* an opponent to beat me at swimming, but I understood the motivation of having someone nipping at your knees. Or ankles. Or some other piece of the leg type parts.

I put my hand on her shoulder and gave her a quick hug against my hip. "You're an idiot."

"You wish," she replied, beaming at me.

"That's true. It might be easier. Now, where do you want to have dinner?"

Jazzy began running through options, but I'd stopped listening after a few names. Walking to the car park ahead was the kid Jacob and I had met at the house in West Bay a few days back. Junk-Dog00. The stuttering kid, Christopher Ellington. Except he didn't look like the meek and sheepish boy with a speech impediment now. He was walking with a swagger, with an arm wrapped around the neck of a friend, dragging him along as they wrestled with each other.

"Hey," I interrupted Jazzy, who was still deciding on dinner. "Is that Chris Ellington?"

Jazzy followed my gaze. "Yeah. He's a *drittsekk*."

"Don't swear. He's the kid with a speech problem, right?"

"Yeah. He talks shi… I mean, trash, to everyone."

"But he doesn't stutter?"

"What are you talking about?" Jazzy asked, looking at me as though I had two heads.

"*Fy faen*," I muttered.

"Don't swear," Jazzy jabbed back, and I rolled my eyes at her.

As I called Jacob.

29

TEST DUMMIES AND WORKING THEORIES

I didn't get much sleep, but as it turned out, I was glad I hadn't slept late or napped yesterday in preparation for the night shift. I wouldn't have had any rest if I'd pre-rested. My mind was weird like that. I was itching to go by and see Christopher Ellington, and Jacob was even more eager, but it would have to wait. I'd arranged to meet Whittaker at Heather Lawson's house at 7:00am, and I had an errand to run before then. But I was still early. Typical of Whittaker, he also showed up a few minutes before the arranged time. And he'd brought Davies along.

"Let's get on with this," the coroner announced the moment he got out of the Range Rover. "I have much to do today."

"Good morning, Constable," Whittaker greeted me, and his message was clear.

Don't be an arse, Davies, and *Be patient, Nora*. It was a valiant effort, but I was pretty sure neither one of us could help ourselves.

"Morning, sir. As soon as Jacob gets here, we can start."

Davies muttered something under his breath to make it clear he wasn't happy waiting, and Whittaker used the key the family had allowed us to keep and opened the front door. I grabbed my ruck-sack full of props and was relieved to see Jacob roll up a few moments later. While I waited for him to join us, I brought up the photos from the scene on my mobile.

"Good morning, Constable Tibbetts," Whittaker said, when Jacob walked in. "Any particular reason why you're not in uniform?"

Jacob looked surprised by the question. He was wearing a track-suit and trainers. "Nora told me to wear dis, sir."

"He's an accessory, sir," I explained, which made them all look at me in confusion, so I guess it didn't explain much. "You'll see," I added. "I didn't want to ruin his uniform."

"You didn't say you were plannin' to ruin anyting," Jacob commented.

I gave him my best shut up and play along stare, then poured water on the tile floor, one metre farther from the kitchen counter than we'd found the puddle last week. I then borrowed a bunch of cushions from the living room sofa and set them on the floor between the water and the counter.

"This is all well and good, Miss Sommer," Davies said. "But we have no actual way of knowing exactly where the victim was when she slipped."

I ignored him and continued preparing the scene. The last part of which was to zip tie Jacob's wrists together in front of him.

"Do I get to know what you gonna do to me, Nora?" he whispered.

"*Nei.* Better you don't know what's coming any more than she would have done."

Although, once I took the next step, I couldn't imagine it wouldn't be obvious.

I manoeuvred Jacob into position and looped a rope around the back of his legs then dropped the coil by his feet.

"I'll finish tying your legs in a minute," I told him as I stood and addressed the others. "To slip on the water, the victim had to be moving, so Jacob is set as though he was walking from the kitchen side of the island counter. He's wearing trainers which have a rubber sole similar to the Skechers worn by the victim." I turned to Jacob. "Show us how slippery the floor is."

Jacob tried sliding a foot forward. The rubber juddered along the tile.

"Not very slick with the rubber soles," Whittaker commented.

I stepped onto the sofa cushions behind Jacob and put my arms under his. "Let yourself fall backwards. I've got you."

He let me drop him to the floor, where his head missed the counter by a good margin.

"I set up one metre farther away so Jacob can't bash his head," I pointed out. "But at this angle, you can see he wouldn't have hit the counter, anyway. Same would be true if he was coming around from the living room side, slipped, and fell backwards."

I helped Jacob to his feet and repositioned him, crouching down and setting his feet where I wanted them. As I stood, I kept the end of my rope in my hand, but held it behind my leg out of Jacob's view.

"It would be completely unnatural to walk directly away from the counter, but if she did," I continued, stepping away. "Then it's possible…"

While still talking, I leaned in and shoved Jacob's chest, while at the same time pulling the end of the rope with my other hand. With his weight over his heels, I was able to easily wrench his legs out from under him, and he crashed to the cushions with a loud gasp.

"Notice now his head is within less than a metre from the counter," I said.

"Are you okay?" Whittaker asked, leaning over my groaning partner.

Jacob nodded as he couldn't speak yet with all the wind knocked out of him.

"Roll over," I instructed and twisted his ankle so he had no choice.

I pulled up his trouser leg. "See the marks on the back of his ankles?"

"Are you sure you're okay, Jacob?" Whittaker asked again, and I wondered if he was paying attention at all.

"How would the perpetrator get the victim to stand still where he wanted her?" Davies asked, and I was pleased to see at least he was following along.

"Gunpoint," I replied. "Or threatened her in some way. Or her cat. People play along when the alternative appears to be worse."

I took cutters from my bag and snipped the zip tie from Jacob's wrists.

"I didn't have time to find some, but I think the killer used soft restraints on his victims. Maybe the furry handcuffs kinky people like. Until Renae Waybridge. That's why I think he was rushed with her. Not fully prepared."

Jacob sat up and I offered him a hand to pull him to his feet.

"You could have warned me," he muttered.

"That would defeat the exercise," I replied. "You were perfect."

"I tink I broke someting."

"Well, the next one's in water, so you'll be fine."

He rubbed his wrists while I picked up the cushions and returned them to the sofa. I was keen to get to the next location. That little shit Chris Ellington would be at school, but I planned to have him picked up and brought home to see us grab his computer under the warrant, which was hopefully in process, while I used Jacob as a test dummy.

It took me another fifteen minutes to clean up the floor, lock the house, and move our little circus to Zara Parsons' backyard. On the way over, Jacob rode with me and made me tell him what to expect for round two. This one didn't require an element of surprise, so I was fine with explaining my plan.

When we arrived and gathered by the pool, I saw the pool cover was back in place, held by the weighted bags. I let Jacob crawl over it on his hands on knees, and even with his extra body mass compared to Zara, the cover didn't sink into the water. It was designed to float on top anyway, but I'd figured it would drag the ballast bags off the patio, and wondered if my theory was right after all.

"Put your hands behind your back, Jacob," I instructed, and he frowned at me.

I may have left the restraints part out of my explanation.

"She didn't have any skin or debris from the cover under her fingernails, only a few scuffs," I pointed out. "So she must have been tied up."

"We can just pretend," Jacob replied.

"*Nei*. We're doing it right."

"She drowned, Nora."

"Not that much right. Just hold your breath, and I'll get you out."

"I don't think it's going to sink under his weight," Davies chimed in. "These covers are designed to save children and pets and what have you, as well as keep the pool clean."

"This style?" I questioned. "I thought they had to be fixed to anchors in the concrete to hold that much weight?"

I'd read a few articles about them instead of sleeping last night, but as usual, the internet provided conflicting reports. Regardless, Jacob was bone dry on top of the cover, and even wriggling around, he hadn't pulled the ballast sacks into the water.

"Fine. Come out," I told him. "We'll have to do this exactly as I think it happened."

Jacob scrambled to the patio. "I don't like da sound of dat," he muttered, but I was already heading for the Jeep.

"Straighten the cover out," I ordered when I returned, deciding I'd keep him busy so he couldn't fuss too much.

"I was going to explain this part, but we'll just do it anyway," I said, and heaved a scuba diver's weight belt around Jacob's waist.

"Not a chance, Nora," he complained, but I slapped his hand away and fastened the clasp.

"How much weight you got on dis ting?"

"Twenty kilos, I think. I grabbed all Reg would spare me this morning."

"That's the bruising," Whittaker said, pointing to the weight belt.

"*Ja,*" I replied, putting a zip tie around Jacob's wrists this time.

"Seriously now, Nora. I'm a little worried about dis," Jacob jabbered.

"You can swim, can't you?" I asked, tying his ankles.

"Not wit my hands and feet tied I can't."

"I mean, you're not scared of water."

"Not till now, no," he said, looking anxiously at the cover over the pool.

"Don't worry, I'll be right here," I assured him, urging him closer to the edge.

"Nora," Whittaker said, standing close by. "Please don't hurt your partner showing us this. I think we get the picture."

"I'm not convinced the cover will give," Davies countered, which is when I gave Jacob a good shove.

I must say, I was just as surprised as the coroner at how well it worked. Jacob yelled and thrashed as the impact dragged a bunch of the ballast bags to the very edge, allowing water to flood into the indentation made by his body. The puddle wasn't more than five or six centimetres deep where my partner was cocooned in the loose cover, struggling to keep his nose and mouth clear of the water. Between the indentation, weight belt, and restraints, he couldn't roll his body to either side, and it was obvious he'd wear himself out in no time.

"What an awful way to go," Whittaker sighed.

"Quite so," Davies agreed. "I must say, this does explain how it could have been done."

I took that as high praise from the man.

"Nora!" Jacob yelled and spluttered.

"*Ja, ja,* quit crying like a baby. You can get out now."

I'm not completely sure what he said next, as he was swallowing and spitting water, but I leaned over and cut the zip ties so he could lift his face out of the puddle.

A few minutes later, sopping wet, and very pissed off, Jacob sat on the patio muttering to himself, while Whittaker helped me straighten out the cover and reset the ballast bags.

"I assume we don't need to throw Tibbetts down the stairs," Davies quipped. "So just the Dilbert incident to cover?"

I offered Jacob my hand. He glared at me, but finally took it, and I hauled him to his feet.

"*Takk*," I said, and squeezed his shoulder.

"We're certainly not electrocuting anyone," Whittaker said. "So perhaps we can just discuss what could have happened."

That would be great, but I didn't actually have a great explanation. The wiring was old, and according to Whittaker's electrician, who checked it out, none of it appeared to be recently tampered with. It was patched together years ago and never updated.

"Dat one seems different to da udders," Jacob said, and I was glad to hear him getting involved. Maybe he'd forgive me.

And he had a good point. One that had been bugging me for days.

"It is," I blurted, and looked at Whittaker, who I could see had just come to the same conclusion.

"The woman falling off the ladder and Dilbert electrocuting himself were both unfortunate," he said. "But they were accidents."

"No trophy taken, and he was a married guy," I added.

"Da udders are all single women," Jacob pointed out.

"Recently divorced, single women," I echoed, as the pieces fell into place. "The killer starts eighteen months ago with the man who slept with his wife. His anger builds, and now he's taking it out on women who leave their husbands."

"That's a lot of assumptions," Davies said sceptically.

"It's called a *working theory*, Gareth," Whittaker replied. "It's how we move an investigation forward when we have very little to work with."

The coroner looked indignant for a moment, before his expression softened. "Fair enough, Roy. Then we have the how. Now you'd better find the who."

"Before he do it again," Jacob said, still rubbing his wrists.

"Indeed," Whittaker replied, and we hurried to the cars.

30

SHOCKING PLANS

As I reached the Jeep, I realised I'd forgotten about Christopher Ellington. I checked my mobile. The warrant to search and seize his and his immediate family's computers and mobile devices had been issued.

"Sir!" I called out, catching Whittaker before he got in his SUV. "We have the warrant for the kid I told you about."

The detective looked at his watch. "What do you need?"

"An hour, and an officer to pull Ellington out of school," I replied, looking at Jacob, who nodded his agreement. "We can meet you at Central afterwards, sir."

Whittaker thought for a moment. I knew what was going through his mind. *Was it worth losing an hour chasing an internet scammer when a killer could be eyeing his next victim?* My own answer was no. Except our next steps were to visit the independently owned paramedic service station near the airport and speak with the manager. Whittaker had tried yesterday afternoon, but the manager had been out and no one else could access the personal data. Having Jacob and me there looking over his shoulder wouldn't get us further ahead, and I'd bet at least one of the EMTs we needed to visit lived in West Bay, so we'd be in the right area once we were done.

"Fine. But I'll call Detective Weatherford and see if he can help you. Pass it over to him as soon as you can, okay?"

"Sir," I replied in agreement.

I had no problem with that. Weatherford might, as he'd get all the paperwork, but the important part to me was having Jacob there to make the arrest. I knew how much it would mean to him. But first, we had to get my partner home to change out of his wet clothes.

Jacob had invited me around to his home a hundred times, but I'd never set foot in the house. I'd picked him up and dropped him off at various times, but I'd always declined to go inside or attend one of his family gatherings. He had a lovely family who didn't need me in their lives, and I didn't want anything to affect our partnership. If his wife thought I was weird, or not very nice, then it would be pressure on Jacob he didn't need. And that's exactly what I expected his wife to think if she met me.

"I'll arrange for Ellington to be picked up," I told him as my excuse to stay outside today.

He didn't argue, which wasn't a surprise. I'd needed a prop for my re-creations, and I'd abused his willingness to help the case, and me. Again. I should have apologised more, but I didn't want to hear him say that I'd do the same thing again if the need arose. Because he was right. I watched him leave wet footprints as he trudged up the driveway to his front door, which opened before he reached it. His wife stood there looking him over, then glanced my way. I waved. She herded him inside without acknowledging me.

"*Fy faen,*" I muttered to myself as I called Weatherford.

"Nora, Whittaker gave me the briefest of briefs. What do you need?"

"Are you in George Town, sir?"

"Yeah. I'm at Central," he replied.

"Can you pick up a seventeen-year-old student from the high school named Christopher Ellington?"

"Sure. Bring him to West Bay?"

"*Ja.* I'll text you the address. Don't let him make any phone calls. I'm hoping his parents are home when we get there in ten minutes. We're arresting them for cybercrimes."

"Okay," Weatherford said. "Should we bring in the cybercrimes unit?"

"*Nei.* You can drop all the computers on Luke's desk when you get back to Central. It'll be a nice surprise for him."

Weatherford laughed. "He'll love that."

"Don't tell Ellington he's under arrest, sir. Just say there's an issue at his home and you've been directed to pick him up. Let him talk as much as he likes."

"Okay. I assume you'll clue me in a little more at the house?"

"*Ja. Takk,*" I said, and hung up as Jacob came out of his house, still buttoning his uniform shirt.

I waved to his wife again. This time, she lifted a hand in return, but it was hardly a warm greeting. Her expression remained stern.

"Weatherford is picking the little shit up," I said, as Jacob climbed in the Jeep.

Jacob nodded.

"I'm sorry for this morning, okay?" I said, despite having told myself to move on. "It was shitty of me not to clue you in a bit more."

He looked over at me with a pained expression. "I was scared, Nora. All tied up like dat, I couldn't save my myself. I trust you, but it hard to have blind trust when my face is sucking in water, you know?"

I bit my lip. "I get carried away sometimes," I admitted.

"You tink?"

"I really am sorry. I'll explain everything next time."

"No you won't," he scoffed. "Dere ain't gonna be no next time."

Dritt. I walked right into exactly the scenario I'd told myself I would if I opened my mouth. I'd spent the morning using more words than I usually expended in a month, and I still let myself use a few more for no good reason.

Jacob's face eased into a grin. "Can we go arrest the Ellingtons now?"

"*Ja,*" I replied and fired up the engine.

Maybe the extra words were worth it after all.

After grabbing the signed warrant from West Bay station and collecting the patrol car from outside Heather Lawson's house, we parked around the corner from the Ellington's place. I didn't want to give them any opportunity to destroy or hide the evidence on the slim chance Christopher had been able to warn his parents. They obviously knew what their kid was up to, as they'd allowed him to fake a speech impediment to the police. At least the mother had. With warrant in hand, we marched up to the front door and knocked.

After a few moments, the father, Trent Ellington, opened the door and looked us over in surprise.

"Back again?"

"Yes, sir. May I ask who else is in the house?"

"Why? What's going on? Is Chris okay?" he asked, his voice getting more panicked with each question as his concern grew.

"Your son is fine. A detective is bringing him here shortly. Who else is in the house, sir?" I asked again.

"Just the missus," he responded, looking over his shoulder.

His wife appeared in the living room and I watched her eyes go from minor concern to major panic of her own. For a different reason. She bolted down a hallway.

"*Dritt,*" I hissed, and shoved the paperwork into Jacob's hands. "Serve it," I added as I bowled past Trent Ellington.

"Hey!" he yelped, and I heard Jacob beginning to explain why we were there as I shot around the corner after Mrs Ellington.

The first door on the right was swinging closed, so I barged it open to reveal a bedroom with a neatly made queen size bed and not much else. I darted back into the hallway and tried the handle on a closed door on the left. It was locked. Frantic bashing and crashing sounds came from inside, so I backed up and charged the door, leading with my shoulder. Wood splintered, and the door shuddered, but didn't open.

"What the hell's going on back there?" I heard Trent yell, followed by Jacob ordering him to stay put.

My shoulder stung, but I backed up again and took a second run. This time, the lock broke out completely, and I stumbled into the room. From the sci-fi movie posters on the walls and a pile of clothes on the floor, I figured I'd found Christopher Ellington's bedroom. His mother was halfway out the open window, clutching a laptop computer which trailed wires and cords from where she'd wrenched the device from the desk.

"Stop!" I shouted, but she lurched through the window, disappearing from view.

Rushing over, I peered outside and saw her lying in a heap on the ground.

"Police. Stop running. You're under arrest," I said, knowing I was wasting my breath.

She struggled to her feet and started to run, before dropping like a sack of cabbage. Or some other vegetable. Maybe potatoes?

I ejected the Taser cartridge out of the window and holstered the weapon, then walked back through the house. Jacob had moved Trent Ellington into the living room.

"Where's Melanie? What's going on? I heard a scream," the man blustered.

"Yeah, that was your wife. She's fine," I replied, although I doubted the woman felt fine at the moment. "She's waiting for me in your back garden."

I walked through the living room to a glass slider leading to a patio and the lawn beyond.

"Hey, Mr Ellington," I said, pausing. "Where were your wife and son last Monday afternoon?"

"Last Monday? Chris would have been at school. Why?"

"Are you sure?" I asked. "In the afternoon."

The man thought for a moment. "Wait. I think Melanie picked Chris up early. He had a dentist appointment."

"In George Town?"

Trent nodded. "Just south of downtown."

I looked at Jacob. "That'll be the cruise ship horn in the background."

"Probably hear it from da school too," he replied, shaking his head. "Everyting okay out dere, Nora?" Jacob added, and I knew what his question really meant.

What have you done now and will I get in trouble for it? was what he wanted to ask, if a suspect hadn't been present.

I opened the door and looked back at Jacob as I stepped outside. "She was shocked to see me, but we're going to have a chat now."

I'd been dying to use that line.

Five minutes later, with a frazzled and shaky Melanie Ellington sitting next to her thoroughly confused husband, a text buzzed on my mobile from Weatherford, letting me know he was walking up to the house. I went to the front door and paused by the photographs I'd noticed before. Several more I hadn't noticed were of the mother on stage performing. She and her son had certainly put on an award-winning performance when we'd dropped by last week.

I swung the door open and let Weatherford in, along with a concerned looking seventeen-year-old.

"You?" Chris Ellington blurted.

"Come in. I'm glad to see your speech therapy must be working."

Weatherford threw me a questioning glance.

"Did Chris have a stutter on the ride over?" I asked him.

"No," the detective replied. "And he wouldn't be quiet."

"He must have overcome the stutter he had the other day when we first met him," I explained, leading them into the living room. "I'm guessing he's pretty good at putting on accents, too."

"Fuck," Chris muttered when he saw his computer on the coffee table.

"Someone needs to tell me what the hell is going on here," Trent raged. "You've barged in here, assaulted my wife, and dragged Chris out of school like we're all criminals."

"Shut up, Trent," Melanie snapped. "Don't say anything. We need a lawyer."

"A lawyer?" her husband said, pulling his consoling arm away from her shoulders. "Why on earth would we need a lawyer? We haven't done anything!"

"Actually, you're all being arrested for cybercrimes, Mr Ellington. And I don't care if you talk or don't talk. The evidence on that computer, and from your bank accounts we're seizing, will prove you've been ripping off old ladies."

"Doing what?" he bellowed, looking from me to his wife and then his son. "What the hell have you two done?"

"Shut up, Trent," Melanie said again, while staring at the floor.

I looked over at Jacob and gave him a nod. My partner stepped forward and pulled his handcuffs from his belt.

"Christopher Ellington, you're under arrest for fraud," Jacob announced with pride in his voice, and as he continued cautioning the son, Weatherford and I did the same with his parents.

Although I suspected Trent Ellington was guilty of nothing more than paying too much attention to his football team and not enough to what his family was up to.

I bagged the computer, along with another laptop we found in the master bedroom, and all three of their mobile phones. We loaded the electronics into the detective's car while Jacob walked the family around the corner to his patrol car. I could have brought the car to the house, but I figured it served them right to be paraded down the street with their neighbours pulling their curtains back to witness the show.

"Call me when you're done," I said, as I climbed into the Jeep. "I'll tell you where to meet us."

"Don't do nuttin' crazy till den," he replied, and I gave him a wave.

Sitting in the Jeep with the tropical sun sending a trickle of perspiration down the side of my face, I called Whittaker's phone, and wondered why Jacob had felt the need to tell me that. I had no plans to do anything crazy.

31

WHO THE HELL IS MR BEAN?

"I'm just leaving the paramedic service office now," Whittaker said, after asking how our arrest went. "I'm on my way to meet Mrs Sanchez. Her husband's at work."

"Where does she live, sir?" I asked, wondering if I could meet him there.

"East of town in Prospect. Why don't you two visit Gates's ex-wife? Iris Perkins. She works in West Bay."

I was about to correct him and let him know Jacob was processing the arrests, but I stopped myself in time. Whittaker wouldn't let me go alone. He'd insist I had a partner with me, and who knew how long that would take going through Sergeant Redburn.

"Can you text me the address, sir?"

"I'll send it over as soon as we hang up. And Nora, the manager here told me Jimmy's divorce was not amicable. He took a bunch of time off dealing with it."

I'd had a bad feeling about the guy since our eyes met outside the grocery store. Nothing I'd seen since had eased that concern.

"What about the third one?" I asked.

"His ex returned to Hawaii," the detective replied. "I have a constable at the station tracking her down. It'll have to be a phone call. Okay, I'm sending the address, and Nora, touch base after you've met with Miss Perkins."

"Sir," I replied and ended the call.

Within thirty seconds, my mobile buzzed with the message, and I opened the address in Maps. It was a sports shop on West Church Street, not far from where the lady fell off her ladder in her back-yard. I'd been in the shop before with Jazzy. The drive took me less than five minutes, and I pulled up out front to an empty car park. It appeared I'd arrived at a good time, when no one else was shopping for sports gear.

I walked inside and stepped around a sale display full of shoes, balls for a variety of sports, and one of those runners' timing systems I'd looked at online. I paused. It was discounted down from $499 CI to $299 CI. That was still a lot of money for replacing my finger pressing an app on my phone.

"Is Iris Perkins here?" I asked a man behind the counter when I moved on.

He looked towards the far end of the store where a woman turned at the sound of her name. She was probably my height, but broad in the shoulders, with a sturdy frame and strong legs. I figured she could bench press me all day.

"Constable Sommer with RCIPS. I have a few questions for you, Miss Perkins. Can you take a break for five minutes?" I asked as I walked her way.

"What's this about?" she asked in a London accent, dropping a shoebox onto a trolley loaded with more items she'd been stocking.

"Better we talk in private," I replied.

Maybe she didn't mind airing her personal life in front of co-workers, but I wasn't about to start rumours about this case by letting uninvolved people overhear. She nodded, and led me to a small office in the back, where she closed the door behind us.

"What's going on?" she asked again without taking a seat or offering me one.

"You were married to Jimmy Gates, correct?"

"Something happen to him?" she fired back.

"Not to my knowledge."

"Oh, okay," she said, her shoulders relaxing. "Not that he doesn't deserve a dump truck full of shit landing on his head, but I guess it's bad form to wish it upon him."

I fought back a grin. I might like this woman.

"Why did you divorce?"

"So, what's this about?" she baulked. "I mean, that's a strange question for a copper to ask me, isn't it?"

"I'll get to that in a minute. Divorce?" I asked again.

"He's a wanker. That about sums it up," she replied.

"Can you be a bit more specific? Abusive? Drunk? Cheat on you?"

She laughed. "Have you met him?"

I nodded.

"Then I think you'll agree that I could kick his arse, so no. Not abusive. He has a pint or two, and would rather hang out with his mates, but he's not a drunk or a gambler, or anything like that. And as for cheating…" she laughed again. "I'm no prize, but I traded down with that one. I can't imagine he'll find another sucker out there."

"Did you cheat on him?" I asked, knowing I wasn't being very subtle, but I didn't feel like I had the time.

Iris frowned at me. "No. I just woke up one day and looked at him lying there in bed. Made me wonder what the hell I was doing. I didn't even like him anymore. Know what I mean?"

I'd never looked at someone I'd chosen to go to bed with in that way, but I'd certainly looked at too many people I'd been *sent* to bed with in that manner. Or worse. But I didn't like to think about my past at The International Fellowship of Lions.

"Did you know Philippe Girard?"

She frowned again. "Yeah. I mean, I met him a few times through Jimmy's work. Why?"

"But you weren't seeing Girard?"

Iris put her hands on her hips. "Listen here, Constable…" She squinted at my badge. "Sommer. I don't know why you're asking me all this shit, but I didn't run around on Jimmy, alright? And what does the French bloke have to do with anything?"

"We've learnt Girard may have been seeing the wife of one of his fellow EMTs," I said, being guarded about giving away too much.

"Well, that ended when the car fell on the poor bugger, so what's any of this got to do with the price of tea in China?"

I wasn't sure what to say. I guessed the last part was another one of those English expressions, but I couldn't fathom out what it meant.

"What does who Girard was sleeping with two bloody years ago have to do with me, love?" she said, obviously seeing she'd confused me.

"Because there may be a tie to a current, ongoing inquiry. A murder inquiry."

"Bloody hell," she muttered. "And you think whoever was sleeping with the Frenchy has something to do with whatever's happening now?"

"We need to urgently speak with them," I said, leaving out the part about their husband being the one we were really interested in.

But I believed Iris, so I hoped Whittaker was faring better. I knew tracking down the woman in Hawaii could be a wild goose chase. I did remember that phrase.

"Thank you for your time," I said and opened the office door.

I felt a hand on my arm.

"Hey," Iris said quietly, and for a moment I wondered if the reason she'd left her husband had more to do with her tastes changing beyond a better man.

"Ja?" I responded, turning around.

"You might want to speak with Darcy Lockwood."

"Who's she?" I asked, not recognising the name.

"Rowan Lockwood's ex-wife."

It took a few moments for my brain to catch up. I knew that

name. Rowan. Maya's regular partner. *But why didn't Maya mention him?*

"She was sleeping with Philippe Girard?"

Iris shrugged her shoulders. "I don't like to gossip, but that was the rumour."

"You said ex-wife. When did they divorce?"

"A year or two ago, I suppose."

"Was it a year? Or two years?" I pressed. "Before or after Girard was killed?"

Iris looked annoyed. "I don't remember. I had my own shit going on."

"Okay. Thanks again for the help," I said, eager to find out why Maya hadn't mentioned her partner.

Back in the Jeep, I couldn't decide who to call first, so I settled on Jacob's cousin, figuring I'd rather speak to Whittaker with more info than simply a rumour.

"This is Maya," she answered the phone.

"This is Constable Sommer, Jacob's partner."

"Hey girl, what's up?" she replied, and I could hear road noise in the background. Her voice also echoed a bit.

"Am I on speaker?"

"Gotta be hands free. Only way we s'pposed to take calls in da wagon."

"Are you alone?" I asked.

"No one in da back, if dat's what you're askin'"

That wasn't my concern, and from her answer, I deduced her partner was in the passenger seat.

"Call me back as soon as you can once you're alone. It's about Jacob," I lied.

"What da hell, Nora? What's happened to him?"

Dritt. This is why I liked to tell the truth instead of making up shit.

"He's fine. Just call me back."

"Okay," she said, sounding anything but okay.

I hung up and called Whittaker. It went to his voicemail. I hung up again. That knotted feeling in my stomach was in full twist mode. I felt like time was a luxury we didn't have and I was sitting in my Jeep getting nowhere. I called Sergeant Redburn's mobile.

"I thought you were Whittaker's problem for a few days," he said in way of a greeting.

"Yes, sir, but I need to check a name on DMV and I'm not with the patrol car."

"Oh, so I'm your personal assistant now?"

Fy faen. "No, sir. But I have a new suspect in the murder inquiry, and I need to track him down. And his wife. I mean ex-wife."

I heard a deep sigh. "It's become a murder inquiry?" he said in a more serious tone.

"Yes, sir."

"Name?"

"Rowan Lockwood."

"Spelling?"

"I don't know. He's English. I thought you'd know. Sir."

Another sigh.

"I have a Rowan, spelt like Rowan Atkinson. Sound right?"

"Who? Sir."

"The comedian. Mr Bean."

This was one of those stupid television/movie-type references I never understand, and didn't have time for.

"Is his last name Lockwood?"

"Yes."

"Then that's probably him, don't you think? Sir."

One more deep sigh and I could picture my boss shaking his head.

"I'll text you his address. It's Courtside Apartments on the south side of West Bay. Wife's name?"

"Darcy Lockwood, sir. But they're divorced. I don't know her maiden name."

"DMV records should connect to her current surname if she used Lockwood while they were married," he replied as I heard him tapping keys.

"Darcy Vaughn. She lives on Canal Point Drive. That's a swanky neighbourhood," he commented.

"Sounds like she upgraded from an EMT driver," I responded, thinking about the location in my head.

Canal Point Drive was in what was called Seven Mile Corridor, the long and narrow strip of land between Seven Mile Beach and the North Sound. Courtside Apartments were closer, and on the way to the wife's location if I took a longer route.

"Sending the second address," Redburn said. "Anything else?"

"No. Thank you, sir," I replied and ended the call.

My phone buzzed a couple of times as I turned around and sped down the road. It would be the addresses, but I knew the location of Courtside off West Bay Road, so I didn't need the details until I arrived. But I needed to speak with Whittaker. Just as I picked up my mobile, it rang in my hand. It was no surprise that the number wasn't one of the handful in my contacts.

"*Ja.*"

"It's Maya. What's goin' on with Jacob?"

"Nothing. Are you alone?" I shouted to be heard over the wind noise and deep tone whirring of the Jeep's off-road tyres.

"Nuttin'? You said someting was up wit my cousin."

"I couldn't say what it was until you were alone," I replied, annoyed at having to explain a bunch of shit that had no bearing on catching a killer. "Was Rowan Lockwood with you?"

"Yeah."

"But you're alone now, and he can't hear you?"

"Yeah. He's in da shop buyin' us a soda. What you got goin' on, Nora?"

"You didn't tell me Lockwood was divorced," I said, sounding more challenging than I'd intended.

"He got divorced before dat French fella died, dat's why. He was da one I meant when I said dere were four."

"Do you know his ex, Darcy?"

"Not really. Met her once or twice a few years back. He don't talk about her none. But he's a pretty quiet guy anyhow."

I wanted to share more with Maya, but there was no way she'd be able to act normal if I did, and the last thing I needed to do was spook Lockwood. He couldn't do any harm while he was on duty riding around in the ambulance. My mobile buzzed, and I saw it was Whittaker trying me back. I declined the call.

"When's your shift over?" I asked.

"Seven tonight. Hey, he comin' outta da shop. What I s'pposed to do?"

"Tell him I'm arranging a surprise party for Jacob, or some shit like that, okay? And let me know if Lockwood leaves work for any reason before seven."

"Okay, Nora. He'll love dat," she said, her tone changing. "Keep me posted."

The line went dead. Juggling the phone in one hand, while indicating and downshifting, kept me busy while I drove slowly down March Road until I reached Courtside Apartments on the right-hand side. Parking, I dialled Whittaker back. I barely resisted launching my phone across the car park when it went to voicemail again. This time, I left him a message.

"I think our suspect is Rowan Lockwood, sir. His ex-wife, Darcy, may have been the woman who had the affair with Philippe Girard. Lockwood's an EMT and they divorced before Girard was killed. But our guy is a planner, so it may have taken him a while to figure out how to get back at him. Or he found out later. I'm at his apartment now. We need a warrant, sir. I'm texting you the address. I'll take a look around and wait for you to call back."

I ended the call and took a deep breath. There were way too many words coming out of my mouth lately. It was exhausting. I longed to be back underwater where everybody had to shut up.

Climbing from the Jeep, I checked the apartment number from Redburn's text. Lockwood's was the end unit. There were only six of the two-storey residences. I peered through the front window into a clean and tidy living room. Beyond, I could see a dining area, then the kitchen in the back. Stairs on the left side of the living area led to the first floor.

I walked around the side where there weren't any windows, just a set of air-conditioning compressors and a tall white privacy fence which extended a short distance to the rear wall. The backyards were tiny. I tried the gate, but it was locked from the inside. Looking up, I could see a window, which I guessed from the size of the unit to be one of two bedrooms. I clambered on top of the big steel casing of the air-conditioning compressor, which allowed me to see into the backyard. It was a basic concrete patio with a single lawn chair next to the rear door.

I shook the fence, which was made of sturdy plastic. Looking up, I figured I might be able to see into the bedroom window if the fence would hold me. If it wouldn't, I'd come crashing down onto the patio. I placed my phone on top of the compressor so it couldn't fall out of my pocket.

Using the corner of the building as support, I stretched my left foot onto the fence, and heaved myself up, wobbling and teetering as I tried to balance on the narrow top. The plastic creaked and groaned under my weight. Below me, my phone buzzed as a call came in. I glanced down and watched the device vibrate itself over the edge of the compressor case, and hit the concrete pad below. So much for keeping it safe.

The window was about a metre in from the end of the building, and I reached out with my left hand until my fingers gripped the edge of the frame. From the building beyond the rear wall, I heard a patio slider open, scratching along its track. I dared a glance over my shoulder. A girl, probably around four or five years old stared at me from a deck.

"Mummy!" the kid shouted. "There's a lady dressed like a policeman breaking into the neighbour's house!"

Fy faen. Bloody kids. I ignored her and leaned towards the window, risking more and more of my weight on my outstretched arm. Finally, I could peek through the lower corner into the room. It took a moment for my eyes to adjust from the bright sunshine to the dim interior before the details came into focus. The room was set up as an office, with a desk against the wall to my right, and a rectangular table in the centre. On the table was what appeared to be a scale model of part of a house with the roof and two walls missing. Lying on the table were two action figure dolls. One male, one female. I didn't recall hearing anything about Lockwood having a kid. And there was no bed in the room.

The mirrored door to a built-in wardrobe to my left was half open, revealing shelves. I pressed my face closer to the glass and stared into the shadows of the closet. There were more models made from the same white foam board used for the mock-up on the table. One appeared to be a swimming pool instead of a room. These weren't doll houses, and they certainly had nothing to do with a child. Rowan Lockwood had indeed carefully planned his attacks. Scanning back to the desk, I noticed a map of the island pinned to the wall above. Small, red handwritten Xs appeared all over the place. From a few of the locations I knew, I determined the man had noted the positions of official CCTV cameras.

My eyes tracked the floor, where a gas bottle rested against a table leg.

"Hey there!" came a voice from across the way, making me jump.

The fence creaked, cracked, and my hand slipped.

32

"I THINK THAT LADY'S A GONER"

If my feet had snagged on the top of the fence, I would have hit the concrete head first. Fortunately, they didn't, and somehow I managed to get them underneath me, so I landed in some kind of crashing, tumbling front roll. I lay still and waited for a moment to see if the pain of broken bones would hit me while I caught my breath.

"Mummy, I think that lady's a goner," I heard the little girl announce.

"I'm calling the police," the mother said, which prompted me to my feet.

By standing with my back to the house, I could see over the wall to the balcony where the kid's eyes went wide as I appeared in her view.

"She's alive again, Mummy!"

The mother's face craned over her daughter, and I waved.

"I am the police."

"You don't look like the police," the mother shouted back.

I took my badge from my belt and held it up. "Royal Cayman Islands Police Service, ma'am."

"Then why are you breaking into somebody's house?"

I'd recovered my breath, and outside of a scuffed knee, I appeared to have survived the fall, but I really didn't have time for this shit. Opening the gate, I walked out of the backyard, picked my mobile up off the ground, and called Whittaker. This time, he answered.

"Nora, I need something more to get a warrant. A judge won't issue one based on what we have."

"He has a model of a house and dolls in his spare bedroom, sir. Looks like he's planned out each of the kills."

"You broke into the house?"

"*Nei.* I looked through the window."

"I've called the police just in case!" the mother shouted from her balcony.

"Me too!" I yelled back, holding the phone down, so I didn't blow Whittaker's eardrums out.

"What's going on there?" he asked when I put it back to my ear.

"Just a concerned neighbour, sir. Do you think you can get a warrant now?"

"Maybe. I'll try."

"Okay, sir. I'll pay the ex-wife a visit."

"You're leaving Tibbetts there?" he asked, and for a moment I'd forgotten the lie I'd told. "You should stay together. Take him with you," Whittaker continued. "I'll send someone to watch Lockwood's place until we get the warrant."

"Yes, sir," I replied, wondering how I could get myself out of this mess without another 'official hearing' about my behaviour. "We'll check in after visiting Darcy Vaughn."

I ended the call and walked to the Jeep, dialling Jacob as I went.

"I have pictures of you!" the mother yelled as I walked away.

I gave her a thumbs-up. The little girl waved goodbye.

"Jacob, where are you?" I said before he had a chance to waste time with niceties.

"Still at West Bay station. Everyting okay?"

"I think the killer is Maya's partner, Rowan Lockwood. I need you to meet me at his ex-wife's house."

"What, now? Rowan? He's da nicest guy. Are you sure?"

"No, but he's at least guilty of being a weirdo."

"Can't really arrest da man for dat, Nora," Jacob replied. "Or you'd be behind bars."

"Whittaker's getting a warrant to search his house, which should provide the evidence we need to arrest him. So I need you to meet me at the ex-wife's house where we can get her side of things."

"I'm almost done here," he replied. "Want me to call when I'm all set?"

"No!" I said, louder than I intended. All these long-winded conversations were driving me nuts.

It would all be a lot easier if people just did what I said instead of needing to know all the stupid details.

"Leave the Ellingtons with the sergeant and meet me at the address I'm sending you, okay?"

"I can't just leave, Nora. We're in da middle of doing all da paperwork."

"*Fy faen*, Jacob. Whittaker thinks you're with me, so get there as soon as you can."

"Den wait a while till I'm done, Nora," he replied. "Hey, where is Rowan now? Is he working with my cousin today?"

"Yeah. I spoke with her," I replied, starting the Jeep. "And I can't wait, so hurry up."

"Then…" Jacob began, but I hung up.

I could wait. But my stomach was still twisted in knots and a thought bounced around in the back of my mind. *Why hadn't Lockwood taken out his rage on the one person who'd caused his angst?*

I backed out of the spot and sped down Marsh to West Bay Road. It could be that his attacks were deranged demonstrations of the depth of his affection for his ex, although I couldn't imagine how even a nutjob could think killing other women would win her back. Or more likely, it was something else. He'd planned on killing Renae Waybridge, but my investigation had rushed him and now Darcy would be his grand finale. I turned left on West Bay Road

246 | NICHOLAS HARVEY

and grabbed my phone between gear shifts. Finding the number I recalled belonging to Maya, I hit redial. It rang until it went to voicemail. I hung up.

Jacob had probably freaked out and called his cousin, so she was now talking to him. Or she could be busy doing EMT-type stuff. Either way, I'd made it clear that she should warn me if Lockwood took off for any reason, so I felt like we had until 7:00pm tonight until we had to worry about him roaming free. With a bit of luck, we'd be arresting him before then.

At the Yacht Club roundabout, I joined the Esterly Tibbetts Bypass and headed south. My stomach moaned and I checked the time. It was almost one, and I'd skipped lunch. Three roundabouts later, I indicated for Canal Point Drive, which was up ahead on the left. Just as I reached the turn, an ambulance pulled to the stop, leaving the neighbourhood. My eyes met Rowan Lockwood's as he quickly took off down the bypass.

With only the briefest moment to decide, I kept turning into Canal Point Drive, flooring the throttle. The old inline six-cylinder engine responded, and I grabbed third gear before fumbling for my hip radio. So much for not worrying about what Lockwood was up to. I now had Maya to worry about, too. There was only one person sitting upfront in the ambulance.

"Dispatch, this is PC277. We have a potentially armed and dangerous suspect driving an ambulance south on Esterly Tibbetts, last seen heading towards the Foster's roundabout by Camana Bay. Over."

I threw the radio down on the passenger seat and picked up my mobile, searching my texts for Darcy Vaughn's house number as I shifted to fourth and kept accelerating, hoping I wasn't speeding past her home. The places were all huge, on large lots, with little cul-de-sacs between short canals which extended to a wider waterway leading to Man O War Cay. I found her street address and braked hard, sending the radio tumbling into the footwell while dispatch asked me to confirm the details.

Screeching to a stop, I checked the house number on a small

plate on the pillar beside the grand front entranceway. I turned right, pulled into the semicircular brick-paved driveway, stopped again beside a slick-looking yellow sports car, and groped for the radio. After quickly confirming the details of the ambulance, I asked for backup at my location as I ran to the front door. It was locked. I wanted to call Whittaker, but I couldn't dial a phone while running around the side of the house, and right now, finding Darcy seemed a bigger priority.

The home was huge. White, with a beige Spanish tile roof and dark brown window frames. The gate in the fence blocking off the rear patio was open, and I ran through, finding a pool and a lush lawn extending to the sea wall along the canal. At the rear of the house, several glass sliders allowed access to the patio, but they were all closed. I tried each one and found them to be locked. Peering through the glass, I could see most of the open plan living room, kitchen, and dining area. The place looked deserted, with no signs of any trouble. Maybe she wasn't home.

Staring at the sliding door handle, I contemplated picking the lock, but there were bound to be security cameras, and capturing me breaking in didn't seem like a great idea when there weren't any signs of distress. I turned and looked around. To one side of the pool was a building about half the size of my shack. I could see a large outdoor grill under the extended roof and a door into what I assumed to be bathrooms, or maybe a games room. I ran over and put my face to the window. To my left, by the door towards the pool, was a full kitchen, and to the right there were doors labelled as restrooms. Between two large sofas in the middle of the room, a woman sat cross-legged on the tile floor with a hand to her face.

I banged on the window, and her head slowly turned my way. She looked completely stoned and appeared to have vomited down her shirt. Her eyes widened as she squinted to focus on me. If she'd taken drugs, it didn't look like she was enjoying her trip. I sniffed the air, and the bottle in Lockwood's planning room flashed through my mind. I could smell gas.

Running around to the door, I tried the handle, but it was also locked. The woman, who I presumed was Darcy Vaughn, watched me and tried to speak, but if any sound came out, I couldn't hear her. The gas smell was far stronger now. I stepped back and kicked the glass panel in the door above the lock, and it shattered into pieces, falling to the tiles. A wave of stinky fumes assaulted me. The little room was full of natural gas. No wonder she looked stoned.

With a hand held across my nose and mouth, I reached inside and unlocked the door, swinging it open. My eyes stung, and I caught my breath. I took a few steps back and inhaled cleaner air before moving inside to get Darcy out. But as I approached, she looked up in horror and struggled to wave me away.

"Stop," she gasped. "Trigger... I'm sitting on... a trigger."

Dritt. She was booby trapped.

"Okay. Let me get the windows open to let more of this gas out," I said, then coughed and gasped a few times.

"The timer..." Darcy spluttered, pointing to a built-in oven in the kitchen. I hadn't noticed before, but the oven door was tilted open. "No time," she wheezed.

I ran over and looked at the display. A clock told me it was 1:13pm, and the only other item illuminated was a stopwatch icon. There was a timer set to start the gas oven at some point. Which would ignite the gas under the oven's floor panel, as well as the rest of the flammable gas in the room.

"What time?" I said, before choking on the fumes.

Darcy shook her head. Perfect. We had no idea. Most people would choose a round number, which in this case would probably be fifteen, but that was a guess. We could have an hour, or only a minute. I was betting it was closer to the minute mark.

I gasped and tried to close the oven door.

With it sealed, the oven could come on, but the electrical igniter wouldn't light up the room. Except the door wouldn't close. I shook and rattled it, unsure why. And then I noticed a small piece of metal in the hinge channel at the base of the oven door. It fitted so perfectly that I couldn't get at it with my fingers.

I coughed again.

How could I be so stupid? All I had to do was turn the start timer off. I pressed the control panel, but nothing happened. I jabbed at it with my fingertip on every function button, but nothing lit up or changed. The prick had disabled the panel. He really did plan this shit. The clock changed to 1:14pm. I started counting down in my head.

Dritt. I could find the gas supply and shut it off, but all the fumes in the room wouldn't clear for a while. Grabbing a tea towel from the counter, I held it over my nose and mouth, and rushed back to Darcy, kneeling before her.

"We have to figure out the trigger," I wheezed through the cloth. "What is it?"

"It's a... vape pen," she managed to splutter.

"Yours?" I asked, wondering how he would rig one of those stupid things to create a spark. They had an internal heating element but no igniter or flame.

She shook her head. "He took... mine."

This guy had thought of everything. After this little building went boom, all evidence of his presence would be burnt into oblivion. The oven would be turned to shrapnel, and if they ever found the remains of a vape pen, it would be assumed it was Darcy's. I'd paused my mental countdown to think and talk. I guessed it had been at least twenty seconds.

"Is there a separate button you're sitting on?"

Thirty-seven, thirty-six...

She shook her head. "Just the... the pen."

Darcy retched, but she'd already emptied her stomach, so she dry heaved. I'm sure it would have reeked if the gas smell wasn't already overwhelming. Thirty, twenty-nine...

"Did you see it? Did it have extra wires or anything?"

Another shake of the head. "He said... it would..." she said, then succumbed to a coughing fit.

"He told you..." I started, but the gas was starting to really irritate my throat now. After a few coughs, I tried again. "He told you it would spark if you mov... moved?"

Darcy nodded and began to slump forward. She was about to pass out, and I'd forgotten to count again. I held her by the cheeks and shook her face.

"Stay awake!"

We both coughed and choked. I grabbed her by the arms and pulled her to her feet.

"No!" she screamed, and I saw the vape pen on the floor, as I dragged her towards the open door.

Half there, she stumbled and fell to her knees. "Don't, don't... leave me," she gasped.

I tightened my grip on her arm and towed her across the tile floor, her body falling limp behind me. When I reached the doorway, her legs hit the threshold, and I jarred to a halt. I glanced at the oven clock. It was still 1:14pm.

"Get up," I yelled, and Darcy tried to stand.

I wrapped an arm around her and we staggered across the covered outdoor kitchen, where I chose the best cover I could think of. I hauled us both into the pool with a big splash. When I bobbed up to the surface, I grabbed Darcy and made sure we could stand. She sucked down gasp after gasp of fresh air.

"Maybe it wasn't one fif..." I began, but that was as far as I made it.

Flames blasted the glass from every door and window as the ground shuddered and a blast of hot air hit me in the face. The surface of the pool rippled and slurped over the sides onto the patio, and pieces of debris rained down around us.

"How did we outrun the trigger?" Darcy wheezed, her voice scratchy, but returning. "I thought it would blow me up right away."

I ran a hand over my head, sweeping my hair back, where my ponytail had succumbed to the blast and the dunking. "The vape pen wasn't a trigger. He'd set the oven for 1:15."

"I sat there all that time for nothing?" she fumed, coughing a few more times with water running down her face.

"*Ja.*"

"How did you know?"

"I couldn't figure out how I would have made a trigger from a vape pen without using some kind of dead man's switch on the outside."

"Really? Holy shit."

"*Ja.* But mainly I figured we were out of time, so it seemed like it was worth the gamble."

"Shit," she mumbled. "You're crazy."

"My partner thinks so," I confessed.

33

ERRANT BABIES, STAR WORLD EMPIRE, AND RETURNING SHOES

Whittaker kept looking from the burnt-out shell of the pool house and back to me. He was clearly upset about the near miss.

"Rasha and her group will go through the remains with a fine-toothed comb, but quite honestly, the case will rely mainly on your testimony about what he'd set up here."

I nodded. This was good. Not the rely on me part, but the Whittaker obsessing over the case part. At some point, he'd circle back to the fact I'd led him to believe that Jacob was with me, and I hoped to push that pram as far down the road as I could. *Pram?* What a weird saying. *Why would you shove a baby-carrying device down the road?* Maybe it wasn't pram. It was something that sounded like pram. Regardless, I hoped he'd forget about me lying to him for as long as possible.

Apart from not being blown up in the pool house, my biggest relief was that Maya was okay. A touch traumatised as Lockwood had tied her up in the back of the ambulance and she'd thought he'd kill her at some point. But we all have our demons to bear. She was alive. In actuality, I didn't think he would have harmed her. His misguided anger lay with women who had left their husbands.

I had no idea if Heather, Zara, or Renae had left their spouses for another man, or whether simply leaving was enough in Lockwood's deranged mind, but Darcy clearly had. She'd admitted to me that she and Philippe Girard had indeed engaged in a brief affair, but to the best of her knowledge, Rowan never knew that. I was able to explain that he did, and that her lover's accident wasn't an accident at all. Also, her moving in with a rich financier a month ago was probably the trigger which set Lockwood off on his killing spree. That made her burst into tears, so I was glad the ambulance crew took her away before I revealed any other upsetting truths.

I looked at my watch. *Dritt.* "I have to go, sir."

Whittaker looked surprised. "You don't want to join me in interviewing Lockwood?"

I absolutely did, especially as he'd not put up a fight when the patrol car had pulled him over on the bypass near George Town. He seemed resigned to the fact that he'd be caught at some point, so I figured he might be keen to tell us all the details, which interested me. While I wished he hadn't killed anyone, he was a really smart guy who'd meticulously planned and executed multiple murders while covering his tracks. If he'd been patient and spread the incidents out over months, I wasn't sure we ever would have figured him out.

"I have to be somewhere in an hour, sir. I can meet you at the station afterwards."

"Something I should be aware of? Has it a bearing on the case?" he asked.

"No, sir. Personal. But it's important."

He nodded. "Everything okay?"

From his tone, and knowing the man, I knew his question was coming from concern rather than prying or displeasure at me leaving.

"*Ja.* I'll call you when I'm done, sir."

He nodded again, and I walked over to where Jacob stood, chatting to a fireman and looking at the smouldering remains.

"I have to go," I told him, and he turned to walk with me.

"Dat's some timely karma, huh?" he said.

"What do you mean?" I asked, unsure of what he was referring to.

"You gettin' soakin' wet," he chuckled.

I looked down at my soggy uniform and laughed. I'd towelled myself as best I could, but I was still a mess.

"This make us even?"

"No," he quickly replied. "I owe you big time."

"What for?" I replied, stopping by the Jeep. "I figure it's the other way around."

"I shoulda bin here, Nora. You asked me, and I didn't come quick enough."

I shrugged my shoulders. "If you'd left the second I'd called, you still wouldn't have been here before the timer went off," I said. Which was true.

"Den I shouldn't have left you in da first place. We gotta stay together in da future. I don't wanna hear da radio call about an explosion and tinking it were you."

"You'd rather blow up with me?" I asked. Then grinned at him.

"Someting like dat," he laughed.

"Okay," I said, and climbed into the Jeep. "I have to go."

As I backed up and started down the road, I wondered what would have been different if Jacob had been there with me. I wasn't sure I would have risked running out the door and gambling on the vape pen being a decoy. It was only a hunch that the timer was set for 1:15pm. A guess based on Lockwood's eye for logic and detail. Setting it for 1:16pm would have been awkward for him. I knew that, because my own brain craved that kind of order. If Jacob had been there, we may well have all been blown up, simply because I wouldn't have taken the gamble with his life on the line. A strange irony.

It took me thirty minutes, and some persuasive talking at one stop, but I managed to round up what I needed and drive across town. I hoped I wasn't too late. We weren't. As Jazzy, Rabbit, and I entered the check-in area of Owen Roberts International Airport, Mrs Barker was pushing Robbie towards the doors for security. She looked surprised, and his face lit up.

"Here to tell me you can't bear to see me leave?" Robbie greeted us, and laughed.

"This is a lovely surprise," his mother added with a broad smile.

"Hi. This is Jazzy, who you spoke with," I said, with a hand on her shoulder. "And this is Rabbit. I wanted you both to know, because of your help, we arrested the internet scammer this morning."

"Really?" Robbie enthused, looking at Rabbit, who looked uncomfortable with the compliment.

In addition to her basic discomfort with being out in public and dealing with other humans.

"Good to meet you in person," Rabbit said, her hands stuffed in her jeans' pockets.

People walking by kept looking at us, and I guess we were a strange sight. A tall Scandinavian in a damp police uniform, accompanied by two dark-skinned girls, both with wild hair, all chatting with a young guy in a wheelchair. His mum was the only normal-looking one amongst us.

"We thought we should see you off, and tell you we expect you back at work in a few days," I said, and Robbie laughed some more.

"I don't have my computer, but Mum can check my email if you need me."

"We'll manage as best we can," I assured him. "You worry about keeping the doctors inline."

"I have a project for you when you get back," Rabbit said.

Robbie couldn't stop smiling. "Cool."

"We have to go," his mother said, resting a hand on my arm. "This whole process takes a few extra minutes. Thank you all so much for coming."

"Have a good trip," Jazzy said. "I don't play video games, but I need to get better at computer stuff. Maybe you could help me sometime?"

"That would be fun," Robbie enthused. "And I'll show you how I beat Rabbit at Star World Empire."

"In your dreams, Woof on Wheels," Rabbit grinned.

Robbie's whole body shook as he laughed even harder.

His mother squeezed my arm and then wheeled her son away. I could hear him talking excitedly all the way through the automatic doors for security.

After dropping Rabbit by her apartment, I considered stopping by the station, but I still had the kid with me. It was too late to drop her back at school, so I called Whittaker.

"Hi Nora. Everything go okay?"

"Yes, sir. Thank you."

"Good to hear. We're waiting on Lockwood's lawyer, so based on the time, I don't see anything happening until tomorrow."

"I'll be there first thing, sir. How did the house search go?"

"Maybe he planned on being caught at the end of all this," Whittaker replied. "He hadn't hidden anything. They found the dolphin pendant and chain, the pink bracelet, and the class ring. There was also a small gold hoop earring which I'm betting belonged to Philippe Girard. Plus all the models of the crime scenes and detailed notes on how he planned it all. Plenty of evidence."

"I'm pretty sure that nitrile glove I found on Renae Waybridge's patio was dropped by Lockwood, too, sir."

"I dare say you're right."

"Okay, I'll see you tomorrow, sir."

"Bright and early," Whittaker replied. "And Nora. Good job on this one. If you hadn't been like a dog with a bone, I doubt Darcy would be alive. Your instincts were spot on."

"Okay," I mumbled, and hung up. It was hard to feel good

about the case when Lockwood had killed four people, but I guess four was better than five.

"We gotta go by your work?" Jazzy asked in her best *I don't want to stop at your work* voice.

"*Nei.* Just one quick detour on the way home."

I didn't need to look her way to know she had just rolled her eyes, and I grinned.

Thirty minutes later, we made it home, and after I poured myself a glass of wine, and the kid a glass of juice, we sat on the deck, where I watched Jazzy unpack her new track timing kit. I sat quietly while she narrated her thoughts on every part and piece, asking me how each component worked and not expecting a reply.

Before too long, I was struggling to keep my eyes open when I heard rustling from the end of the deck. After a moment, a prehistoric-looking little head popped into view.

"Edvard!" Jazzy whisper-shouted, and carefully moved to the door, where she snuck inside the shack in search of iguana snacks.

I looked at the stupid lizard heaving himself over the edge of the deck and slowly walking my way with his weird, exaggerated leg movements, which looked like he was stepping over invisible obstacles.

"About time you came home," I said, and surprised myself by how happy I was to see the ugly bugger. "You're still not big enough for a pair of shoes," I pointed out.

He wiggled his way closer, only pausing when Jazzy returned with a leaf of lettuce. She went back to her new toy while Edvard chewed on his supper, and I sat back, taking another sip of wine, feeling quite pleased that I didn't get blown to pieces today.

Thank you for reading *Relentless Sommer*!

Not ready to be done with Nora?
In return for joining my newsletter list, I've written a fun bonus scene you'll find by using this QR code…

Grab the next book in the series, *Festive Sommer*

ACKNOWLEDGMENTS

My sincere thanks to:

My incredible wife Cheryl, for her unwavering support, love, and encouragement.

My family and friends for always being there.

My marvellous editor Andrew Chapman at Prepare to Publish for his diligent work and wise suggestions.

Andy and Ethan Stansbury for their video game advice.

Lily at Orkidedatter for her Norwegian advice.

Casey Keller, Craig Robinson, and Alain Belanger for their help with all things Cayman Islands related.

Shearwater Research and Dive Rite for their friendship and support.

The Tropical Authors group for their advice, support, and humour. Visit and subscribe at www.TropicalAuthors.com for deals and info on a plethora of books by talented authors in the Sea Adventure genre.

My beta reader group has grown to include an amazing cross

section of folks from different walks of life. Their suggestions, feedback and keen eyes are invaluable, for which I am eternally grateful.

Above all, I thank you, the readers: none of this happens without the choice you make to spend your precious time with my stories. I am truly in your debt.

LET'S STAY IN TOUCH!

To buy merchandise, find more info or join my newsletter, visit my website at
www.HarveyBooks.com

If you enjoyed this novel I'd be incredibly grateful if you'd consider leaving a review on Amazon.com
Find eBook deals and follow me on BookBub.com

Catch my podcast, The Two Authors' Chat Show with co-host Douglas Pratt

Find more great authors in the genre at TropicalAuthors.com

Visit Amazon.com for more books in the
Nora Sommer Caribbean Suspense Series,
AJ Bailey Adventure Series,
and collaborative works;
The Greene Wolfe Thriller Series
Tropical Authors Adventure Series

ABOUT THE AUTHOR

A *USA Today* Bestselling author, Nicholas Harvey's life has been anything but ordinary. Race car driver, adventurer, divemaster, and since 2020, a full-time novelist. Raised in England, Nick has dual US and British citizenship and now lives wherever he and his amazing wife, Cheryl, park their motorhome, or an aeroplane takes them. Warm oceans and tall mountains are their favourite places.

For more information, visit his website at HarveyBooks.com.

Made in the USA
Middletown, DE
29 April 2024

53652620R00149